BONECHILLER

GRAHAM McNAMEE

Hodder
Children's
Books

A division of Hachette Children's Books

First published in the USA in 2008 by Wendy Lamb Books,
a division of Random House Children's Books

First published in Great Britain in 2009
by Hodder Children's Books
A division of Hachette Children's Books
This edition published 2013

The right of Graham McNamee to be identified as the Author of
the Work has been asserted by him in accordance with the
Copyright, Designs and Patents Act 1988

1

A Catalogue record for this book is available from the British Library

ISBN 978 1 444 91282 1

Typeset in Caslon by Avon DataSet Ltd, Bidford-on-Avon, Warwickshire

Printed and bound in Great Britain by
CPI Group (UK) Ltd, Croydon, CR0 4YY

The paper and board used in this paperback by Hodder Children's Books
are natural recyclable products made from wood grown in
sustainable forests. The manufacturing processes conform to the
environmental regulations of the country of origin.

Hodder Children's Books
a division of Hachette Children's Books
338 Euston Road, London NW1 3BH
An Hachette UK company
www.hachette.co.uk

One

Don't look for it on the map. This place is so small it doesn't even get a dot. Once a year they get a new 'welcome to' sign put up, but it doesn't last a week before it's so full of buckshot holes you can't even tell the name of the place, and you sure don't seem welcome.

Nowhere – officially known as Harvest Cove. Tucked away in the Big Empty that makes up most of Canada. On the shores of Lake Simcoe, the Cove is summer-cottage country, or at least it's trying to be. Only it's a little too far from anywhere to be popular. Off-season, the population shrinks by two thirds and the place turns into a ghost town.

Turn off Highway 11, north of Barrie, then follow the road as it goes from paved to gravel to dirt.

If you're looking for somewhere to hide, this is it.

Two

'Wild!' Pike shouts, his foot on the gas. 'We're gonna die!'

We're flying down some unnamed backroad in the deep black of the country night. The world through the windshield is a midnight blur lit only by the shaky beam from our one working headlight. Our speed is infinite, unmeasurable by the cracked speedometer on the dash.

It's freezing out, and this piece of crap's got no heating. You can see Pike's breath steaming as he laughs like a lunatic.

'Hope this thing's got power brakes,' I yell from the back.

Gravel ricochets off the sides of the car like hail.

'What brakes?' Pike fights the shuddering steering wheel. 'We'll stop when we hit something.'

Meet the guys. Pike's behind the wheel. His little

brother Howie's riding shotgun, feet braced up on the dash like that's going to keep him from going through the windshield on impact. I'm in back with Ash – technically not a guy, but she still acts like one.

My heart's ramming against my ribs.

'Buckle up,' Pike calls out.

'There's no seatbelts,' I tell him.

'So, sue the manufacturer. Oh, wait. That's me.'

Pike's the mad mechanic who built this monster from the graveyard of dead and mangled cars out by Sunset Speedway, where they have stock-car races and demolition derbies in the summer.

These roads weren't meant for speed. I'm banging my head off the roof as we're tossed around like loose change in a dryer. The only thing distracting me is Ash's hand on my right knee. She's trying to hang on as we slide around. I've got a shiver running up my thigh that's got nothing to do with the arctic blast outside.

I look over and see Ash laughing in little swallowed gasps. And I know why she's laughing. Because I can feel it too, that roller-coaster freefall that rips the laughs right out of you.

The car fishtails and we do a full doughnut before stopping in the intersection of two empty roads.

In the sudden quiet, I get a grip on Ash's hand. She shakes me off and gives me a little backhand punch in the chest. Like I was making a move, like it wasn't her with a death grip on me.

Pike looks out through the trees at the lights from a building about a hundred yards away.

In the dim interior of the car, the brightest thing is his red hair, catching some of the shine of the headlight reflecting of the snow. Pike's got a regulation army haircut like his father's, just a wide mohawk strip of red bristle. When the sun catches his 'hawk he looks like a lit match.

Pike brushes his hand over it now, thinking.

'Perfect. Wait here.' He pulls a pair of leather gloves out of his pocket.

'Bad idea.' Howie's voice is soft in the nervous hush of the car. 'This is a real bad idea.' He's staring at those lights shining through the trees. 'Let's just go, Pike. Don't do this. Let's go.'

'We'll go, bro. After I'm done.' Pike gets out, letting in a glacial gust. 'Kill the headlight, Howie. But keep the motor running.'

The door slams shut, and we watch in silence as he makes his way through the grey skeletons of the bare trees.

Those lights he's aiming for shine from the windows above the Stony Creek Convenience Store. Run by a fat old guy named Bill Clayton, who lives in the apartment above the store. The place is on its last legs. Peeling paint, with spiderweb cracks in the corners of the windows and sun-faded signs.

I can't make out Pike any more from the shadows.

'What's he gonna do?' I ask.

A shrug from Ash, a head shake from Howie.

What am I doing here?

All Pike told me on the phone was the guys were going out for a spin, and I was coming. I tried to get out of it, saying it was like twenty below outside and I had stuff to do. He told me to grow some balls, they'd be picking me up in half an hour. I asked who *they* was, and when I heard Ash's name I said why not. Me and her, we've got a thing going. Only she doesn't know it yet.

Howie leans forward, breathing hard like he might puke any second. The guy's a walking panic attack.

While we're waiting, let me tell you why Fat Bill's got it coming to him.

When I say *fat*, we're talking close to three hundred pounds of blubber on a five-and-a-half-foot frame. The guy's a midget whale, with yellow teeth and stained fingers from chain-smoking. And he's got a thing for young guys.

Stockboys, he calls them. They don't last long, so he's always got that sun-bleached 'Help Wanted' sign in the window. As pervs go, he's mostly an over-the-clothes groper. From what I hear, Fat Bill even pays you for the 'overtime' afterward. It's not something you're going to brag about after, so there's always fresh meat applying for the job.

Which is where Howie comes in. He wanted to make some extra money to get a new hard drive. Howie was there less than a week when he noticed how Fat Bill was always brushing up against him. But he thought it was because the guy was so huge he couldn't help it, trying to squeeze by in the tight aisles and behind the counter.

I'll skip the details. But anyway, Howie freaked and quit.

Fat Bill put the sign back in the window and hired Jeff Cameron, thirteen years old. But it turned out Jeff's mother is an Ontario Provincial Police officer. And Jeff wasn't going to keep his mouth shut like all the other humiliated kids over the years. Cop Mom went ballistic and now Fat Bill's out on bail and under house arrest till his next hearing. Can't go near schools, can't be alone with kids, can't run his store. The cops have been interviewing other stockboys, finding more victims.

Howie wouldn't talk to them, wouldn't talk to anybody, except Pike. His big brother.

I look past Howie shivering up front, toward the darkened store and the glow from the apartment on top. There's no movement above or below.

We've been idling here a few minutes, and the exhaust is starting to leak in through the rusted holes in the floorboards. The fumes are making me dizzy.

'Can't you kill the motor?' I ask Howie.

He meets my eyes in the rear-view. 'Pike wants a quick getaway.'

'Then I'm cracking open a window.'

I'm reaching for the handle when a thump on the roof makes us all jump. A face appears a couple inches from mine on the other side of the glass. I flinch back from Pike's deranged grin.

'Got ya!' His breath clouds in the frigid air. 'You're dead.'

'Right. And you're nuts.'

He's always sneaking up to scare you.

Pike opens my door and tosses a pile of boxes in my lap. Mars bars. Mr Bigs. Juicy Fruit. 'Don't say I never gave you nothing.'

He slams the door and gets in front.

'Got your favourite, bro.' Pike turns to Howie. 'Kit-Kats.'

I hand that box over to Howie.

Pike takes a piece of jerky out of his pocket and starts gnawing on it.

'How did you get in?' I ask.

'I'm a ninja.'

Ash rolls her eyes. 'A ninja nutcase.'

She cracks the box of Mars bars and takes one. I try a Mr Big.

We sit here chewing, getting high off the fumes. Then Pike hands out some 'scratch-em' lottery tickets.

'We'll split the winnings,' he tells us. 'Eighty-twenty. Me getting the eighty.'

'Can we get out of here first?' I ask.

'Not yet,' Pike says.

'What are we waiting for?' Ash wants to know. 'Let's go.'

'You'll see.' Pike looks off toward the store.

We follow his stare. There's nothing moving in the gloom of the store, or in the apartment above.

The car windows are starting to steam up from our breathing, so Howie wipes a patch of the windshield clear.

'See what? I don't . . .' My words die off.

Because there's a flicker of something inside the store. A flashlight? Or a candle? The light seems to grow.

Not a candle. More like . . .

'Fire in the hole!' Pike laughs.

I open my mouth to say something, but nothing comes out.

'No way. No way,' Howie mumbles.

The flicker expands to a torch-sized glow. Too stunned to even blink, I see the flames start to consume the front counter.

Howie's box of Kit-Kats falls to the floor. He whimpers in the back of his throat.

'Oh, man,' Ash groans. 'What the hell did you do now?'

Pike wipes away the condensation on the glass with his sleeve. 'Just warming things up for Fat Bill.'

'I can't believe you did that?' I say. 'You total psycho.'

A minute passes in shocked silence as we watch the fire eat its way through the store.

'We gotta get out of here,' Ash says.

But Pike doesn't move, hypnotized by the blaze.

Black smoke leaks out through cracks around the door. The place is going up fast, the flames feasting on the old wooden building.

Now a shadow moves past one of the windows in the apartment above.

'Should we uh . . . ?' Should we what? Call the cops? The fire department? Harvest Cove is so tiny they don't even have 911. The fire truck is parked in the garage of the community centre, with one guy who sleeps on the couch inside overnight. If there's an emergency, he calls round to the volunteers and they meet at the scene. By that time there's usually nothing left but charcoal.

A figure shows up around the side of the store. Short and wide. Fat Bill. It looks like he's holding a cellphone to his ear.

Pike snorts happily, shifting into drive. 'Okay. Fun's over. We can go.'

He pulls out slow, with the headlight off. Me and Ash watch the blaze out the rear window. We don't have to worry about Fat Bill seeing us. He's busy watching his life burn down.

'Never again,' I say. 'Never going nowhere with you again. What if he didn't get out, eh?'

'What if he was sleeping or something?' Ash snaps at him. 'You think of that?'

Pike shrugs. 'I guess then we'd have us a pig roast.'

After the glow of the fire is swallowed by the dark, we pick up speed. Pike leaves the headlight off, driving by the faint shine from the sliver of moon playing hide and seek with the clouds. The road's a grey smudge in the blackness.

I feel a trickle of sweat icing down my spine. That Mr Big bar I ate ain't sitting right.

'Man,' says Ash. 'That was extreme.'

'Want to know how I set it?' Pike asks. 'Best way is to always use stuff that's already there at the scene. Then they can't trace anything back to you, right? So I used a Marlboro, just like Fat Bill smokes.'

Now I realize why he brought us all along. Pike loves an audience. He needs someone to shock and awe.

'I left the Marboro on top of a stack of newspapers behind the counter. Even if they find the source, they'll just figure Fat Bill got careless.'

He pauses. Waiting for applause?

But the only sound is the rattle of gravel against the floor of the car.

'And don't think about saying nothing to nobody. Because technically you're all accessories.'

'We didn't do squat,' Ash says.

'You ate the candy bars, didn't you? Stolen goods.'

'We're not accessories to anything,' she says. 'Just witnesses to one of your psychotic episodes.'

He shrugs and keeps on smiling.

I slide around in back, bumping into Ash as we hit teeth-cracking ruts and potholes. The gravel's slick with snow and ice, and the tyres on this junker are nearly bald. It's a miracle we haven't rolled into a ditch.

Just as I think that, Pike makes a sharp turn and the car tilts to the right. For a second we just hang there, riding the edge. I hold my breath, waiting for the world to turn upside-down. But the tyres find some traction and we swing away from the drop.

'Pull over,' Howie moans. 'I'm gonna be sick.'

He's got a real nervous stomach – it's why they call

him Howie the Hurler. The car skids to a stop as Howie throws the door open and leans out.

The sound of him retching makes my own guts start to heave.

Ash nudges me with her elbow. 'Come on, let's go.'

'Go? Go where?' I ask. 'I don't even know where we are.'

'That was Cove Road back there. We can walk home from here.'

'That's like two miles back to the lake. Ever heard of hypothermia?'

'Don't be a pussy,' she tells me. 'We can jog it in no time. Besides, you want to keep riding with him?'

I get out, feeling the arctic wind on my face. I pull up the collar of my leather jacket and yank the zipper to just under my chin. I would have worn a toque, but I didn't want to mess my hair – gotta look slick for Ash. So now my frostbitten corpse will win best hair.

I glance over at Howie, spitting up into the ditch. He's a skinny little stick insect, lost in the bulk of his parka.

Pike climbs out to check on him. 'You okay?'

Howie answers with a groan.

'Come on, bro. Let's get you home. I'll take it slow.'

Ash tugs my sleeve and we start walking.

'See ya, Howie,' Ash says.

He gives her a little wave. 'Sorry, guys. I didn't know he was gonna do that.'

Me and Ash crunch through the icy muck to Cove Road.

'See you in hell,' Pike yells to us. His way of saying bye. Guess he thinks it's funny.

When I glance back I see he's got his arm around Howie's shoulders. Somewhere under the rage there's something human. Barely.

Me and Ash reach Cove Road and start toward the lake. She turns to me.

'Hey, Danny. Wanna race?'

'Okay.' It beats losing my toes to frostbite.

'On three.'

Just as I nod, she barks, 'Three!' – and bursts ahead.

I sprint after her into the inky black.

Three

First time I set eyes on Ash was in the gym on the base. That's Canadian Forces Base Borden. Ash is an army brat, like Pike and Howie. Their fathers are instructors at Borden.

Call it temporary insanity, but I thought it might be a good idea if I took some boxing lessons. Most of the time I feel like hitting something, so I thought I'd learn how. I'm not a rage-aholic or anything, but I've had a real bad run these last couple years, and sometimes you gotta let the beast out before he eats you alive.

So I took it out on the punching bag they kept for the amateurs. Rips in the old leather had been sewn up in half a dozen places, duct tape holding it together in others. You might almost even feel sorry for it. But everything I hated was stuffed into this faceless bag. I worked it till my wrists went numb and I could barely hold the soap in the shower after.

One night at the end of August, a couple of weeks after I arrived in Harvest Cove, I got my chance to hit something real.

'Hey, kid! Get over here,' the voice of Sergeant Owens cut through the gym.

I looked up from my assault on the bag.

'Yeah, you. Blondie,' he said, waving me over to the boxing ring. 'Move it!'

There were some girls sitting in folding chairs nearby, Army brats and townies. They let local civilians come on the base without a hassle. No terrorist has ever heard of Borden. Not exactly a prime target.

The only thing the girls were working out was their mouths. Here to check out the guys, I guess.

My T-shirt was soaked with sweat, and I could feel a fat drop hanging on the end of my nose. My frayed shorts showed off my pale, skinny legs. Real sexy.

'That bag don't hit back,' Owens told me. 'Might as well be jerking off. Let's get you in the ring and see what you've got.' The girls' laughter made my face go red.

He'd shown me some basic moves in the beginners' class. I'd done some soft sparring, but mostly shadow boxing and bag work.

'Put this on.' He handed me a face-guard.

Basically a cushioned helmet, it left my face

open from brow to chin, but blocked any chance of serious damage.

'Remember what I showed you? Jabs, hooks and cuts. Focus on the jabs.'

Owens checked to see my gloves were laced up right, then held the ropes apart so I could slip into the ring. The mat was stained with sweat, brown sprays of old blood and other mysterious substances.

I was trying not to look at the girls, just kind of rolling my shoulders and stretching my neck to loosen up.

'Go easy on the cherry,' the Sarge was telling my opponent, who was stepping into the ring. A cherry is a ring virgin, never had a fight. I winced a little at the name, hearing a spatter of giggles.

Shorter than me by a couple inches, slim but wiry, the other guy was no cherry. He stared at me with intense dark eyes, the left one ringed by an old bruise, yellow at the edges. A Band-Aid stretched over the bridge of his nose. Couldn't see much of his face. Spiky black hair stuck up from the open patch at the top of his headgear. He was wearing a T-shirt with the emblem of the 441st Squadron – the head of a black fox, grinning with hungry white teeth. Below was the squadron's motto: *Stalk and Kill*.

Great, a hardcore brat.

'Protect yourself at all times,' Owens shouted. 'Got it? Good. Touch gloves, and get it on.'

I can do this, I told myself. I've got a couple inches and maybe twenty pounds on him.

We touched gloves. I stepped back and we started to circle each other. *Focus on the jab*, Sarge said. So I closed in, guarding my head with my left and striking out with my right.

My jab hit empty air, where the brat's head had been a millisecond ago. And then—

Then I was staring at one of those mysterious stains on the mat. Up close, because my face was resting on the canvas. I didn't remember anything in between. No impact, no falling. Didn't even see the punch.

'On your feet, soldier.'

I heard the voice past the ringing in my ears. The brat stood over me. His eyes were black pits. *Stalk and Kill*.

My eyes rolled over to the girls, some wincing sympathetically, some shaking their heads. Get up, I thought. But I couldn't tell which way *up* was, like the floor and ceiling had reversed themselves. I clung to the mat to keep from freefalling toward the glare of the lights on the ceiling.

Hardcore helped me up, heaving me vertical and leaning me on the ropes. I expected him to lay me out again with another shot. I tried to lift my gloves, but they hung like dead weights.

'You're all right,' his voice echoed inside my shattered skull. 'Just breathe. In. Out. In. Out.'

'You okay, Blondie?' Sarge called.

I tried nodding, but that sloshed my brains around too much. 'Uh-huh.'

'Rest up a minute,' Sarge said. 'Then hit the showers.'

'Uh-huh.'

I looked from him to Hardcore, who was yanking off his headgear. I blinked, my eyes going wide. He was a *she*.

'How many fingers am I holding up?' she asked, a thin smile stretching her lips.

I stared at the hand she stuck in front of my face. But she still had her gloves on. How many fingers? What?

'It's a joke,' she said.

'Uh-huh.'

She laughed at me a second, then took my arm.

'Come on, killer. Walk it off.'

So that's how I met Ash. Concussion at first sight.

She's toying with me even now, on our night-run down the gravel road back to the lake. Ash lets me close the distance just enough to get my hopes up, then pulls away again.

The crescent moon is hiding behind the clouds. It's not like in the city, where the sky never goes completely dark, just a deep grey. Here, I can barely see the road. Only the paleness of the snow keeps me from falling off the edge into the deeper shadows of the run-off ditches that border the road. Those ruts are filled with tangles of bushes and tumbleweeds of trash frozen in the muck.

All I can see of Ash up ahead is the white blur of her running shoes.

'Move it, Danny!' She's not even winded. 'Catch me, and maybe I'll let you cop a feel.'

I let out a wheezy laugh. Reaching deep down, I gather up enough juice for one burst of speed, and close in on those flying white runners. I stretch my arm out and just graze the back of her jacket with my fingertips.

Then my motor dies. I stagger to a stop.

Gasp. Wheeze. Gasp. Wheeze.

Her shoes keep going, eating up the road. I watch them grow smaller and smaller as I hunch over.

That girl's got lungs. And legs. She can squat two hundred pounds, she keeps telling me. I guess that's a lot. I can't squat *squat*.

At least I'm not cold. I'm dying here, but not from frostbite.

Ash's shoes shrink to white smudges, on the brink of vanishing in the black. Then they stop moving. As I suck in the frigid air those smudges grow bigger. I hear the snow-dusted gravel crunching under them as she jogs back.

'Giving up?' She's not even panting.

'I surrender. What are your terms?'

'It's gotta be unconditional. Your butt is mine.'

'Be gentle,' I wheeze.

'Man, you are such a pussy. But I'll let you live.'

We just walk the rest of the way.

As we get closer to the lake, more cottages start to appear down the roads that branch off. These backroads don't have names, only numbers. We just passed Tenth Line. As we get nearer the water, the Lines tick down to First. The little houses we go by are flickers of light in the winter gloom. Like arctic fireflies. We lean into the wind, speeding the pace.

'Think there's gonna be anything left of Fat Bill's?' I ask.

'Nothing but dust. They'll have to crack the ice on the creek just to get enough water to keep the fire from spreading.'

'Pike should be locked up.' I blow into my cupped hands. 'It's just a matter of time before he adds "spree killer" to his résumé.'

In the darkness I see her shrug. 'Pike has to go around being Pike every second, every day. That's punishment enough. Besides, you ever met his dad? He used to be a drill sergeant. We're talking *intense*. If you had to grow up with that your brains would be scrambled too.'

Through a break in the clouds I see a cluster of stars. Growing up in Toronto, I only ever saw the brightest dozen or so. Out here, the longer you look, the more you see.

We reach the Fifth Line, where Ash turns off for her place.

In the moonlight I can just make out her face. Ash is half-Indian, half-Whitey. But it's the Ojibwa that shows in her features – high cheekbones, strong nose, and a wide mouth with a razor-thin scar on the lower lip, where it got split during one of her fights. When I'm trying to get to sleep lately, restless in the new bed, the new town, I've been thinking about that scar. Thinking about tracing it with my tongue.

'What are you staring at?' Ash asks. Her black eyes are even blacker now in the dark.

'Do I still get to cop a feel?'

She snorts. 'You never caught me.'

'I was close.'

'Close only counts in horseshoes and hand grenades.'

She starts to turn away. But then she grabs me by the collar of my jacket and yanks me in close. Her lips collide with mine. They're shockingly warm, a little chapped, and totally amazing. I reach to put my arms around her, then feel her palms hitting my chest, knocking me back.

'Tell anybody,' she says, 'and I'll kill you.'

I stand stunned, trying to think of something smooth to say.

But then she's gone, sprinting up Fifth Line and leaving me with a great big stupid smile on my face. She's already invisible in the night.

'See you at school,' I say finally, to the empty air.

Four

I stumble on home in the dark, dizzy and delirious.

The wind whips up, cutting right through me. So I start to jog. Back at the house, Dad will have a fire going and the place will be nice and toasty.

He's the caretaker at the Harvest Cove marina, for the off-season, while the owner winters down in Florida. Staying at the small marina house comes with the job. There's a bait and rentals office on the ground floor, with the living space up top.

It's a temp job. Everything's temporary for us. In the spring we'll be moving on to the next town, next life. I'm not going to think about it.

I think about Ash instead.

Back on the first day of school, I was slouching in my seat. Trying to lay low. New place. New faces. Same old same old. Then in walks the boxer-girl who knocked me out. I slouched some more, hoping she didn't see me. I was staring at the floor when a pair of black army boots stopped beside me. I looked up into the dark eyes of my assassin.

'Hey, killer. Ready for a rematch?' She was grinning wide.

Then she grabbed the seat right in front of me, and I had to stare at the back of her neck the rest of the day. A very nice neck, I discovered. And a very nice rest of her too.

Now, licking my lips as I jog, I can taste her Mars bar. So what do I do when I see her at school tomorrow? She's going to act like nothing happened. Guess I'll play along with—

What's the hell is that? Out of the corner of my eye, I catch something big moving in the ditch on the right side of the road. I only get a blurry glimpse before it dips out of sight. Something pale and quick. And big!

Slowing to a walk, I try and focus in the dim light from the crescent moon. Without moving too close to the ditch, I can only make out shades of grey – dark, darker and darkest.

Nothing's dumb enough to be out on a night like this. Like my grandfather used to say – a night not fit for man or beast. Or me.

So I start jogging again. All the insanity that's gone down tonight has got me wired and twitchy. That, and a case of hypothermia, must be toying with my brain.

Coming up to Fourth Line, I pick out the firefly lights of houses set back from the road. The wind brings the smell of burning wood from cottage fireplaces. The taste of smoke in the air teases me with a promise of warmth, making the cold seem even colder.

Passing the Line, I catch a flash of something pale in my peripheral vision, emerging from the right-side ditch to cross Fourth Line, then diving back into the deep shadows of the ditch on the other side.

That was something – definitely something!

I slow to a stop, listening hard. But there's nothing past my own panting, and the hollow whisper of the wind.

Maybe it's just a plastic bag. There's tons of trash blowing around out here, with the local dump only a mile off. But even I know that's weak. It would have to be one huge bag. And whatever it is, it's going against the wind coming off the lake.

Might be one of Mangy Mason's big Alaskan huskies. He's this ancient guy who lives in a rusting trailer on the lakeshore, and lets his dogs run wild. They're harmless, right?

Should I take a peek?

There's a shiver doing laps up and down my spine, from the cold, but also from that phantom itch you get when you feel someone staring at you. Someone, or something.

Take a peek? Hell no!

Just as I'm going to bolt, I hear it. A growl, so deep it shivers my eardrums. Like when you max out the bass on your speakers.

I'm paralysed for a long moment. Then I force myself into a staggering jog, eyes locked on the far side of the road.

I stick to the left side. The edge next to me drops off into the deep dark.

Just as I hit Third, I see it.

And it's no dog.

It's big! And long. And fast. It isn't much more than a blur as it flashes across Third Line and vanishes back in the ditch on the other side. It looks eight to ten feet long.

That can't be right. There's no way.

It's running on all fours, I can tell that much. But running silent as it speeds through the debris in the ditch. Not a sound – no scratch of gravel, cracking twigs. Nothing.

My brain stalls on me.

Stunned, I slow down and try to remember what you do when confronted by a wild animal. Make some noise? Try to scare it off?

Then I hear that growl again, keeping pace with me in the dark. Shivering me bone-deep.

Just run!

At top speed, I can make it home in five minutes.

But that's a long time on a dark road, too far from the nearest house for anyone to hear me scream.

Shut up and run!

I sprint against the wind, arms pumping. My runners chew up the gravel. I'm flying now. Raw fear makes me ignore the burning in my chest as I heave for more oxygen.

Up ahead, I can just make out the light at the end of the road, marking the turnoff for the marina. First Line, finish line.

Crossing Second, I can't help looking back. My vision is blurred with tears from the frigid wind.

Nothing. Nothing. Maybe it's had its fun, and now—

No. Diving from ditch to ditch, it clears the Line without even setting foot on it this time. My eyes must be screwing with me. There's no way anything can move like that. If it's making any noise now, I can't tell past my own gasping and my shoes pounding the snowy gravel.

Focus on the light! Eyes on the prize.

That beacon in the black grows slowly. So slowly. As

I close in on it a few more lights from the marina wink in and out through the trees.

I might just make it.

Then my foot hits a patch of ice. Staggering wildly, I fight to stay vertical. But I go down hard. Hands out, I barely avoid bouncing my head off the ground.

I crouch on my knees, dazed, sucking air into my starving lungs.

I'm dead!

That thing's going to come leaping out of the ditch now that its prey is down.

The growl rises up from the shadows. *Hungry.*

Seconds tick away, marked by the ragged wheeze of my lungs, and the low rumble in the dark.

Is it getting closer? I strain to see. Ten feet in any direction and the black is absolute. I can feel that ghost itch again, the sense of being watched. What's it waiting for?

Wide-eyed, I search the gloom.

There! Its breath rises in wisps over the far edge of the road, like grey smoke. The growl rolls with the rhythm of those breaths.

I get back on my feet, stumble the first few steps and keep going. I fix my gaze on the light at the end.

The wind tries to blow me back, but I fumble on. So close now.

The light-post comes into view, and a glowing circle of snow at its base. Like a little island of safety, of sanity in this crazy night.

I grab the post, leaning against it to face the dark. Outside the edge of my little island, the world disappears.

The turnoff for the marina is a stone's throw away. Two lines of lights run along the twin piers that stretch out onto the frozen lake. I can pick out the yellow glow from the windows of the marina house.

A hundred yards away. A million miles away.

Behind this post, the two run-off ditches tunnel under First Line, merging into one big ditch that feeds into the lake. I shoot a glance over my shoulder. Did that thing get past me?

The night waits. I strain to hear, but there's only the hollow rush of the wind.

I can't just stay here, turning into a human popsicle, pretending this pool of light is any protection.

Then I feel it, the vibration before the growl. I swing my head around.

I almost piss myself. The sound is all around, echoing inside my skull.

Screw this!

One last sprint to the house. My only shot. But is that thing still in the ditch? Or circling my little island, waiting to take me down?

The growl turns my legs to rubber.

Come on! You can do this. Ready? On three.

Three!

I push off and burst down First Line.

Just as I cross the border from the light into the black, a pale blur rushes at me in an avalanche of speed.

Then it hits! The impact knocks me off the road. As I tumble, the black ditch yawns wide to take me. I'm falling into nothing.

Then the ground hits me like a frozen hammer. My left shoulder slams against ice-hard muck, my head cracking with an explosion of red sparks behind my eyes.

I slide to the bottom of the ditch.

What? What? What?

Focus! Gotta focus.

But my brain's whipping around in a blender. I try and slow that nauseous spinning.

It's so dark. Like the whole world has been snuffed out. Like I'm blind.

Rolling onto my back, my shoulder screams in protest.

I catch some light leaking down from the post on the road above. The bulb is just visible over the rim of the ditch, like a moonrise.

I'm staring at that glow, the only thing keeping me

from getting swallowed by the black, when a shadow moves across it.

The night is dead quiet. No wind, no rustle of tree branches. Nothing but the thud of my pulse in my eardrums. The shadow has melted into the dark again.

I look at the wall of the ditch. How fast can I climb it? And what's going to be waiting for me up there when I get out?

But I have to try. Or I'm dead meat.

I push up on my elbows, about to make my move.

Then the light is blocked out by a huge form leaping into the ditch.

The ground shudders under me when it lands.

What I'm seeing can't be real.

It's on all fours – but its shape is almost *human*. The thick trunks of its arms rise to hugely muscled shoulders. There's a torso and ribcage wide as a horse's, ending in legs that are flexing now, ready to pounce.

The air is electric. Every hair on my body is standing straight.

What gives it even more of a human look is its bald *skin*. No fur. Ghost-pale, like something that's never seen the sun.

It moves toward me. I scramble backwards on my butt, scratching my palms on the branches and trash frozen in the mud.

With one step the beast closes the distance.

I freeze, propped on my elbows, staring up at its head looming over me.

Not human, but some twisted freak-show nightmare. The face is deformed, like a reflection in a warped mirror, with the nose pinched tight into two long slits, and the mouth stretched so wide its edges touch the flattened bony curves of the ears. There's a broad hump of a forehead, and jutting brows above the eyes.

And the eyes. Nowhere near human. They gleam silver in the weak light from the road above. Like perfect round mirrors, they bulge from under the brows, the size of softballs in that huge white head.

My gut twists, the breath shivering out of me.

It sniffs at me, steam trailing from the nostril slits, then rises up on its back legs to its full height.

Towering over me, its wide mouth opens with a roar that flattens me. Just when I think my eardrums are going to rupture, it cuts off.

Holding my hands up, I press my spine deeper into the muck.

The beast falls back down on all fours, quaking the ground.

This is not happening. Not real.

It lowers its head, and I see reflections of myself in those silver eyes, tiny as an insect.

That mouth gapes open. And I see the teeth.

Gleaming rows of eight-inch teeth, like long thin blades. Those vicious jaws stretch farther apart, showing more, row after row of curved white blades reaching all the way down into its throat.

My arms are frozen in place, hands held up to shield me. Can't shut my eyes. Can't even blink.

A tongue emerges from the mass of teeth, like an albino eel. It stretches all the way out of the mouth and hangs above me. On its tip is what looks like a scorpion's sting.

In a whipping blur the tongue stabs the back of my hand with its sting, so deep it feels like it's going to come right through my palm.

A jolt of pain shoots up my arm and into my chest, a hundred icy needles jabbing into my heart.

I get a blinding flash of white light.

Then deepest black.

My eyes open on nothing. I blink them wide, straining to see. I try moving my head, wincing as a jolt of pain pierces my skull.

But past the pain, I see something now. The sliver of a crescent moon hangs above me, white as a tooth. I make out walls of earth on both sides of me, stretching up a good eight feet.

33

A grave! I'm in a grave, waiting to be buried. I'm dead!

I hyperventilate puffs of steam into the night air. Then my breath catches in my throat.

Wait! I'm still breathing. The frosty air smells like dead leaves and dirt.

Slow and aching, I sit up. I see more light now, shining down from the post on the road.

In a rush, everything comes back.

I crawl onto my knees and do a quick scan of the ditch. I'm alone. Somehow I manage to get to my feet.

I brace myself with a few deep breaths, then stumble over to the wall of the ditch. I search the shadows for a handhold, find a cluster of roots and climb up. I heave myself over the edge of the ditch and roll onto the ground.

Getting on my feet, I peer into the night till I find the marina lights through the trees. Then I lurch into a jog.

I don't look left or right, and definitely not back. My shoes crack through iced puddles. The uneven ground tries to trip me up.

There's the house. So close.

Thirty feet. Twenty.

I can sense that thing behind me, insanely quick and

huge. Reaching out to claw my back and swat my legs out from under me.

Ten feet.

I lunge at the back door and twist the knob with my frozen fingers. Thank God nobody locks their doors around here.

Slamming it shut with my shoulder, I turn the deadbolt.

Can't believe it. I'm still breathing.

There's a window beside the door. I pull back the drapes and peer out into the dark, leaning away from the glass, half expecting that beast to crash through.

But the night is empty. At least that's what my eyes tell me.

Only I know better.

Five

Sleep. The big eraser.

Cutting off one day from the next. Making yesterday history. Giving you enough distance to shake your head and say – what was I thinking?

Last night was a really bad dream, a psychotic nightmare. Judging by the headache hammering my skull to the beat of my heart, I might even have a concussion.

My memories are broken in pieces. What's real, and what's hallucination?

I've been lying in bed here trying to glue the pieces back together. I keep getting these crazy images flashing in my head, of this massive, albino-skinned thing. Of silver, mirrored eyes. And teeth. Endless rows of blade-like teeth.

These images are scattered like shrapnel in my head. Jagged pieces that won't fit together in any *sane* way.

I cracked my head pretty bad – that I'm sure of.

The rest must be delusions caused by head trauma.

I must have looked like an escaped mental patient racing down the road last night, wild and breathless. Chased by some stray dog I hallucinated into a freak-show monster from hell.

Blame it on the concussion, or just the weirdness of the night – the death-defying joyride, the overdose of exhaust fumes, the fire, the kiss.

Right. The kiss. I didn't imagine that too, did I?

Swinging out of bed, I set my feet on the frigid floor and shiver. The furnace in this place is moody, some nights sweating you out from under the covers, other times leaving you to freeze. I put my hand on the radiator. Man, you could make ice cubes on this thing.

Parting the drapes, I find my window frosted over, leaving only a small clear patch in the centre. The lake looks grim in the grey morning light, with snow devils chased across its frozen surface by the wind.

I'm about to turn away and steal another half-hour of sleep when I see a figure in a parka walking along one of the wooden docks, past boats hibernating under their tarps, locked in the ice. The wind pushes back the parka hood and I recognize the orange wool cap underneath.

What a lunatic! Sun's barely up and Dad's out there in the polar chill. He's a borderline insomniac, can't sleep more than a couple hours a night, since . . .

Since Mom died.

No! Not going to think about that.

I stand with one foot on top of the other to minimize contact with the hardwood ice rink of my room. I'd love to slip back under the sheets and find the sweet spot, the little hollow of leftover body heat. But if I crawl back in now, I ain't coming out till spring.

Before hitting the bathroom I have to kick away the doorstop I wedged under my door last night to keep out demon dogs and other delusions. I couldn't get to sleep until I'd checked the window latch a half-dozen times, and even looked in the closet to make sure it was unoccupied.

I shake my head at my insanity, but the ache inside my skull flares up. Take it slow.

Shuffling down the hall, I decide it must have been some overgrown stray dog. A Great Dane on steroids. Or maybe a moose. I hear they still wander into town sometimes, in the winter months when good grass is hard to find. Do moose growl? Chased by a moose, I have to laugh at that.

Skipping a shower – takes too long for the water to heat up – I scrub most of the debris off my teeth and squint in the mirror to make sure I still have a reflection. Feeling like one of the undead this morning.

Last night I checked myself out for bite marks, blood

or claw tracks. Any physical proof of my hallucination. But all I had were minor scratches on my palms from crawling out of the ditch.

In one of those nightmare flashes, a snake-like tongue lashes out and stabs me in the back of my hand with some kind of sting. But the only mark I find there is a tiny blue dot, like I got jabbed by a pen. I've got freckles scarier than that.

Dad's back by the time I drag myself to the kitchen.

'Hey, Danny,' he says, tossing his cap on the table. 'Feeling better?'

'Better than what?'

'You seemed kind of shaky last night.'

Dad was crashed on the couch watching TV when I got in. I was shivering so bad all I could manage was to stutter one-word answers to where I'd been, what I'd been up to. *Nowhere. Nothing. Night.*

'Ten below will do that to you.' In the light of day I feel stupid about my mad dash.

He goes over and opens the fridge. Dad's side of the family is what they call *Black Irish*, meaning the black hair and eyes. He's a big guy, played linebacker on his high school football team. Wish I'd gotten more of his muscle and less of Mom's delicate bird bones. I've got her pale skin too, her blond hair, snub nose and blue eyes.

'Eggs?' he asks.

'Sure. Scrambled.' Like my brains.

I grab a Coke from the fridge. Caffeine – quick!

The smell of eggs and melting cheese fills the kitchen.

When I head off for school, he'll be back out checking stuff, fixing things that don't need fixing. Now that it's December there isn't much action at the marina. Just patching up the walkway on the main dock, tying down the tarps covering the boats, renting out the occasional snowmobile or ice-fishing hut. But he'll keep himself busy, so he won't think about anything deeper than the weather, what's for dinner and the hockey game on TV tonight.

'It's gonna hit twenty below,' he tells me, 'with the wind chill.'

'Another day in paradise.' I glance at the frosted window over the sink.

Dad hands me my plate. 'There's a game on tonight. Leafs are playing.'

'Sounds good,' I mumble around my eggs.

No way I want to be out again after dark. Only problem is the sun sets just after four, when school lets out. And night falls fast around here with no city lights to hold it back. Maybe I can bum a ride off Pike.

'Forgot to tell you,' Dad says, tossing some slices of rye in the toaster. 'Your aunt Karen called when you were out last night.'

'What she want?'

'You know,' Dad shrugs, watching the toaster with his back to me. 'To talk.'

'So did you? Talk?' I already know the answer.

He waits for the toast to pop up. 'I wasn't in a talking kind of mood.'

Dad never is, when it comes to Mom's sister.

'Anyway,' he says. 'You should give her a call.'

I push my eggs around on my plate. Talking to Aunt Karen kills me. She looks so much like Mom it hurts. On the phone, her voice even sounds like Mom's. It screws with my brain, and my heart.

Maybe it does the same for Dad.

I'm thinking too much. Quit that!

The toast pops up, and so do I, leaving my plate in the sink.

'Gotta go.'

I escape before we start showing emotions. Not something we do real well.

I go get dressed, grab my gloves and my pack. I'm walking back through the kitchen when I hear a car pull up outside.

Dad peeks through the clear patch on the frosted

window over the sink, then ducks his head down. 'What's she doing here?'

'Who?'

'I think she saw me.' Dad stays clear of the windows. 'Who?'

'That woman from the Red and White.'

Andrea. She runs the Red and White grocery store, the only one in Harvest Cove. Dad's been driving all the way to Barrie for supplies just to keep clear of her.

It started last month when Andrea was bagging up our stuff.

'You staying the winter?' she asked. 'I thought maybe you guys were just summer folks.'

'No,' Dad grunted. 'We're staying on.'

'Deer hunting season starts up soon. Or are you sticking around for the ice fishing?'

She was taking her time with the bagging, doing some fishing of her own. Dad wasn't taking the bait though.

So I jumped in. 'We're caretaking at the marina, over the winter.'

Dad looked at me like I'd just betrayed a national secret.

Andrea paused in her packing. 'Oh, right. Ray Mitchell's place. First frost hits and he's on a plane to Florida.'

Dad nodded reluctantly. 'Guess so.'

'Well, you need anything special, I'll order it in. Is it just the two of you?'

Dad looked cornered.

'Just the two of us,' I said.

Then Dad was heading for the door.

'Be seeing you,' she called after us.

And she has been seeing us ever since, popping by for any reason she can make up. She's pretty enough, maybe a little on the heavy side, with long dark hair and nice laugh lines around her eyes.

Now there's a knock at the door downstairs.

'I'm not here,' Dad tells me.

'What if she saw you?' I try to swallow back a smile.

Dad winces. 'Just say, um . . . tell her . . .' He looks to me for help.

I shrug. 'I got nothing.'

'Thanks! Thanks a lot.'

I start down the stairs. 'Come on,' I call back. 'She's harmless.'

'Yeah, right.' But he follows me down to the front door.

I open it, letting in an icy gust. Andrea looks way too bright-eyed for this early in the morning. She's got a warm smile, holding a bag from the Red and White.

'Hey there, Danny. Where's your toque?'

I hate wearing those wool caps. They get my hair all staticky, make it stand up so I look like a retard.

'Don't think I need it.'

'You know, you lose eighty per cent of your body heat through your head,' she says.

'Good to know.' I step out. 'See you later.'

I glance back at Dad with a 'good luck' look. Walking away, I hear an awkward silence before Dad says:

'So, what brings you out?'

Whatever brought her, I'll hear about later. I abandon Dad to the torture of small talk with a friendly local.

In the blue light of morning Harvest Cove looks innocent and harmless.

Not a soul in sight. No monsters either.

Looking down, I see my shoeprints in last night's snow. I follow them back down the marina turnoff, scanning the ground for any sign of my beast. But all I find are tyre treads, and my own marks.

I walk up to the light-post where I huddled last night.

From here the landscape stretches out flat for miles, the sun glaring off the snow. Only the caws of crows in the bare trees break the silence.

I can pick out the tracks I made running up to the post in a blind panic, criss-crossed by a few new tyre treads.

Nothing more. No monster tracks.

I stare into the big ditch behind the post. That's a deep drop. Lucky I didn't break anything. Except my brain!

From up here, it's hard to see much. I think I can spot where I fell and skidded to the bottom. The snowcover is scraped away, showing the stiff brown muck beneath.

Can't see any sign, print or track of anything but me.

Should I take a closer look?

Turning in the intersection, I do a quick three-sixty, packed snow crunching underfoot. The roads stretch white and empty into the distance, running through fields of unbroken powder.

I have to know. How much of last night was real?

So I go around the side, where I climbed out of my moonlit grave not ten hours ago. I use the same roots I grabbed on to then to get down now, my backpack swinging on my shoulder.

I recognize the tread of my runners pressed in the snow, and follow them to the cleared patch where I fell. The ground is like concrete. If my skull collided with this, you can't blame my poor brain for freaking.

I glance up at the sound of a car whipping past on the road above.

Maybe it was a car that hit me last night, knocked

me airborne and down into the ditch. It was so fast. I don't remember hearing a motor, or seeing headlights. But I was in a blind panic. Who knows?

If there was a struggle here, you'd expect the ground to be torn up. Or *something*.

Enough! Let's go.

But then I see it.

About four feet from the cleared patch where I fell there are some marks in the snow. I crouch for a closer look.

There's a row of holes stabbed through the light snow into the frozen mud underneath. They almost look like they were made with an ice-pick. I count eight of them, curved in an upside-down 'U' shape, cleanly jabbed into the powder.

Claw marks? Eight of them means, what, eight toes? That can't be right.

Behind these holes, the snow has been pressed down to an icy crust by something heavier than me. The impression stretches long and wide. Pacing it off with my own size-ten runners, I could fit four of them inside this – this what? Pawprint? Footprint?

What am I seeing here?

Who knows? But what I do know is I wasn't totally out of my mind last night. There was some kind of animal down here with me.

I find another track. Identical to the first, this one is set on the other side of where I'd been laid out.

I get a flash of that thing leaning over me. The gaping mouth. Razor teeth. And a long pale tongue striking out.

Panic works my heart like a speed bag. My breath comes in short gasps. I'm back there again – in the dark.

I hunch over and force myself not to think. Just breathe. A cold sweat runs icicle fingers down my back. Takes a minute before I can get a grip.

Time to go.

But first I pull out my cellphone and take a few quick shots of the tracks, setting my own foot beside them to show how big they are.

I'm a city boy, so I don't know squat about wildlife. But I can't imagine any kind of animal leaving tracks like these. Whatever left them was real, though. This was no nightmare.

I pocket my cell and climb the overhanging roots. Back on top, I breathe a little easier.

Already late for school, I start to jog, burning off some adrenalin.

I glance over my shoulder a few times as I head for the turnoff for school. That ghost-itch feeling of being watched by hidden eyes is gone. Still . . .

But there's nothing out here except blowing snow

under a steel-blue sky. The big empty. So big it could swallow you without a trace. So empty, nobody's going to hear you scream.

My headache throbs to the beat of my feet, snow crunching under my runners.

None of this makes sense.

What I need is a bigger brain. And I know where to find one.

Six

Like a name on an old grave, the date carved into the cornerstone of the school has been erased by a century of hard winters.

But the place was made to last, a stubborn, red-brick building that has survived everything from fires to blizzards, to a tornado that touched down where the baseball diamond sits right behind it.

I'm running through the outfield now, making for the back door. Fifteen minutes late.

I throw the door open and step from the chill into the dusty dry heat. I stand there shivering a moment, my ears tingling back to life. Then I climb the stairs to the first floor.

There are only three classrooms in the school, with grades seven through twelve. We're talking *small* town. So my class has the eleventh and twelfth graders squashed together, all fourteen of us. It makes for kind

49

of a split-personality classroom. It's either this or you take the forty-minute drive into Barrie every day.

I make the top of the stairs and I'm just starting down the hallway when I see the cop outside my classroom, talking quietly with Miss Mercer.

I stop dead. My confusion and panic over what I found in the ditch drop away.

Their backs are turned to me. They haven't spotted me yet.

This looks bad. Somebody must have seen us last night at the fire, or recognized Pike's car. We're in deep crap.

Should I take off? Before they see me.

What good will that do? Then I'll be the only one missing from class. They'll put me on Harvest Cove's Most Wanted.

But, come on, I didn't do anything. Wasn't even driving. And there's no way eating a Mr Big makes you an accessory to arson.

So I start down the hall again. Dead man walking.

They both glance over.

'Sorry I'm late,' I tell Miss Mercer. 'You know, the snow.'

A weak excuse, but she just nods. 'Take your seat, Danny. We'll be in in a second.'

Avoiding eye contact with the cop, I slip past into the room.

A low mumble of conversation inside pauses momentarily when I come in. I catch Ash's gaze first, and make a little head gesture toward the door, mouthing 'cop'. She gives a tiny nod. Howie's got his head buried in his arms on the desktop. I glance at Pike, who sits right behind me. He's got a crazy smile, like this is funny.

I drop my pack on the floor and plant myself at my desk, staring at the back of Ash's neck. Everybody's talking, except my row by the window, with Ash in front and Howie bringing up the rear.

Death row. We sit silent, waiting for the verdict.

Miss Mercer walks in with the cop. 'This is Officer Baker, with the Ontario Provincial Police. Listen up now. Officer?'

He looks us over. He's got wolfman eyebrows – big, black and bushy – giving him a natural scowl. Which he focuses on us.

I hold my breath. He knows! In the sudden quiet, I think I hear Howie sniffling at the back.

'Some of you may already know why I'm here.'

I stare at my desk. Here it comes.

'Raymond Dyson, a student in the tenth grade class at this school, has gone missing.'

I let my breath out, too stunned to be relieved.

'As you may be aware, he's been receiving treatment

at the Royal Victoria Hospital in Barrie. He's in pretty rough shape, suffering from some kind of infection. Anyway, he seems to have wandered away from the hospital last night, and we need your help finding him. He may be confused, or delirious. Has anybody seen or heard from Raymond in the last twelve hours?'

Nothing from the class.

Then Janey Carlyle sticks up her hand.

'Yes?' asks Officer Baker.

'Okay, I heard he has rabies or something,' she says. 'Someone said he got bit by one of Mangy Mason's dogs.'

Another girl jumps in with: 'No, it was a raccoon.'

That opens the floodgates.

'I heard it's West Nile virus.'

'No. It's Lyme disease. You get it from ticks.'

'It's a superbug. The kind that resists antibiotics.'

'They had him in quarantine. He's contagious.'

Baker's scowl deepens. 'Enough! There's no need to speculate. He's not contagious. We just need to locate Raymond before he gets himself hurt or frozen to death. Keep your eyes open. You see or hear anything, call the OPP, Barrie detachment. The kid's very sick, and needs to be back at the hospital.'

Now he holds up a sheet of paper with a photo of Ray. 'I'm sure most of you know what Raymond looks like, but I'm going to leave some flyers. Our number is at the bottom.'

He turns to Miss Mercer, who says, 'Thank you, officer. We'll definitely keep our eyes open.'

Then the cop leaves and I sag back in my seat.

The teacher pins one of the flyers up on the bulletin board. Ray Dyson. We just call him *Raid*, after the bug spray. It suits him – that guy's toxic. A real psycho bully. He makes Pike look sane. Last time I saw Raid was a couple days ago when they took him off to the hospital.

The day he went nuts.

I was sitting at my desk, dozing off as Miss Mercer went on about the retreating glaciers and the end of the Ice Age. Heading into the third week of a killer cold snap, it was looking like the Ice Age was back with a vengeance.

'What the hell's that?' Pike blurted out.

I snorted awake with the rest of the class.

'Watch your language!' Miss Mercer told him.

Pike was staring out the window.

Right in the middle of the frost-covered baseball diamond, there was a guy standing in his underwear. No socks or shirt. Just briefs and bare skin.

Miss Mercer peered out the window with us. 'Good lord.'

Then she made for the door, telling everybody to

stay in their seats. Which nobody did, of course.

The crowd by the windows watched as the guy in his tidy-whities flashed his pale body to the trees and the snow.

'Who is that?' Ash asked.

'Ray Dyson,' Howie mumbled. 'Raid.'

I don't know how he recognized him from that distance, but Howie always knows the right answer.

Raid wasn't hugging himself against the cold, like you might think. He actually had his arms held out wide, like he was waiting to hug something.

A minute later, Mr Cunningham, who teaches the ninth and tenth grade class, was running out to the diamond, with Miss Mercer hustling after him. Mr Cunningham tried talking to Raid. But he just stood there, arms out like he was going to fall back and make a snow angel any second. They managed to get him walking finally, back toward the school, with Miss Mercer gathering up the clothes and shoes he'd stripped off.

That was the last we saw of Raid. Word was he'd been bit by some stray dog, bat, raccoon, coyote or deer tick, depending on who you talked to. They took him to the hospital for rabies shots, and observation I guess.

Now, as Miss Mercer tells us to turn to our Canadian history texts, I stare at the face on the bulletin board.

Ray Dyson. The photo they used for the flyer might be one of his mug shots the cops have on file. He's a local legend, local loser. Dark little pit-bull eyes glare out from under his caveman brows, cheeks and forehead cratered with acne. Greasy hair hangs down over his eyes. More muscles than brain cells, he's already failed a couple grades, or he'd be in our class.

I picture him escaped and running wild through the snowy fields, in some hallucinatory fever. Wearing a flimsy hospital gown, out in a ten below chill, he's not going to last long. I almost feel sorry for the guy. But he's one missing person nobody's going to miss much.

Still, I hope he's holed up somewhere. You don't want to be wandering around here at night.

'Can I tell you something?' Howie's working on his third doughnut.

We're having lunch at the Tim Hortons fast-food dive. It's either that, or eat at the tables they set up in the gym. The school's too small for a real cafeteria. So we walk the three blocks here most days, get a sandwich or soup. Or in Howie's case, doughnuts and Coke.

'Sure,' I tell Howie, chowing down on my meatball sub. 'What's up?'

'I don't know if it means anything . . .'

'Try me.'

He looks around to see nobody's listening. Ash is in the can, and Pike's over at the counter.

Howie sips his drink. 'The day Ray Dyson freaked, I sort of ran into him in the washroom. I was taking a leak, when I heard this voice. Whispering. I thought I was alone in there, so I kind of jumped and wizzed on my shoe. This is probably more detail than you need.'

'Probably.'

'Anyway, so I finished up and saw there was one stall door closed. I could see his shoes under. At first I couldn't tell what he was saying. So I went closer. And he was whispering: "It's sleeping. It's sleeping."'

'What's sleeping?' I ask Howie.

'I don't know. I'm just telling you what he was saying. So then he goes like: "Thought I got away. Thought I got away. But it was just letting me think that."' Howie raises his eyebrows. 'So, by then I'm thinking this guy's playing with me. Screwing with my head. I couldn't tell who it was yet. But everybody knows how jumpy I am.'

Jumpy is putting it nice. He's a panic attack waiting to happen.

'I ask him through the door – *you okay?* And he doesn't answer, but he says like: "When it wakes up, it'll come for me." So I'm pretty freaked out. Then the door opens and I see who it is. I was in Raid's class last year. Before I skipped, I was one of his favourite victims.'

He's already skipped two grades, which is why he's in twelfth with his brother. Howie's scary smart.

'By then, I'm sure Raid's playing mind games with me. But man, he didn't look good. He looked . . . *blue*. Like he just walked out of a freezer. So I say to him – *maybe you should go home, you don't look so hot*. But he's not even hearing me, not even seeing me. He just keeps going: "It's sleeping. Sleeping."'

Howie finishes off his doughnut, shaking his head.

'What?' I ask. 'That's it?'

'Pretty much. I didn't know what to do. I said his name a few times, trying to snap him out of it, get him to wake up. But then he walked out. The last thing I heard him say was: "Nowhere to hide. Nowhere."'

Pike drops his tray on the table. 'Who can't hide? What are we talking about?'

'Ray Dyson, freaking out,' I tell him. 'You know, on the diamond.'

'That was one strip show nobody needed to see.' Pike looks over at what Howie's eating. 'You gotta have some real food, bro. Can't live on that. Eat some of my sandwich.' He drops half in front of Howie.

Hard to believe they came from the same womb. It's like when Pike was born, he took all the muscle, anger and balls, so there was none left when his brother came along.

Their father, former drill sergeant and now a captain assigned to Base Borden, thought it would be a great idea to name his boys after weapons. A *pike*, Howie tells me, is a kind of spear with a long shaft and a nasty, razor-edged head. *Howie* isn't short for Howard, but for *Howitzer*, a type of artillery gun that fires heavy-calibre shells.

The weapon-naming thing suits Pike. But Howie wouldn't hurt a fly – the fly would hurt him.

Ash comes back, crowding up against me in the booth – not that I mind. 'You get my lemonade?'

I pass it over. 'You're not eating?'

'Nah. Gotta make weight for my fight tomorrow. I don't drop two pounds by then, that bumps me up a class and I'll have to fight with the middleweights. Those bitches are fierce.'

In Barrie, they're hosting the Canadian Junior Boxing regionals. If Ash wins tomorrow, she's got a shot at going to Toronto for the next round of eliminations.

'How you going to lose two pounds in a day?' I ask.

'Sweat it off. Got this thermal suit I work out in. You wear it in the sauna, you can lose four pounds easy.' She stares at Howie's sandwich with lust. 'You guys coming to the fight?'

'Course we are,' Pike says. 'Gotta get you a name, though. Something catchy. Like, I was thinking – *The*

58

Indian Assassin. Or how about – *Red Death?*'

Ash glares at him. 'Maybe something a little less, I don't know, racist.'

Pike grabs one of Howie's doughnuts. 'My genius is wasted on you slobs.'

Something that's been bothering me since the cop showed up this morning comes back to me.

'So why were you smiling?' I ask Pike. 'When that cop was out in the hall? Before we found out he was just there about Raid, and not, you know . . . last night?'

Pike gives me a sample of that lunatic grin now. 'It tickled me. The way you guys were all pissing your pants.'

Ash drains her lemonade and belches. Her warm leg is pressed up against mine in the tight booth. She throws off a lot of heat. After the kiss last night, I'm still kind of stunned. Where do we go from here?

'What happened with those meds you were taking?' she says to Pike. 'For your anti-social, insane homicidal rages.'

He shrugs. 'I quit them. They made me numb. Weak. I lost my edge. No edge – no Pike.'

It feels like I've known these guys a lot longer than the few months I've been here. The thing with army brats is they're drifters too, moving from base to base, town to town. And drifters never fit in, except with each

59

other. Guess that's why we're so tight, so quick. But they pretty much grew up together. I'm still the new recruit.

Howie mumbles something.

'Huh?' I ask.

'Wonder where Ray is now,' he says.

'Frozen stiff.' Pike licks powdered sugar off his thumb. 'They're not gonna find him till the spring thaw. Then they'll find him by the stink.'

Howie turns a little green.

Wish I had him alone, so I could show him my cell shots of the monster tracks. See what he makes of them. But right now there'd be too many questions.

Looking out the window I watch the wind blow swirling snow devils down the road.

Not fit for man or beast.

But maybe there's one beast out there who doesn't mind the chill.

Seven

I'm sitting on the couch, half watching the hockey game, half trying to finish the chapter I'm reading. I dog-ear the page, close the paperback and squeeze it to see how much there is left. I've barely made a dent.

Frankenstein. Sounds action-packed. Some monster pieced together from a dozen corpses, brought to life with a bolt of lightning. In the movie there was a massive body count. Decapitations. Stranglings. Miscellaneous slaughter. But the book – anaesthesia. And it's written in this English nobody talks any more.

Right now, some guy's been writing a letter for the last ten pages. This guy never heard of postcards? Enough! Less scribbling, more killing!

Miss Mercer gave us a choice for our English essays. We could do one of the Romantic poets (gag!), *Frankenstein*, or some epic poem called *The Rime of the*

Ancient Mariner. The Rime's about some crazy guy who stops strangers to tell them what's haunting him. No thanks, I'm haunted enough already. So I took Frankie, expecting killing sprees.

But I'm twenty pages in and the only thing that's died so far is my brain, from boredom.

Dad's on the other end of the couch, drinking a beer. I count the empties on the coffee table. Only his third. If he hits six, I know he's in a mood. Trying to *drown the demon*, as he likes to say.

Looking up from the empties, I notice something new on the middle shelf of the fishing trophy case. Sitting between two mounted trout is a midget ceramic Christmas tree with tiny lights.

'What the hell is that?' I point at the tree, with its lights blinking red, green and blue.

'That woman from the Red and White, Andrea, thought it would bring some cheer to the place. Tis the season, eh?'

I go over and take a look at the incredibly tacky, incredibly sad little tree.

'You plugged it in?' I'm surprised he didn't banish it to the basement the second she left.

Dad takes a swig of beer. '*She* plugged it in. I'm afraid to go near it. My heart might start expanding like the Grinch's, and before I know it I'll be shouting out carols, running down the street screaming – *it's a wonderful life.'*

I stare at the little lights, winking on and off. 'That's the most depressing thing I've ever seen. We should take it out back and shoot it. Put it out of its misery.'

Christmas decorations were always Mom's thing. She was a wizard with tinsel, stringing lights up everywhere, spraying fake snow in the windows. We even had a doormat that 'Ho Ho Ho-ed' when you stepped on it.

Me and Dad don't do Christmas any more. A few presents on the day, okay. But unwrapped, no cards.

Now I shake my head. If Dad's not touching this sad little tree, I'm not either.

'Hey, I need you to give me a hand in the morning,' he says, eyes on the game. 'Before school. I have to tow a couple huts out onto the ice. Got tourists coming to try out the fishing. I'll give you ten bucks for an hour's work.'

'That's like minimum wage. You running an arctic sweatshop here?'

'Can you have an *arctic* sweatshop?' He peers into the bottom of a newly emptied empty.

I shrug. 'Sure. Bunch of Eskimos making Gucci knock-offs.'

He smiles and sets the bottle down with the others.

'Shouldn't call them Eskimos, you know. It's like calling a black guy *coloured*. *Eskimo* is what white people always called them, because *they* thought the name meant "raw meat eater". Doesn't even really mean that, but that's what everybody thought. You want to be called "raw meat eater"?'

'Guess not. Wouldn't get many dates.'

Dad's showing his Irish side. I grew up on stories of how the Irish were treated like dirt back in the old country. Dad had this postcard framed on the wall when I was little, of a sign you used to see outside English pubs that said: 'No Dogs. No Blacks. No Irish.' They were the lowest of the low. So he's always sticking up for other screwed-over minorities.

'They call themselves *Inuit*,' he says. 'Just means "The People".'

I yawn. On TV, the Leafs are losing. Again! And the curse goes on.

'Yeah? Well, this *people* is hitting the sack. Gotta be up at dawn. The old man's a slavedriver.'

I go down the hall to my room.

'Night, Danny-boy.'

He calls me that when he's tired, a little sad, or a little drunk. It's from some old Irish song, where a mother calls out for her son, who's wandered far away, to come home. Her Danny Boy. Dad wouldn't be calling me that if he wasn't three beers into a buzz. See, Mom's the one who named me. The one who used to sing the song to me when I was little. It kills me when he calls me that.

My room is one of the guest bedrooms the owner of the marina rents out to tourists in the summer. It's decorated by someone with a serious fish fetish. Framed photos, yellowing behind the glass, show prize-winning catches from years past. Guys in angling gear holding up trout, bass and carp. For me, fish come frozen and battered, in stick form.

Above the bed there's a historical photo of ice-cutters out on the frozen lake. That's going back a century, when Lake Simcoe Ice was big business. Before people had fridges, the only way to get ice was from nature. Ice from the lake was tested as one hundred per cent pure, and was shipped by train halfway across the country. The photo shows a team of horses out on the frozen lake, pulling a long scraper to smooth the surface for cutting into blocks. The ice *harvest* is what gave the cove its name.

I toss *Frankenstein* on the little desk by the window. My cellphone sits there beside the lamp. I've gone over those shots I took of the tracks a dozen times now. And I'm still clueless. I thought about just e-mailing them to Howie, with a little note saying: *look what I found, what do you think made these?*

Howie's a walking encyclopedia. His room is like a museum. He's got a library bigger than the school's, and all kinds of animal bones, bird feathers, rocks, shells, and jars of 'specimens' collected from around the Cove.

A 'mad scientist' in training.

But I hold back from sending them. That whole twisted scene down in the ditch is still broken up in jagged little pieces in my mind. Still unbelievable. God, I wish I'd never found those tracks. Then I could write it all off as some hallucination caused by a concussion.

Finding the tracks was bad enough. But when I show them to Howie, that'll make everything real.

Tomorrow, I tell myself. I'll show Howie.

I kill the light and crawl in bed.

Seems like as soon as I get used to a new bed, we're on the move again. This one's got a sprung spring on the left that pokes me in the ribs all night. So I huddle on the right, and beat my pillow into submission before resting my head. The radiator makes muffled whispering sounds as air moves through the pipes.

I remember my old bed, where nobody had ever slept but me. Back in Toronto, another life ago. Mom always used to tuck me in, even when I was way too old for it. I'd fake sleep, feeling her pull the covers up to my shoulders and making sure my feet didn't stick out. *Don't want your feet to catch cold* – she'd say, when I was little – *then they'll start sneezing all over the place.* And she'd give them a tickle before turning out the light. Some nights, near the end, I'd fake sleep for a different reason. To hide from her. I could feel when she came to sit on the edge of my bed, late at night. Feel her weight settling there. Hear her breathing. Her crying sometimes.

Just as I'm drifting off now, the whispers from the radiator seem to be almost forming words. The pipes breathing, talking to themselves.

The flash of light is so sudden and intense it hurts. Makes me gasp.

What's going on? What's that?

I wake to a blinding whiteness, and try to shut my eyes. Only they won't shut.

Where am I?

Wherever I am, it's cold. A deep, stabbing cold. I turn my head to look around . . .

I try and turn my head . . .

I can't move my head! Wait. I can't move at all!

Can't even blink.

Only my eyes can move. From the corners of my eyes, I see white on white on white. Pure and harsh, it jabs at the back of my sockets. My head is slightly raised, not on a pillow, but something that feels like steel. Icy against the back of my neck.

The bed, the room, the house are all gone. Leaving nothing but white.

I'd shiver if I could. But even that movement is impossible.

Peering out of the bottom of my eyes, I can see my bare chest going up and down, slow and steady despite my panic. My breath steams in the frosty air.

Hey! Anybody there? I try to call out. Can't even whisper.

Between breaths clouding my view, I see something wrong with my chest. It's been cut. Beginning at my shoulders, two straight lines are sliced into my skin, meeting in the middle right above my stomach. No blood. The edges of the cuts look almost blue, and my skin is snow-pale. Where the two lines meet, they turn into one, a single line aimed down at my groin.

With a rising panic, I recognize that cut from TV cop shows. It's called a 'Y' incision. They make it to open you up for autopsy.

Get a grip! This is a dream. I'm dreaming. Dreaming a seriously twisted nightmare. But that's all.

It can't hurt me! There's no pain in dreams, right? Nothing physical anyway.

Stop looking at the cut! You can't close your eyes, so just lose yourself in the white.

I stare snowblind into the bright nothing.

I'm still in bed, in my room. Safe. Nothing to be afraid—

Then something touches the top of my head. A hand? Brushing over my hair? Fingers? Are those fingers?

Who's there? I ask silently.

Straining my eyes up, I can't see back far enough.

There's a sudden buzzing sound by my ear, shockingly loud in the absolute silence of this place. Then cold metal presses against my temple. I feel a tugging on my scalp, of tiny steel teeth combing through my hair. A tuft of cut hair falls against my left ear. The electric hum moves back and forth, like a circling mosquito, as my scalp is buzzed bald.

I don't like this. I really don't like this.

Time to wake up. Now! Please.

I try. Nothing happens. I'm trapped.

The buzzing stops, followed by a deafening quiet. My eyes roll back and forth, trying desperately to pick out anything – a glimpse, a shadow, a tiny sign of what that thing is behind me.

Then I feel it. On the bared flesh of my skull. A hand, but not a hand. Rough and spiky, pricking lightly over my scalp. Like it's searching, probing.

Whatever I did, I'm sorry, I yell without a voice, hysterical. *I swear. Just let me go.*

The hand that's not a hand goes away. Maybe it heard me. Maybe it'll let me go now. Let me wake up.

Then a sharp metallic noise rips through the silence. The electric whine jabs my eardrums. Sounds like something from Dad's workshop.

Like an electric saw.

Wake up, now! Please! Please! Please!

I can see just past the blur of my brows. I make out the silver glint from the spinning edge of a circular blade, as it lowers to bite into my forehead.

My scream is mute.

But there's no pain. Only the sensation of my skin separating, and underneath that the indescribable feeling of bone being violated, cut through smoothly, like a knife through butter.

I go blank then, my consciousness retreating, hiding as far back inside my head as it can go.

An eternity passes until the whine of the saw stops.

I lie numb, inside and out, waiting for this to end.

It's gotta end, right?

But not yet.

I feel the strangest tugging sensation on the top of my head. I get a memory-flash of some TV show with a baby being born and the doctors using this suction cup thing on the head to pull the newborn out.

Not happening. This is not happening. I'm in my bed, in my room. Alone.

I hear something that makes my eardrums tremble. A growl, so low and deep my bones ache as it rumbles through me.

Then a gust of air like a frozen breath caresses the exposed surface of my brain. Paralysed, I can't even shiver at the touch.

With the breath, I hear a whisper. Not through my ears, but spoken directly into my mind.

Danny-boy, it says. *My Danny-boy*.

Wake up. Wake up! WAKE UP!

I come out of it with a strangled shriek. Struggling out of the straitjacket tangle of my sheets, I stumble out of bed and crash into the wall, staring wide-eyed into the darkness of the room.

I shove my hand up under my shirt and feel the smooth, unmutilated surface of my chest. With both hands, I frantically check my head. Still intact. Hair and all.

My heart's beating so fast it's making me dizzy. I'm shivering like crazy. I must look like I'm having a seizure as I make my way over to the shadow of the desk and turn on the lamp.

The room is empty. Just me. Alone. Nobody else.

I tell myself that as I lean against the desk and force my lungs to breathe slower. I try and wake all the way up. Make sure I'm out of reach of that nightmare.

Where did that come from?

It's that stupid *Frankenstein*, mixed with the wild weirdness last night, and memories of Mom buried in my brain. Topped off with Dad calling me Danny-boy. Splice it all together for one warped slasher dream.

After a while, I go from panicked to pissed off. Pissed at everything. At Dad, and our life as drifters. At this pit of a town. At Mom, for dying and leaving me alone.

And that book! I grab *Frankenstein* off the desk and tear it in half, then in quarters. I don't stop till it's shredded into confetti.

Shivering, I lean my palms on the flat top of the radiator, trying to suck all the heat out of it. I notice that tiny blue dot on the back of my hand. I try to rub it off with my thumb, only it won't rub away. But really, it looks like nothing. Maybe it's been there for a while and I just never noticed. Like a freckle – who remembers all their freckles? It's probably some old pen jab that broke the skin and got tattooed into me. I quit trying to erase it.

Muffled hissing sounds and gurgles rise from the radiator pipes. Sounds that could be mistaken for voices in other rooms. Or whispers from outside.

Pressing my thighs up against the radiator, I look out the window. But all I can see is my reflection in the night-black glass.

Just after dawn, I hear Dad heading out to drill the fishing holes.

Couldn't get back to sleep for more than a couple minutes at a time. I've been lying here, listening to the night sounds of the house, paranoid about what's waiting for me in my dreams.

Outside, the snowmobile starts up. Dad revs the engine as he speeds onto the lake. It'll take him about an hour to drill the holes in the ice.

I get up and squeeze in a shower before he returns. Letting the water run till the furnace wakes up and gives me some heat, I hop in and try to melt away the nightmare.

By the time Dad gets back, I've got the coffee ready.

'Cold as a witch's kiss out there,' he tells me, tossing his gloves on the table and gripping the steaming mug I give him with both hands. 'But drilling holes warms you up. The ice is a good ten inches thick.'

I went ice fishing once. Not my idea of a wild time.

After a couple mugs of coffee, I'm wired enough to brave the witch's kiss.

The door opens on a wind that stings my eyes and sucks my nostrils in tight. I scan the snow-whipped stretch of shore and ice.

What are we doing here? I ask myself for the millionth time. Dad's answer to that would be: 'You gotta go where the work is.'

Like there were no jobs back in Toronto? I've been in three schools in two years. I barely find out where the cafeteria is before we're packing up. What's next? A nice little shack at the North Pole? How far do we have to go?

We're on the run. Running from a ghost, a memory. But you can't give your memories a 'no forwarding address'. Just like you can't lose your shadow – it knows where you live. We've got to face what happened to Mom sometime. We're out of places to run. Harvest Cove *is* the end of the world. But when I try to tell Dad this he shrugs it off.

'Hold on tight,' he yells to me now over the snowmobile's motor. I climb on behind him. We pull out, with the sun slanting a white glare off the ice. The stinging wind wakes me all the way up.

The huts are wooden shacks on sleds the marina rents out. Me and Dad tow them a couple hundred yards from shore, teaming up to shove and shift them into place over the holes he's made. Then he anchors them in the ice with drilled spikes.

When we're done, we hop back on the snowmobile. Dad revs the motor, making the thing quiver under us like a horse ready to run.

'What do you say we set her loose?' he calls over his shoulder. 'See what she's got?'

'Let's do it!' I squint against the blowing snow.

'Grab on tight, now.'

I lock my arms around him.

'Unleash hell!' I tell him, quoting our favourite movie, *Gladiator*.

Then we launch.

Hanging on for my life, we fly across the ice. I'm laughing breathless, cheek pressed against Dad's back.

We speed into the blinding white of the rising sun, outracing the wind and the cold – and for a while, even the past.

Eight

I wince in sympathy as the middleweight's head bounces off the mat. I know what that feels like. He pushes himself to his knees, but that's as far as he gets. The ref waves him out, and the winner pumps his gloved fist in the air.

It's Friday night, and the Molson Centre in Barrie is packed for the regionals of the Canadian Juniors bouts. It's like a greenhouse in here, warm and humid from the press of the crowd and the battles in the ring.

'Ash is up next.' Howie leans forward.

Me, him and Pike are sitting two rows back.

'See that blonde sitting ring-side?' Pike mumbles around a mouthful of hot dog. 'She's checking me out.'

The blonde is looking at Pike in shock. Probably because he eats like a starving hyena. Except instead of a blood-covered muzzle, he's got ketchup smeared all over his face.

'She's just stunned at how many dogs you cram down.'

'Here comes Ash!' Howie says.

I stand up to see over the crowd.

Ash strides toward the ring, her spiky black hair springing out the top of her headgear. She's followed by her father. He's a foot taller than her and twice as wide. A full-blooded Ojibwa with a weathered face, and an intense black heat in his eyes. He's Ash's trainer. I've seen him at the gym out at Borden, running drills with her, working on punching combinations. They call him Nick, because his real name is Indian and hard on the tongue – something like Nishkahdze. It means 'angry one'. Ash says he got it because he was born screaming and throwing punches in the air. He's got one of those faces you can't read. You never know if he's pissed, or just laughing at you.

Ash has the same heat in her stare now, as she passes by us to climb the steps to the ring. She doesn't see us, or seem to notice the crowd at all – she's psyching herself up.

Her dad follows her into the ring. Ash shrugs her shoulders and rolls her head, shaking out her arms to loosen up. Nick rubs the back of her neck, talking in her ear.

Ash has on a crimson, knee-length boxing robe. On the back there's this Indian design with a pissed-off-looking bird of prey. Ash looks wild and dangerous. I can't take my eyes off her. If I touched her right now it would be like kissing lightning.

The other girl climbs in the ring.

'Somebody beat that girl with the ugly stick,' Pike says.

Harsh, but true. The pale redhead's nose is a lump, squashed down where it's been broken before. And her eyes are too close together.

Nick takes off Ash's robe and puts it over his shoulder. She's all in red, trunks and top, with crimson-tasselled boxing shoes.

The announcer moves to the centre of the ring.

'Our next match is a four-round girls' lightweight. In the black trunks, from Muskoka, with a record of six wins, two losses – Jennifer Mankowski.'

There are scattered cheers for her, and boos from the three of us.

'And in the red trunks, from Harvest Cove, with a record of five wins, no losses – Ashley Animkee.'

A roar from the crowd, with all the people from the base who showed up to cheer Ash and the other army brats boxing tonight.

The trainers leave the ring. Ash's dad comes over to us and tosses her robe in my lap. 'Hold that. And let's hear you make some noise, boys.'

He takes his station by Ash's corner, setting his black leather bag down on a stool. His bag of tricks, with towels and water bottles as well as mystery creams and stuff.

Ash's mom stays away from her fights. She can't take seeing her girl get smacked around.

I look down at the bird of prey's eyes on the robe in my lap. Still feels warm from her.

Ash goes to centre ring. The fighters do their staredown as the ref tells them the rules. Then they touch gloves and go to their corners to wait for the bell.

Ash's dad calls up to her. It's hard to make out what he's saying, but it doesn't sound English. He repeats it before the bell dings and she goes out to do battle.

The first round, the redhead holds Ash at a distance with her longer reach, jabbing and keeping away from the inside power-punches Ash wants to throw.

When the bell ends the round, Ash comes scowling to sit on the stool Nick sets down. He squirts water in her mouth. She rinses and spits into a bucket. He's talking to her the whole time as she glares at the other girl.

Then she gets up for the second round, and he steps back through the ropes. Before the bell, he calls to her: '*Nataga wab moodoo.*' Something like that.

Pike gives me a nudge. 'They're talking Injun.'

He's way too loud. Always too loud.

Nick turns and gives him a killer stare. Pike looks down at his hot dog till the bell sounds.

The second round starts like the first, with Ash held off by the long arms of her opponent. But then Ash catches her on the side of the head.

I've felt that hook before. It's a stunner. The other girl staggers and backs off. The redhead sticks to long-range jabs, trying to keep clear of Ash's inside power. Ash absorbs the jabs without effect, like they're mosquitoes.

Then she bursts in, catching the redhead with a combination that knocks her head from side to side. She tries to retreat but Ash stays on her, up close.

She grabs on to Ash, one arm holding her in tight while the other works body shots to Ash's ribs.

'Break it up.' The ref moves in.

They step away. Ash has her fuse lit now. She's says you have to take a few hits, and taste some of your own blood, before you really get juiced.

She comes up under the redhead's guard to catch her chin with an uppercut. When the other girl falls back on the ropes Ash stays with her, knocking her head around, keeping her off-balance.

The other girl grabs on to her, trying to pin Ash's arms against her body. Then she shoves her glove up inside Ash's headgear.

Ash stumbles out of the hold, shaking her head and squinting badly.

'Gouge!' Nick yells at the referee. 'Thumb gouge. Come on, ref! You blind?'

The bell rings and Ash goes over to collapse on the stool in her corner. Her dad kneels and holds her head to get a look at the gouged eye. He flushes it out with some water.

'She's losing her legs,' I hear him tell her. 'Desperate. End this now. Quick! Hear me?'

Ash gives a little nod, and he towels her face dry.

When she stands for the third round, struggling to keep her left eye open, her dad shouts to her:

'*Nataga wab moodoo.*'

The sweat is running down her back, making her shine.

Before the echo of the bell dies, Ash is right up on the other girl. She forgets about guarding herself and goes all out. The redhead responds with a flurry of punches.

The crowd is loving it. Even Howie's screaming for blood.

Just as the redhead is pulling back to fire a killer hook, Ash comes in low and puts everything she's got into a wicked uppercut. The other girl falls back on the ropes. She tries to stay standing, but her legs give out and she hits the mat hard on her knees.

The ref waves Ash back to her corner and starts the count.

I count along, trying to hurry the ref.

'Eight. Nine. Ten!'

There's the bell. Ash holds her hands in the air and walks a circle in the middle of the ring. She owns the place. Her dad climbs in and they knock fists, his bare to her gloved. Then he grabs her up, holding her tall in his arms so everybody can see.

'Hoo-rah! Hoo-rah!' chant the guys from CFB Borden. A soldier's salute.

Ash, held high and pumping her fist in the air, squinting and sweaty, is the most amazing thing I've ever seen.

A knockout.

Nine

After the fights, a convoy heads over to the base for the celebration. Two of the three brats boxing tonight won. The third lost a decision on points, leading to a near riot in the stands.

I'm riding with Ash and her dad, with the guys following in Pike's junker.

'How's that eye?' Nick asks, pulling off the highway at the exit for Canadian Forces Base Borden. 'Got her thumb right in there, didn't she?'

'Clearing up. Little blurry.'

'Can you read that licence plate, just with your left?'

I lean up from the back seat, watching her try to focus. She reads out the plate of the car ahead of us, getting it right except for calling a 'B' an '8'.

'Close enough. You'll be okay,' he tells her, reaching across to pat her knee. 'What do you think of my girl?' He glances at me in the rear-view mirror.

I open and close my mouth a couple times, like a goldfish eating lunch. How do I answer that? In front of her father?

'Yeah.' Ash turns back, fixing me with her bloodshot eye. 'What do you think of me now?'

'I – I think – I – uh. She's great. You're great. I mean, uh . . . you know.'

Ash grins, enjoying torturing me.

'Gotta watch out for these smooth talkers.' Nick pulls up to the base gate, and they wave us through.

We park at the Legion Hall. Usually you have to be eighteen, and army, to get in. Tonight they're relaxing the rules for the boxing brats.

The wind chases us across the lot. Stepping inside, I catch a warm breath of beer fumes and greasy fries.

'I'm starving.' Ash leans in close to be heard over the teeth-rattling, sonic boom of the amped-up jukebox belting out a country song. 'Skipped lunch to make weight. Time to binge.'

We squirm through the crowd, Ash getting congratulatory pats and high-fives. Shouts of 'Hey, champ', 'Outstanding' and 'Unbeaten' follow us to the last empty booth.

'What are we eating?' Nick asks.

'Everything,' Ash shouts.

He nods and disappears into the crowd to order the feast.

Besides her bloodshot eye with its puffy lid, her lower lip is swollen where a shot slipped past her headgear. But no new scar to join the old one tracing a pale line on her lower lip.

Those lips are smiling at me now.

'So, what did you really think? First time you've seen me fight. Not counting me knocking *you* down and out.'

I give a little shrug. Don't want to say too much – you know, open my chest, spread my ribs and expose my heart.

'Incredible. There was no quit in you. You took the hits, and kept on coming. And you looked . . . amazing.' I stop. Don't let out too much. 'I mean, with that robe and everything. Where did you get that?'

'My aunt made it for me, on the reservation up at Grassy Narrows. First, I thought it made me look too Indian. That I'd get a lot of crap from everybody for it. But like my dad says – you get crap anyway. If you're gonna be Indian, go all the way.'

'The bird on the robe mean anything?'

'My last name, Animkee, means thunder. So my aunt put a thunderbird on the back. Brings me luck. Hey, I'm unbeaten, right? The T-bird brings on the storm, makes thunder with its wings. Shoots lightning from its eyes.'

Ash makes her eyes go wide, staring me down. Then she breaks into an almost shy smile and looks away. Shy for Ash is still pretty cocky, though.

The guys crash in on us, Pike shoving me over in the booth, Ash patting the spot next to her for Howie.

'You were awesome,' Howie says. 'Best fight yet. And you beat her clean, when she went dirty.'

'You terminated her,' Pike laughs.

The food comes fast. Burgers, nachos, spicy chicken wings, fish and chips. Ash eats like she fights – no stopping, no fear, no quit.

Nick makes it over to the booth after a few congratulatory beers in honour of his girl. He leans in and rests one of his massive hands on the back of Pike's neck, giving it a squeeze that makes him wince, payback for Pike's 'Injun talk' comment earlier.

'Pike, you little pyromaniac.' He fixes him with a cold glare. 'Blow up anything lately?'

'I don't like to brag.'

'Hell you don't,' Nick grunts. 'Shove over.'

He releases Pike, and digs into the feast.

Pike's reputation as a pyro is legendary. If anybody really cared about Fat Bill's place getting burned down, he'd be the prime suspect. Not that they'd ever nail him for it. He's slippery as a greased rat. The back-page story that ran in yesterday's *Barrie Examiner* said the fire was probably the result of a careless smoker. Nobody's going to be crying for Fat Bill anyway.

Pike's need to shock and awe us reached its peak back on Halloween, during the fireworks. The town does a show every year down by the lakeside, with fireworks shot off over the water.

Me, Ash and the guys were watching from the beach. Out on the water, a raft of glowing pumpkins flashed their gap-toothed smiles toward the beach.

'Wait till you see the fireworks finale,' Pike told us. 'I've added my own little twist.'

Then he disappeared before the show even started.

There were oohs and ahhhs, shooting stars, starbursts, and sparkling silver waterfalls in the night sky. When it ended the crowd applauded and cheered. Show over.

Then a row of sparklers flared to life on the raft of pumpkins. Pike's show was just getting going.

The pumpkin on the far left exploded with a red flash and a sound like a gunshot. A second later the next one in line went off, rocking the raft and sending pumpkin shards into the air. One by one they went off with thunderclap booms that made you wince. The last explosion sent pumpkin guts raining down on the beach and people running for cover.

They tried to nail Pike for it after, but how do you

pull fingerprints off a squashed squash?

How he did it was pretty disturbing, using small charges of actual dynamite. He wouldn't tell where he got the stuff. But around here they use dynamite as a fast way to clear stumps. He must have raided somebody's stash.

The crazy thing is, Pike and Howie's dad, Captain Slater, his job during his tour in Afghanistan was clearing land mines, explosives and booby traps. So here's the Captain neutralizing this kind of lethal stuff while his son is building his own home-made versions.

Last week, when we had to pick a favourite quotation for an assignment in Miss Mercer's class, Pike chose one by the guy who invented the atom bomb. After this guy saw his first A-bomb tested out in the desert, he said: 'I am the destroyer of worlds.'

Right now Pike's destroying the nachos.

'Don't steal all the cheese,' I say. 'Leave some for the Champ.'

'The Champ's on her third burger,' Pike mumbles around a mouthful. 'She ain't gonna starve.'

A couple of crew cuts in uniform come up to our table.

'Hey, Captain. One of the new guys wants to try out your arm.'

Ash's dad is a legendary arm wrestler. He won an army competition a few years back.

Nick scowls playfully up at them, flexing his massive right hand. 'You mean, The Crippler?'

'Yeah. We're taking bets. What do you say?'

He makes a fearsome fist, knuckles popping. 'Cut me in.' Nick gets up and follows the crew cuts into the crowd.

'Time to ride the Reaper,' Pike says. 'You guys gonna come watch?'

The Reaper is the mechanical bull over in the corner, roped off and surrounded by cushioned mats.

'We can see from here,' I say. 'But it sounds like a bad idea, man. You're gonna be puking nachos all over the saddle.'

Pike stands on the seat to peer over the mob and see if the bull is free. 'I think I'll try it on five, tonight.' (The thing goes up to a spine-shattering, testicle-pulverizing *six*.) 'Yep. I'm gonna reap the Reaper.'

Pike makes off for the bull, and Howie gets up. 'Somebody has to be there to pick up the pieces,' he says, leaving me and Ash alone.

She finishes off her third burger and leans back.

'You finally full?' I have to shout over the music.

'Just pacing myself.'

'So you have to tell me . . .'

'What?'

I start to lean over the table so she can hear, but she waves me over to her side of the booth. I slide in next to her.

'You have to tell me,' I say, leaning in close enough to smell her shampoo. 'What was that thing your dad was yelling to you during the fight? Something Indian?'

She gives me a small smile, curving her swollen lower lip. 'It's just this thing he says to get me juiced for battle.'

With my leg against hers, I can feel the heat coming off her.

'What was it?'

'*Netaga waab minodoo.*' She twists her tongue around the strange words. 'It's Ojibwa. Kind of an inside joke between me and him. Means: "*Kill the white devil.*"'

'What's the white devil?'

Her grin gets wider, and she hits my leg lightly with her fist. 'You are, man. Whitey.'

'Kill the white devil?' I laugh nervously.

'Don't worry,' she says. 'I'll let you live. You're too cute to put in a coffin.'

I go red and have to look away.

Through the crowd, I see Pike's head whip-lashing around as the bull spins and bucks under him. His red-haired mohawk flashes in the light like a struck match.

Ash stretches her left arm, laying it down along the back of the booth, resting it on my shoulders. I lose sight of everything but her.

'Don't get any ideas,' she says. 'It's just, I think I strained my rotator cuff. Gotta stretch it out.'

'Right. Anything else you need to stretch out?'

She shrugs her 'strained' shoulder. 'I'll let you know.'

We share a nice silence, picking at the remains of the feast.

Howie slides in the other side of the booth. He notices Ash's arm around me and gives a shy little smile. 'Pike's waiting in line to have another go at the bull.'

Ash stuffs some fries in her face. 'Remember back at Gagetown, him and the Rottweiler?'

Howie shakes his head. 'He's lucky it didn't rip his head off.'

'What's that about?' I ask.

Ash, Howie and Pike grew up at the army base in Gagetown, New Brunswick. They've got some serious history together.

'Pike, when he was little,' Howie tells me, 'wanted to run away and join the rodeo. He saw this bull-riding competition on TV, and thought that was like his destiny. So he started out practising his riding technique on the local dogs. He tried this big Rottweiler, named Napalm. A hundred pounds of mean, slobbering muscle. Pike hopped on, grabbed its collar and locked his legs against its sides. That thing spun, twisting and trying to take a chunk out of him. It rolled in the dirt to get him off, but Pike wouldn't let go. Finally, Napalm just gave up and lay down on its belly, exhausted.'

'That was when we knew Pike was kind of wrong in the head,' Ash says.

Howie grunts. 'We knew way before then. But seeing him break Napalm – that was something.'

He's proud of his brother, no matter what.

Ash taps my shoulder. 'Let me out. Gotta take a leak.'

When she's gone, I remember my cellphone pictures. Now that I've got Howie alone, I can't put it off any longer.

'Gotta show you something.' I dig out my cell. 'I found these weird tracks in the snow. From some kind of animal, I guess. See if you can tell me what made them.'

I pull up the shots from the ditch. 'There.' I hand my cell over to him.

Howie pages through the shots on the little screen. 'Where was this?'

I gulp some of my Coke, stalling. I don't want to say too much, don't want to come off like I'm nuts.

'Down by the lake,' I say. 'In a . . . ditch.'

'Hmmm,' he frowns. 'What were you doing in a ditch?'

'Doesn't matter. Long, weird story. But, what do you think? What kind of animal left those?'

He makes more *hmmm*ing sounds, squinting at the pictures. 'The claws marks are bizarre. Eight digits to a paw? And the impression of the pad . . . ?'

Howie keeps flicking back and forth through the photos.

'What size shoe are you?' he asks, looking at the shot where I set my foot down next to the tracks to get scale.

'Ten.'

Howie blinks at the image on the screen. Then he pulls out a pen. 'Give me your shoes.'

'Huh?'

I hesitate as he clears some space on the tabletop. But then I pull them off and hand them over. Never question a genius.

Using the photo and my running shoes for reference, he paces out lengths and widths, drawing lines in ink on the pale wood of the table. Then he draws an outline, adding little circles in a curve at the top to show the position of the claw marks.

The outlines stretch most of the width of the table.

'Wow, that's . . .' He dies off. 'I don't know what that is.'

'How about a bear, or something?'

'Nan. Even if you had one gigantic polar bear on steroids, the structure's all wrong. The heel, the span of the digits.'

'So, what then?'

Howie shrugs, with a puzzled half-smile. 'Bigfoot, maybe? The Abominable Snowman?'

'Any way you can look into it?' I ask, glad that he's not pressing me for the full story yet.

'Definitely. Just let me e-mail these shots.'

He sends the digital images to his own address.

Ash shows up then, and sees my shoes on the table.

'What's this? Strip poker? Can I get in on it?'

I grin, glancing at her sideways as she slips in next to me.

Midnight is closing time at the Legion Hall.

This was a good night. The best in a long long time. As we make our way out to the parking lot, the crisp air shivering in our lungs, we're all flying high.

Ash is pumped with her victory in the ring. Pike's bragging about beating the Reaper, and then getting some girl's number after. Howie's staring into space, focused on the mystery monster tracks.

And me? I'm still riding the electric buzz of Ash's touch. The feel of her heat.

Right now, there's no past, no future. Nowhere else we need to be. Beneath a clear black sky crowded with stars, the shock of the cold braces us, shouting that we're alive. Right here and now.

And we're all feeling – invincible, maybe.

Immortal.

Ten

It always catches me when I'm not expecting it.

I'm getting out of the shower, towelling my hair dry. The mirror is cloudy from the steam. Reaching to wipe a patch clear, I see the marks where Dad has done the same thing earlier. The glass holds the print of his hand where he swiped away the steam.

And just like that, the memories flood back, stopping my hand in mid-reach.

It was something Mom used to do. She was always the early riser, the first to hit the shower. So when I'd get done with mine later on, sometimes I'd find one of her mirror doodles waiting for me. I'm a heat freak when it comes to showers, so she knew I'd find the invisible finger drawings she made in the steam on the glass when I got out.

She'd draw these stick figures with round lollipop heads. Dumb stuff, but it was our dumb stuff. We had a running thing with a stick figure called *Stinkboy*. My alter ego. He was the one who got mud on the carpet, left dirty laundry everywhere, and was responsible for those foul sneakers. Mom drew the evil stick figure with pointy shark teeth, beady little eyes, and wavy stink lines coming off him. Sometimes I'd add another stick figure to the scene, shooting tiny bullets at Stinkboy, or stabbing him to death.

Dumb stuff. Our stuff.

I remember the morning Mom showed the first sign something was wrong, I'd drawn a nuke attack on Stinkboy, surrounding him with little exploding mushroom clouds.

'I think we've seen the last of Stinkboy,' Mom said, coming in the kitchen. 'No way he can survive that.'

I was nodding off into my cereal, but snorted awake at the sound of her voice. 'He's been shot,' I mumbled, 'been stabbed, burned, bombed and decapitated. Still he comes back. The guy's immortal.'

Mom was in her usual crazy rush, eating toast and chugging coffee while texting messages on her cellphone. She was a realtor, always racing around town showing places. Always with a million things on her mind.

So it was almost funny at first. A slip of the tongue.

She'd just downed her second black coffee and set the cup in the sink.

'Toss me the elephant,' she said to me.

'Huh?' I looked up from my cereal.

'Elephant,' she said. 'Elephant.'

I just stared at her, frowning. She pointed to something on the table by my elbow. Her keys were lying there.

'These?' I asked. 'Your keys?'

'Yeah. Toss them.'

I did, and she caught them without even pausing with her texting. Mom was a master multi-tasker.

'You said elephant.'

'What's that, honey?'

'Just now, you said: *toss me the elephant*.'

She glanced up from her cell, raising an eyebrow. 'I don't get it. What's that mean?'

'Hey, you tell me. You said it.'

She gave me a look like I was talking crazy. 'I think you must have inhaled one of those mushroom clouds meant for Stinkboy.'

We shrugged it off. A slip of the tongue. It was almost forgotten when she did it again.

More slips, getting words wrong. Kind of funny at first. Not so funny when the migraines started.

She went in for tests. MRI, CATSCAN, EEG.

Aphasia, they called it. Getting words wrong, forgetting the names of things. It was the first symptom, soon followed by the headaches, nausea, clumsiness and disorientation.

Then they found *it* in the left cerebral hemisphere of her brain. The part that controls speech recognition, balance, memory. Mom said the image on the MRI scan made the tumour look kind of like an octopus, with tentacles reaching out, holding on. The biopsy showed it was bad. Its location, up against the brain stem, was worse.

Then the real nightmare started.

All this flashes through my head now as I'm standing here in front of the mirror.

I use the towel to wipe the glass clear, and catch my reflection. My eyes are tearing up, and my heart feels like a fist inside my chest. A surge of panic rises.

No! Not now. Not now.

I shut my eyes tight, leaning on the sink. Forcing myself to breathe slow, I try to erase my thoughts like I swiped away the steam. Get a grip on the panic before it pushes me off the deep end. Takes a minute, but I manage to flatline my emotions. The wave of raw grief falls back.

I've almost stopped shaking when there's a knock at

the bathroom door. I jump, opening my eyes on my own startled reflection in the mirror.

'Danny,' Dad says, muffled through the door. 'Phone.'

I have to swallow before I can speak.

'Okay. I'm coming.'

I push off from the sink, avoiding eye contact with that mess in the mirror that looks like me.

Eleven

'What are you doing, frisking me?' Ash frowns at me over her shoulder.

I'm sitting behind her on the motorbike, trying to find where I can hold on to her without it seeming like I'm trying to feel her up. I wouldn't mind trying. But she's driving.

'Here,' she says, taking my bare hands in her gloved ones and fixing my grip just below her chest. 'Scoot up closer, or we're gonna be doing wheelies all the way there.'

It's Saturday morning, around eleven. Ash called when I was getting out of the shower to see if I wanted to take a ride. I said yeah, but I had to drop by Howie's first. His call woke me up this morning, out of a deep and thankfully dreamless sleep. He said he'd made some progress on our mystery tracks and I should come over.

I scoot up close, bringing my groin right up against

her tailbone. Not a bad place to be. I press in tight. 'No helmets?'

Ash shrugs, putting on her bad-ass sunglasses. 'You want to live forever? Gotta feel the wind on your face. Feel the speed. Live before you die.'

We tear out of the parking lot behind the marina.

It's a grey day, smells like snow coming. The fields are covered in a thin layer of powder.

The chains strapped on the tyres of her bike bite into the skim of snow and black ice on the road, giving us enough traction so we don't go sliding into the ditch.

The rattling vibration of the bike, together with the bump and grind of me against Ash as we speed over lumps and potholes, are having a *rising* effect in my jeans. I have this powerful urge to let my hands roam from where they're locked just above her navel.

Even if we wipe out, it'll be worth it. Live before you die, right?

I have to fight to keep from leaning in to taste her neck with my tongue. Right now, the happiest place on Earth is inside my pants.

Howie's place sits in a small wooded hollow with a creek out back.

We sputter to a halt in front of the house. I hop off, taking a few steps away with my back to Ash as she rocks the bike onto its kickstand. The bulge in the front of my jeans is screamingly obvious. I unzip my jacket and let the arctic day soak into me. Next best thing to a cold shower.

Ash goes up the stairs to knock on the door, giving me a few more seconds to deflate.

The door opens on a thin, red-haired woman chewing a big wad of gum.

'Hi, Brenda,' Ash says. 'We're here to see Howie.'

'Ashley, honey. Look at your face. Every time you're over you've got some new cuts and bruises. Your mother must get frantic.'

Brenda lets us in and shuts the door against the cold.

'Well, I was never beauty queen material,' Ash says.

'Don't say that. You've got such a lovely bone structure. Don't you think so, Danny?'

I grin as Ash makes a face. Her right eye is real bloodshot from the gouge last night, the lid swollen.

'Girl's got great bones.'

I get a knuckle in the ribs from Ash.

Brenda's a bundle of nervous energy. Maybe it comes from being married to a former drill sergeant who now specializes in defusing bombs. I can see where Howie gets his nerves.

'He's up in his room. Don't bother knocking, he won't hear you with his headphones on.'

We climb the stairs.

Ash pushes me ahead of her. 'You check first. Make sure Howie's not playing with Howie Junior.'

I knock. Getting no response, I turn the knob and peek in. Howie's sitting at his desk, back to the door. *Junior* is safely out of sight.

'Clear.' I step in.

Howie's room is like his own messy museum. Books, of course, shelved and piled and avalanched on the floor. The ceiling is wallpapered with a map of the constellations that glows in the dark. A row of dusty mason jars on one shelf hold specimens of just about every kind of fish, frog, crab and snake that lives in or on the shores of the lake. They're all pickled and pale in their formaldehyde baths. Bowls hold the shells of freshwater clams and snails, a selection of local rocks, and a there's a chipped teacup containing fragments of bird eggshells.

Watching over this collection from the top shelf is Agent Orange, a stuffed ginger tabby cat. Howie's childhood pet. It was taxidermied in a lying-down posture, legs folded under, tail curled around with its tip slightly raised as if in mid-twitch.

'Howie,' I call, trying to get past his earphones.

He's leaning toward his computer monitor, which shows split-screen images of all kinds of animal tracks. He doesn't hear me, so I move over into his field of vision.

Howie jumps, gasping. He pulls off the phones. 'Scared me.'

'Sorry, man. I knocked, I yelled. Fired off a warning shot. What are you listening to?'

'Nothing. White noise. It cancels out external sounds up to forty decibels.'

'Man, only you would listen to static.'

'Hey, Howie,' Ash says, coming up behind him.

He jumps again.

'Just me.' She touches his shoulder. 'Relax.'

'Damn!' He swivels in his chair. 'Is there anybody else here?'

Ash shrugs. 'There might be a terrorist sleeper cell in your closet. Or maybe that's just your collection of blow-up dolls.'

He grins. 'Those are for scientific purposes only.'

'Right.' Ash picks up a glass paperweight. It's got a big black bug frozen inside.

'That's a scarab beetle,' Howie says. 'They've got a taste for rotting flesh.'

'Yum.'

I squint up at the overhead light. It's insanely bright. 'What do you got in there? A thousand-watt bulb? I feel like I'm getting an X-ray just standing here.'

'Oh,' he shrugs. 'That's for my Seasonal Affective Disorder. SAD.'

I give him a raised eyebrow. He's always got some new quirk.

'It's from the short winter days,' he says. 'No sun. You wake up in the dark every morning. Get home from school in the dark. It's depressing. The mega-watt bulbs are supposed to help. Mimicking sunlight, faking out your brain.'

'Right now, it's frying my corneas.' I look over his shoulder at the open books beside his keyboard. Biology. Anatomy. And a guide to animal tracks.

'Where's Pike?' Ash asks.

'He went with my dad to the shooting range on base.'

'When's Pike going to enlist?' I ask. 'Is he like counting the days till he turns eighteen?'

'They'll never take him,' Ash says.

'Why not? The guy's a military fanatic.'

'He's also a Section Eight,' she tells me.

'Huh?'

Army kids talk their own language – Bratspeak. Sometimes I only get half of what they're saying.

'Section Eight,' Howie translates. 'A discharge from service for reason of mental defect.'

'That pretty much nails Pike,' I say.

Howie shrugs. Pike might be a Section Eight, but he's also his big bro. 'Hey, did your dad get those fishing huts out on the lake?'

'We towed a couple out this morning.'

'Great. Me and Pike are going to try for some wall-eye and scrappy. Maybe we'll come by tonight.'

Ash leans over to look at the computer screen. It shows animal tracks left in mud, sand and snow.

'What this?'

'Research. Something Danny wanted me to look into.' He looks at me. 'Does she have clearance?'

'Clearance for what?' Ash shoots me a suspicious glance.

I probably should have come here alone. Explaining the tracks and that nightmare attack would be tough enough just telling Howie. He'd get a kick out of the weirdness of it. Ash will just think I'm nuts.

'I found some animal tracks in the ditch by the marina. I was asking Howie if he could ID them.'

'What are you doing hanging out in ditches?' she asks.

I shrug. 'Long story.'

'So? I got nowhere to be. How about you, Howie?'

He leans back in his swivel-chair. 'You tell me why you were crawling around in the ditch, and I'll show you my findings.'

How much can I tell them?

'Okay. Might sound a little bit crazy.'

'The straitjacket's on standby,' Ash says.

I wander over to Howie's collection, so I won't have to see the looks on their faces.

'The other night,' I begin. 'You know, after Pike torched Fat Bill's?'

'Yeah?' Howie grunts.

'Me and Ash were going home, down Cove Road. She took her turnoff, and I went on toward the lake.'

I pick up a fossil of a winged bug.

'On my way to the marina, there was this . . .' This what? This giant *thing* with a deformed face, and a growl that'll shake the flesh off your bones?

'There was this big . . . dog, or wolf. A massive one that chased me for nearly a mile, all the way to the lake. And it was running in the ditches, hiding and playing with me. Only not, like, throw me the ball playing, more like stalking and hunting, before chowing down on me.'

I hold the fossil on my palm, running my thumb over the impression of the long-dead bug. Who'd think such a tiny thing could leave any mark at all.

'The next day I found the tracks it left behind. Took some cellphone pics of them, and showed them to Howie.'

I set the fossil down and turn to face them. Nothing too crazy about that, right?

'Must have been one of Mangy Mason's huskies,'

Ash says. 'They're harmless.'

'Definitely not a dog.' Howie taps his keyboard and brings up an enlargement of one of my cell shots. 'I can't tell you what it is. But I can tell you it's not canine or feline, not a wolf, a cougar or a bear. Not an ungulate, of course.'

'Huh?' I say.

'Ungulates are hooved animals. So that rules out elk, deer, moose. I've gone through my guides, and net databases of mammal tracks. Nothing's even close.'

Ash studies the image with those spiky claw marks dug in the snow next to my shoe. 'How big is that track?'

'Takes about a size forty shoe,' Howie says. 'I think what we have here is somebody screwing around.'

'Screwing how?' I ask.

'Take a look at this.'

He clicks to another page. This one shows a huge footprint set in mud, with a tape measure stretched out beside it. Thirty inches long, and about twenty wide. Shaped like a human foot – five toes, a heel and all that. But there's something almost cartoonish about it, like a kid's drawing of a foot, with the toe indentations all the same size, and perfectly round.

'This was found in Washington State, near a place called Yakima. Bigfoot country. Tracks like these kept popping up for years on trails and logging roads. Scientists took casts of the tracks and studied them.' Howie pauses, tapping the screen with his finger. 'People were saying, here's proof that Bigfoot's real, living wild out in the forest somewhere.'

He brings up an image of a grinning bearded guy, holding a giant foot-sole carved out of wood.

'Then this guy finally admitted to faking them.'

Howie clicks through shots of the guy showing how he made the tracks, strapping the bigfeet on like snowshoes and clomping through the mud.

'That guy's got way too much time on his hands,' Ash says.

'So you're saying my snow-prints are fakes?' I ask.

'Gotta be. There's nothing in the books, on the Net – on the planet – that leaves tracks like those.'

I wish they were fakes. Wish the whole thing was a twisted joke.

'So,' Howie says. 'Maybe some local weirdo was trying to get their own hoax started.'

'But there *was* something out there chasing me,' I say, wanting to tell him more but knowing he'd never buy it.

'Whatever was hunting you,' Howie says, 'it didn't leave those monster tracks. They're pure make-believe.'

Ash squeezes my arm. 'Guess your stalker figured

you didn't have enough meat on the bone.'

I grumble, feeling like an idiot.

'Next time, try to get it to pose for a picture,' Howie says. Real helpful.

'Right. A picture of it ripping my head off.'

This is a dead end. I can't even write it off as a hallucination, because delusions don't leave footprints.

'What's this?' Ash asks, picking up a newspaper page from one of the piles on Howie's desk.

'That's from yesterday's *Examiner*.'

Beneath a headline that reads *STILL MISSING* there's a grainy grey photo, like it was taken at night. A fuzzy figure, identified as Ray Dyson, exiting a side door of the Royal Victoria Hospital in Barrie. He's wearing some flimsy hospital pyjamas, stepping into the frigid dark barefoot.

'The picture is from a security camera,' Howie says. 'There's nothing new about what was wrong with him. They call it a viral infection, which covers everything from the flu to AIDS, to the plague. He's been missing three days. Not looking good.'

You can't make out Ray's expression in the grainy freeze-frame. Was he delirious? Hallucinating? What drove him out into that icy night, dressed in next to nothing?

It hits me that around the same time Ray was

escaping, I was being chased down a dark road.

The two of us lost in the night.

But I made it home. Ray never did.

Twelve

By the time Ash skids to a stop in a shower of sand, snow and rocks, I feel like I've gone a few rounds with the Reaper over at the Legion Hall. My butt is numb, and my testicles feel tenderized.

I limp around trying to realign my spine.

'Feeling good?' Ash smirks.

'Oh yeah. I never wanted to have children anyway.'

We've ended up on a secluded, pebbly beach on the outer curve of Harvest Cove. From here you can look back on the marina, the broken-down ice factory, and the docks of shoreline cottages. Nothing moves except the blowing snow on the frozen lake.

Ash runs out on the ice now, sliding to a stop about twenty feet away. She waves me to follow. I slip-skate out to her.

The ice is about eight inches thick this close to shore, twelve inches farther out. Thick enough to take your car out for a spin.

'What the hell are we doing here?' Ash gazes across the frozen wastes.

'What do you mean?'

'Harvest Cove. It's like the end of the world. Nothing to do, and nowhere to do it.'

I hunch my shoulders against the wind. 'Tell me about it. Back in Toronto there's always places to go, stuff to do.'

'Is that where your mother is?'

The question sucker-punches me. Coming out of nowhere. I avoid her eyes, hoping it'll just go away.

'Hello?' Ash says. 'I'm talking to you here. What's the deal with your mother? Divorce or something? Your dad get custody?'

'Uh, you know. She's gone,' I mumble.

'Where?'

'You know.'

Why does she have to press me? I slide a few steps away.

'No. I don't know. You're not saying anything. She's gone where? Disneyland?'

'Gone, like in dead,' I snap. 'Okay?'

That shuts us both up. I can feel her looking at me, but I just stare off at the frosty emptiness.

'Wow,' Ash finally says. 'That's . . . Damn, I'm sorry.'

'Yeah.'

Most times, when somebody asks where's my mother, I just say Toronto. I let them think divorce, separation or whatever. I don't care. Technically, it's true. She is in Toronto. Six feet under it.

'You want to talk about it?'

'No!'

'Good,' she says, letting out a held breath. 'I mean, I'm not great with people being emotional.'

'Me neither.'

There's a long, tense silence. Then Ash coughs. 'Race you out to the buoy?'

The bright orange buoy frozen in the ice is the only thing breaking the white expanse. It marks where the shallows give way to deeper water a hundred yards from shore.

'Same rules as last time?' she says. 'You win, you get to cop a feel. What do you say? On three?'

'I don't know.' I scuff my shoes on the ice, faking her out. Then I shout: 'Three!'

And I take off, sprinting to a quick lead. The dusting of snow gives enough traction to keep me from falling on my face. I can hear her right behind me. It feels strange, running out onto this wide empty plain, with only the buoy showing a flash of colour in the whiteness. Below the frozen surface, the bottom of the lake is dropping away with every step I take from shore. Five feet deep. Ten. Twenty.

I'm still in the lead. But Ash is on my tail, near enough to reach out and tackle me if she wanted. I push ahead, on the brink of losing my footing with each slipping step. Leaning forward, I launch myself at the buoy in the final few feet. I hug the orange beacon to keep myself upright.

Ash skates to a stop a few yards past me.

'I win,' I pant, before my feet slide out and I fall on my butt, still hugging the buoy.

Ash comes sliding on her knees to bump up against me. I lie back, staring up at the grey cloudcover.

Ash's face blocks my view, grinning down at me. She straddles my mid-section, sitting on my stomach.

'Did you let me win?' I ask.

'Thought you needed it.'

'Do I still get the prize?'

'What do you think?'

She bends down and kisses me.

God, she's so warm. Always. Like her blood's in a constant fever. I kiss back, her nose snug against mine.

Ash pulls away. Her palms are flat on my shoulders, holding me down. No question who's in charge.

She must see something in my eyes that makes her ask: 'What? What's wrong?'

'Nothing. It's just. Sometimes, you gotta let *me* be the guy.'

She laughs. 'You think you're up to it?'

I try to shrug, but she's still got a hold on my shoulders. 'We'll never know, unless you give me a try.'

She holds her hands up now in pretend surrender.

'Okay. You the man.'

So I twist on my side, taking her with me as we switch positions. Leaning down, I tell her: 'Close your eyes.'

'Why? What are you trying to hide?'

Everything.

She squeezes her eyes shut and I kiss her, tracing the pale line of the scar on her lower lip, finding her tongue with mine.

Scary how bad I need this. Need her. She lets me forget. Lets me be nowhere but here.

Every day I'm faking it. Fooling everybody into thinking I'm not destroyed inside. It's like I'm trying to glue a grenade back together after it's gone off. There's too many sharp and twisted little pieces. It'll never be what it was.

But when I'm with Ash, nothing can touch me.

'Quit thinking so much,' she mumbles, between kisses, reading my mind.

Right. Less thinking. More licking.

Thirteen

The furnace went nuclear tonight. Dad's down in the basement trying to prevent a total meltdown.

A drop of sweat trickles down my temple. I swipe it away with the sleeve of my T-shirt. Sitting at the desk in my room, I've got the window wide open, inviting winter in to battle the heat.

Since I gave up on reading *Frankenstein*, I'm trying to bend my brain around some poetry by a guy named Keats. I've got an essay due in three days, just before the Christmas break – Keats, life and poems of. But man, I need a translator.

Take this line: 'Here lies one whose name was writ in water.'

Huh? You got something to say, just say it! Don't give me riddles. Keats wrote that line for his own gravestone. They probably killed him because of it.

My essay so far: *Keats was* . . . Just another thousand words to go.

I hear knocking from downstairs. Dad's been pounding the pipes so I ignore it.

'Danny!' a voice calls. 'Yo, Danny.'

It's coming from outside. I lean out my window, into the freezing night. In the shadows below I make out Pike.

'Hey, quit playing with yourself long enough to answer the door.'

'What do you want?'

Pike holds up his Thermos. 'Running on empty. Need to reload. Got any coffee?'

'This ain't a Starbucks.'

'Come on. We're freezing our nuts off out there.'

Pike gestures toward the hut on the lake where him and Howie are night fishing.

'Whatever.' I give in. 'Door's not locked. Come on up.'

I meet him at the top of the stairs. 'Where's Howie?'

'Watching the lines. He's got the Leafs game on the radio, didn't want to leave it. Didn't want to leave his electric seat-warmer either.'

Pike's dressed in his usual army fatigues. His favourite colour is camouflage.

'Lose the boots,' I say. 'You're getting slush all over the place.'

'What's with the sauna in here?' Pike kicks his boots off on the mat by the stairs.

'Furnace went psycho. My dad's working on it.'

As if on cue, Dad's swearing rises up the back stairs, followed by hammering.

The kitchen windows are all open to let out the heat.

'Coffee-maker's over there, grounds in the cupboard.'

He sets his Thermos on the table, then roots around in the fridge. 'Howie needs some sugar. How old are these eclairs?' He pulls out a doughnut box.

'So old I forgot we had them.'

'Nothing's growing on them. They'll do.'

'Anything biting out there?'

'Caught a couple scrappies, and a good-sized wall-eye.' Pike fills the coffee-pot with water. 'Howie's hoping to snag a catfish with this bait he made out of rotten meat. His own recipe.'

He scoops grounds into the filter. 'You watching the game?'

'No. I'm stuck doing that English essay.'

'I got Howie to do mine. Only I had to tell him to dumb it down. Nobody's going to believe I know a word like "symbolism".'

He's flicking on the coffee-maker when I hear what sounds like a scream.

We both freeze.

'You hear that?' I ask.

'Yeah? Is the TV on?'

I shake my head. Maybe Dad burned himself on the boiler. I start toward the stairs.

'Where—' Pike says.

Another scream stops him. My breath catches in my throat.

It's from outside.

We rush to the window that looks out on the lake. A yellow glow from the open door of the fishing hut spills out onto the ice, revealing something moving in the shadows.

A strangled shout reaches us.

'Howie!' Pike yells.

He bursts down the hall, yanks on his boots and crashes down the stairs. I'm right behind him, pulling on my runners.

I pause. Should I get Dad? But for what? What's going on? So I follow Pike out into the night. I'm racing across the snowy slope, halfway to the docks, when I realize I'm still in my T-shirt and boxers.

But who cares? There's nobody around.

Ahead, Pike hits the main dock. It juts out onto the lake about fifty yards. From there, it's another sixty or so to the huts.

I slide down the slope and land on the wooden planks. The walkway light-posts shine on small patches of the dock, leaving the rest to the night.

I speed by the boats. Their winter tarps flap and crackle in the wind.

A scream rips through the dark. It cuts off suddenly, leaving dead silence. Even the wind goes still, holding its breath.

Then the night cracks open with a roar of animal rage. The planks beneath my feet shiver under the impact.

I put my hands over my ears, but the roar goes right through me.

It's here!

I want to run. But I can't move. Can't breathe.

The roar breaks off, and I sag to my knees. The echoes ricochet inside my skull.

Pike gets up from the walkway. He must have fallen under the shockwave too. He staggers to the end of the dock.

I want to yell to him. *Stop! Run!* But I can only watch as he climbs down the metal ladder to the ice.

The sweat on my back has turned into a glaze of ice.

'Danny!' Pike yells, out of sight.

I stand shaking, waiting for the scream when Pike sees what's out here with us.

'Danny! Get over here!'

His voice is torn away by the wind. I glance back toward the house. The open door shows a warm glow. But there's an ocean of darkness in between.

The hairs on my bare legs stand straight out, not just from the cold. The air is electric.

'Danny!' Pike calls.

I break out of my paralysis and jog down the walkway, my gaze sweeping the shadows for any movement.

At the end of the dock, I stop by the metal ladder hanging down to the frozen surface. I see Pike on his knees leaning over Howie, who's laid out flat on the ice.

'He won't wake up,' he shouts. 'He's soaked. Freezing. Must have gone through the ice. Help me get him up there.'

Pike drags Howie to the bottom of the ladder.

'I'll lift him, and you get him under the arms.'

I squat, reaching down to get a good grip.

'Got him?' Pike asks. 'Okay. Here goes.'

He heaves and I pull. Soaking wet, Howie's a dead weight. I grunt and fall back on my butt as I yank him onto the walkway on top of me.

His face looks grey in the dim light. Is he even breathing? He's so limp.

Pike pulls Howie off me.

I'm getting to my feet when I hear the growl. Pike's

123

eyes meet mine. He's thinking the same as me.

We're not alone out here.

'What the hell's that?' he asks.

I can only shake my head, my voice gone. I swing around to the ladder, expecting to see something climbing up after us.

The deep rumble floods the darkness. Surrounding us.

Pike's eyes are wide, but not with the panic that's seizing me. He's hyper-alert, ready to fight.

But he doesn't know what he's up against.

'Let's move!' He lifts Howie in his arms as he stands. 'Just watch my back.'

Right! But who's going to watch mine?

We run from the thunder of the growl. My focus twitches left and right. Shadows shift as the wind flaps the tarps on the boats.

The night squeezes in on us. Any second the beast will jump out of the blackness. Or reach up to grab my feet and pull me off the dock. Finish what it started the other night.

I get that nightmare sensation – running and running but getting nowhere. The light from the house promises safety. But it seems to retreat as fast as we run, always out of reach.

My foot catches a gap between planks. I fall hard,

slide on the snow-slicked wood, and scramble to keep from dropping off the edge to the ice below.

Pike's still going, widening the gap between us.

The growling closes in. I whip my head around. Only the empty boardwalk and shrouded boats.

I get up. Pike's almost to the shore. As I'm about to take my first step, I freeze.

About ten feet in front of me, rising up through the cracks between the planks, is a little cloud of mist. As it starts to fade, another puff rises. The growling rumbles with the rhythm of those breaths.

It's down there! Waiting!

This is not real. Not happening.

The growl blinds me to everything else. It owns me.

I can't outrun the beast. But it let me go before. It had me. I was dead. And it let me go.

Images flash behind my eyes. That warped face. Those teeth.

Stop it! I shout at myself.

Make a run for it! Maybe I'll reach the house. Maybe.

That's all I've got. I suck in a deep breath, then throw myself into an all-out sprint. I don't look down, don't think. I leap over the space where the breath mists up through the cracks.

I'm so locked in on the light from the house I

forget to breathe. I pick up speed, ears straining for any sound of pursuit. But the rumble rushes at me from all directions.

I stagger up the snowy incline to the house, using my hands to keep from tumbling back down.

I almost catch up to Pike as he steps through the doorway, slouching under Howie's weight. Pike sets him down on the floor.

I have to reach back out into the dark to grab the doorknob. For a second it feels like I'm sticking my arm into the mouth of that beast. It'll rip my arm clean off.

Then my hand finds the knob and I slam the door. I lock it and stand there, clutching the knob.

I'm stunned by the quiet. I stare at the door, panting. When I get enough breath, I yell.

'Dad!'

Fourteen

In the morning, I catch a ride to the hospital on the back of Ash's motorbike. The blowing snow and black ice on the highway to Barrie keep me wide awake and holding on tight.

Last night was endless. No chance for sleep. I'm still dazed and confused.

This drive with dead shock absorbers leaves me a little saddle-sore as we walk through the parking lot of the Royal Victoria Hospital. I was passing through these same doors not ten hours ago, after Dad raced us up here. With Howie unconscious and half frozen, stripped of his wet clothes and mummified in blankets, we all crammed into the front of Dad's pick-up. The ambulance from Barrie would have taken forever. Howie was shivering like crazy the whole way, which Dad said was good sign – his body was trying to warm itself. Stop shivering when you're that cold and you're dead.

In the emergency room they wrapped him in heating pads and started him on warmed IV saline. Around here they see a lot of hypothermia, so they had him out of danger pretty quick. He woke up for a little bit, but he just stared through us, like we weren't there.

'It's shock,' the doctor told us. 'Don't worry. We'll keep him overnight. It'll pass.'

Dad's back at the lake now, going over the scene around the ice hut with the cops, trying to figure out why the ice gave. Me and Pike never said anything about the growling and the roar. Neither of us actually saw anything. All anybody knows for sure is Howie went through the ice. They didn't find anything else wrong with him, besides hypothermia. No sign of any attack. So I kept my mouth shut, and Pike was busy dealing with his parents.

Everybody's just waiting for Howie to recover and tell us what happened on the lake. Everybody but me. I've got a pretty good idea.

Me and Ash find Howie's room and take a peek.

The lights are off, but the glare from the snowy day comes through the window. Howie lies buried under a pile of blankets on the bed, his eyes shut.

'Still sleeping,' Ash whispers.

'Shhh,' a voice hushes us.

We turn and see Pike slouched in a chair behind the

door. Guarding Howie, like always. He looks wiped out. Been on watch all night. He stands now and jerks a thumb toward the door, kicking us out.

Pike follows us into the hall. 'Howie keeps waking up. Crying out. Nightmares, I guess. He just got back to sleep.'

'But he's going to be okay, right?' Ash asks.

'That's what they tell us,' Pike says. 'My mother just went home to get him some clothes. Dad had to head out to the base.' He tries to fight back a yawn. 'Man, I need some caffeine.'

'There's a cafeteria downstairs,' Ash says.

'I'll keep an eye on Howie,' I tell him.

'Yeah? Stay in the room. Don't leave him alone.'

'Okay. Don't worry.'

'I'll just run down then. But don't wake him up.'

'I won't.'

He stretches his back. 'Later, we gotta talk, Danny.'

'Yeah. I know.'

Ash takes Pike to the cafeteria as I ease the door shut and step quietly over to Howie's bed. Even in this low light he looks pale.

A bare foot sticks out from the blankets. I reach to cover it up.

'Danny?'

I flinch at his voice, scratchy, barely a whisper.

Howie's eyes are open, focused on me. They've got this glazed, feverish look.

'Thought you were sleeping.'

He shakes his head limply on the pillow.

'Can't sleep. When I close my eyes I keep seeing . . .'

I wait for him to finish, but he just lies there. The pile of blankets rise and fall slightly with his shallow breathing.

'You were there?' he finally says. 'Last night?'

'Yeah. Me and Pike heard you yell. And we ran out to get you.'

'Did you see it?'

In the winter light his face is ghost white. His eyes are wide but unfocused. He's seeing last night.

My throat has gone dry. I have to swallow before I can speak. 'See what?'

'That thing. With the teeth.'

I lean against the bed to keep my knees from folding on me. I didn't want to hear that – really didn't want to hear that!

I open my mouth to say something like, *you're still in shock, you were seeing things*.

But I know better.

'We heard it. But it was out of sight by the time we got to you.'

'It was huge,' he says. 'Bigger than anything I ever . . .'

130

He trails off, shaking his head. 'It had these paws, the size of them . . . and the claws . . .'

His breathing's starting to get ragged, scratching in his throat.

'Howie, you gotta rest. Take it easy.'

But he's not listening. 'Those tracks you showed me. That thing, that's what made them. It's real.'

'Don't think about that now. You're safe here.'

'You said it chased you that night. Did you see it?'

I nod, tugging down a blanket to cover his foot.

'Come over here,' he mutters, fumbling with the sheets pulled up to his neck.

I walk around to the head of the bed. 'You need something? Water?'

He stops fooling with the sheets and falls back exhausted. Even his eyes seem a paler shade of brown.

'Look,' he mumbles. 'On my neck.'

'You finally get someone to give you a hickey?'

I was hoping to make him smile or bring some pink back in his cheeks.

'Right here.' He touches the left side of his neck. 'Do you see anything?'

My stomach goes cold.

A pinprick blue dot, as if someone stabbed him there with a pen.

I start hyperventilating, hit by a surge of panic. I

have to sit on the edge of his bed to keep from falling. Closing my eyes only makes it worse.

'That's where it . . . bit me.' Howie feels the spot on his neck. 'What's there? What's it look like?'

Reluctantly, I hold up the back of my right hand close enough so he can see, and point out the small blue mark.

'Looks like that.'

Fifteen

I have to get out of here.

Hospitals are poison to me. Every sound, sight and smell brings back bad memories.

By the time Pike and Ash return, Howie's out for the count. He could barely keep his eyes open as I sketched out my own encounter with the beast. Finally, his eyelids drooped shut.

Pike takes his post by the bed, with a tall coffee and a fistful of candy bars. We leave him thumbing through old copies of *Sports Illustrated*.

'Want to hit the cafeteria?' Ash asks as we walk down the hall.

I'm finding it hard to breathe this hospital stink. It's making me nauseous. 'Can we just get out of here?'

But before I make it to the elevators, my stomach starts to heave. I can't wait for the elevator. Gotta get out. Now!

I clamp my jaws, push through the door to the stairwell and race down the stairs. My guts are trying to turn inside out. Down two flights, I hit the exit door hard and stumble out onto the snowy parking lot.

Cold, fresh air. My freak-out dies off fast with the wind in my face.

Behind me, the door bangs open. 'You gonna puke?'

'Sorry,' I say. 'Kind of lost it there.'

She gives me a moment to get a grip, pulling on her leather gloves and zipping up.

'You want to ride back to the Cove, or what?'

I shake my head. 'I need to stick around town a couple hours. So I can talk to Howie when he wakes up. Maybe we can walk around? Find someplace?'

So we walk for a couple blocks, silently with Ash shooting side glances at me like I might jump into traffic or something.

'So what was that?' she says finally. 'Back there.'

'Just a little temporary insanity.'

'You want to talk about it?'

I shake my head, but I start talking anyway.

Before I can stop myself, I'm telling her about Mom. It all comes spilling out. Mom getting sick, all the tests, and the doctors who couldn't do squat to help her. But they kept finding new ways to hurt her. Useless treatments, burning her with beam radiation.

Implanting radioactive *seeds* into the tumour.

'Always wanted a garden,' Mom joked, when we got her home, with her head wrapped in a turban of bandages. 'Just not one growing out of my head.'

Even under that torture she could still joke. She was so brave. And I was a coward.

It got so I was scared to come home from school, because of what I might find. But I was scared not to rush home too, in case she needed me.

Sometimes I'd look at her and see a stranger looking back. She'd forget my name. Her brain would short-circuit and she'd swear and scream these horrible things at me — words I'd never heard her use before. We were losing her. And she was losing herself.

It felt like it took forever, but really the cancer was quick. It came out of nowhere and ripped her away from us.

I tell Ash everything. I can't quit till she hears it all.

Finally, when there's nothing left, I stop walking. The pavement underfoot has given way to gravel. We've gone from one end of Barrie to the other, with me talking non-stop.

'Sorry,' I say. 'For someone who hates to talk about it, I can't seem to shut up.'

I'm not even feeling the wind, but Ash is hunched against the cold, rubbing her gloved hands together. For the first time since I've known her, she's speechless. Can't blame her.

Then she throws her arm over my shoulder and pulls me in close. 'Come here and give me some heat.'

We turn and head back into town.

We grab some pizza, and Ash does the talking now. No heartbreak or emotional trauma. Just blunt-force trauma. Boxing injuries and broken bones, stitches and scars.

She describes the different grades of concussions you can get, from first to third grades.

'Now a third-grade concussion, that's some serious brain scrambling,' she says. 'I got one of those from a wicked uppercut to the chin. So they tell me anyway. Cause that shot knocked a couple days out of my memory banks.'

I wouldn't mind a little amnesia.

After the pizza, we stroll through the mall, deafened by Christmas carols. I give Dad a call. He wanted to know how Howie's doing.

Then we make our way back to the hospital.

Before he finally gave in to exhaustion and fell asleep, me and Howie decided we had to tell somebody what was going on. What we saw, what happened to us. But who? Not the cops, no way. We'd end up in the psych ward. So I said let's try our stories out on some friendlies first. Pike and Ash. See how they take it.

As we jump slush puddles, crossing the street to the hospital, Ash tells me what it's like trying to breathe with a broken rib.

'Is there any part of you that hasn't been broken or cut or dislocated?' I ask.

'My nose is still in one piece. And all my good bits are still intact. Show you some time.'

Before I can think of a comeback, she pushes through the hospital doors. I'm left stumbling after her. Even when she's not knocking me out, she leaves me punch-drunk.

We catch the elevator up to the third floor and run into Howie's mom in the hallway. She looks tired.

'Hi, guys. I'm just on my way out for a cigarette-break. Howie woke up a little while ago. He's getting some colour back. Don't wear him out.'

'We won't,' Ash says.

Howie's lights are on, and he's sitting up in bed with a food tray in his lap.

'Hey, Howie,' Ash says. 'Back from the dead?'

'Halfway back.' He gives her a weak smile.

Pike's slouched in his chair, blinking bloodshot eyes at us.

'Thawed out yet?' Ash grabs another chair and drags

it over by the bed. 'You look like crap. And so does that meal. What's the brown stuff?'

Howie pokes at it with a plastic fork, like it might poke him back. 'It's either mud or gravy. I'm guessing mud.'

'Here.' I toss him the Kit-Kat bar I picked up for our little sugar junkie.

His eyes show a glimmer of life. 'Real food. Pike, can you flush this stuff? The smell's making me nauseous.'

Pike takes the tray and digs in. 'Mmmm. Roadkill.'

'So, how long you in for?' Ash asks.

Howie breaks off a finger of his Kit-Kat and runs it under his nose like a fine cigar. He sighs and takes a bite.

'Just till tomorrow. They want to keep me for observation. Make sure I don't relapse into shock.'

'So what's the story?' Ash says. 'What happened last night? You go for a polar bear swim?'

Howie looks over to me for help.

'You want me to go first?' I ask him.

He nods, carefully breaking off another chocolate finger.

'Go first with what?' Pike glances back and forth between us. 'What's going on?'

'What's going on is pretty crazy. Just warning you up front. Ash, I told you part of the story the other day. But

138

I gave you the censored version.' I suck in a deep breath. 'Okay. So, here goes. Flashback with me to the night Pike did his pyro act on Fat Bill's.'

Starting there, I take them through my run home after I parted ways with Ash. I wander around the room, not meeting anybody's eyes. I describe the beast, knowing how delusional it sounds. But I rush ahead before I can chicken out. And when I end with me reaching the house after the attack in the ditch, I'm near breathless.

'I don't get it,' Pike says. 'What's the punchline?'

'No punchline. No joke.'

He sets the tray down on the bedside table. 'What the hell were you smoking that night? And where can I get some?'

I look over to Ash, but her eyes give nothing away. 'What's this got to do with Howie going through the ice?'

I gesture to Howie, passing it over to him.

'I, uh . . .' Howie scratches at the mark on his neck. 'I saw it too. I mean, the thing that went after Danny. That's what attacked me on the ice.'

Howie gets a little twitchy with all eyes on him. He ran through it with me briefly before, when we were swapping stories, but now he's choking up.

'Go from the beginning,' I nudge. 'From when Pike

left you in the hut, and came up to the house for coffee.'

'Right. Yeah. I stayed to watch the lines. We were doing pretty good. The fish were biting.'

He tells his story slow, like he's trying to delay the nasty parts. Even safe and surrounded by the three of us in the light of day, he gets shaky as he relives it.

After Pike left, Howie was sitting on the little wooden bench built into the hut, listening to 'Hockey Night in Canada' on his radio.

He was staring at the black hole cut in the ice near his feet when he felt the bump.

'I thought somebody'd skidded their snowmobile into the hut. The whole thing shook with a thud. Then I thought maybe Pike was screwing with me.'

So Howie started for the door to peek out. From the corner of his eye he caught sight of something jumping up out of the fishing hole. For a split second he thought it was a fish.

But then he saw the size of it, and it was no fish. In the light from the bulb hanging from the ceiling, he didn't know what he was looking at. Until it moved. And he saw the claws digging into the ice. Then he realized the thing was attached to something below the surface. It was some kind of enormous paw.

'Bigger than a polar bear's. Way bigger.' He holds his

hands about three feet apart. 'And no fur on it. Just this pale white hide.'

Howie backed out of range of those claws as they raked into the ice, leaving deep grooves. He was frozen watching, scared and fascinated at the same time, knowing whatever was attached to that thing wasn't going to fit through his fishing hole. He figured out too late what it was trying to do. Make a bigger hole.

Then the ice gave. A chunk the size of the door to the hut fell through, sending out cracks across the frozen floor. Howie jumped up on the bench, watching his fish bucket and rods sink into the water after the hunk of ice and the disappearing paw.

Huddling on the bench, Howie searched for a path to the door on the frozen rim that still held up along the walls of the shack.

But before he could try, there was a spray of water as something emerged from the black depths, breaking through more of the ice. Not just a paw this time, but a massive head surfaced inside the hut.

Howie's description of it is *too* good. My legs get shaky.

Howie stutters big time now, remembering.

That's when he screamed the first time. Me and Pike heard it in the kitchen at the house.

In the hut, Howie was so fixed on those eyes, he

barely caught sight of the paw shooting up from the dark water. He jumped out of the way as it landed on the bench beside him, and he kept going along the rim of ice, hit the door and crashed out.

Howie got about ten feet away when the ice behind him exploded, knocking him to his knees. The cracked surface slanted under him. He slid backwards.

He screamed the second time. Just before he went under.

Howie shivers as he tells it, even buried under all his blankets in this overheated room.

As the lake swallowed him he threw his arms out, splashing in the blackness, searching for solid ice. The cold knocked the wind out of him.

Then something bumped his legs under the surface. Struggling wildly, Howie managed to get his elbows up and heave himself out of the lake, rolling away from the open water.

He crawled, and was pushing himself to his feet when the ice shook under him. Looking back he saw something huge and pale burst upwards, spraying water into the air.

Howie turned and ran for the dock. The ladder was in sight, leading up to the house and safety.

But his legs were knocked out from behind. He rolled onto his back and saw that thing looming over him.

What happened was like with me and the beast down in the ditch. It let out a roar. The tongue stabbed him.

Then it was lights out for Howie. Nothing more till he came to in the hospital.

He sags back on his pillow, forehead shiny with sweat.

The room is dead quiet. Pike rubs his hand over his mohawk, frowning at his brother. Ash looks from Howie to me, her face unreadable.

'Sounds like a *Windigo* story,' she says finally.

'A what?' Pike grumbles.

'Kind of an Indian ghost story. Windigos are demon spirits that roam the wilderness, eating up lost souls.' She widens her eyes at us. 'Spooky stuff. My dad used to tell me about them.'

'But they're not real?' Pike asks.

'Well, no. It's just stories. I mean, come on.'

'What are they supposed to look like?' Howie says.

'Big, ugly things. Bulging eyes. Lots of long nasty teeth. They have a chunk of ice for a heart. And when they shout they grow taller than the trees.'

'Right,' Pike grunts.

'You heard it,' I say to him. 'Remember that growling in the dark, and the roar?'

'Could have been a wolf – a bear? Hell, I don't know.'

Howie's head turns on the pillow, eyes on his brother.

143

Pike shrugs. 'It's not that I'm not believing you, bro. It's only . . . this is some insane stuff.'

If it was just me and my ditch story, Pike could dismiss it. But he trusts his brother. And Howie's the only one on the planet who believes in Pike, who knows him as more than the nut everybody else sees.

'I don't know, guys.' Ash gives us a look like the show's over, now let's get a grip. 'Where's your proof?'

'Our stories back each other up,' I say.

'Don't mean squat. Come on. They brought Howie in unconscious, in hypothermic shock. He still looks out of it. And you say you hit your head and blacked out in the ditch. Maybe you got a concussion. Definitely not thinking straight.'

'Yeah, I hit my head and everything. But me and Howie saw the same thing. I mean, two people can't have the same hallucination, right?'

'If there's some big nasty monster hunting out there,' she says, 'and it had you guys cornered, then why didn't it just chow down on you? Why are you still breathing?'

I've been wondering the same thing.

'The footprint.' Howie speaks up. 'Danny's cell-shot of the print he found in the ditch.'

'But you said that was some kind of fake,' she says.

'I was wrong. Way wrong. And there's this.' He starts pushing the blankets down his chest. 'When that thing caught me it bit me. Or stung me – whatever. It left this.'

Howie stretches out his neck to show her. She leans over, and Pike comes in close to take a look.

'Where?' Pike asks.

Howie points out the blue dot.

'That looks like an old zit or something.' Ash squints.

Pike pokes it gently. 'A sting? Like a needle jab?'

Howie shrugs. 'I guess. Something like that. But that's proof.' Howie looks to me for back-up. 'It bit Danny, too. Show them.'

Reluctantly, I hold out my hand. Looking at the blue dot under their sceptical stares, I realize how unimpressive it seems.

'I don't know,' Ash says, sympathetic but still not buying this. 'That's it? That's all you've got?'

'That's evidence,' Pike says, standing up for Howie now.

'That's a dot. A blue dot. Like you poked yourself with a pen. Sorry, but it looks like nothing.'

She's not trying to be harsh, just real.

'Howie's not crazy,' Pike says. 'And he's not lying.'

'I'm not saying nothing like that,' Ash says. 'But, give it a day or two. Let him recover. Then, both you guys, we'll see where your heads are at. You go telling the doctors your monster stories, they'll think you've lost it.'

She's reading my mind. Nobody's going to believe us. Hell, I wouldn't.

'But that thing,' Howie mumbles. 'It's still out there. If it comes back—'

'It'll have to get past me,' Pike breaks in. 'And that ain't gonna happen.'

I heave a sigh, sitting on the foot of the bed. I feel like curling up and sleeping for a couple days.

Ash and Pike know us and they still aren't buying it. Pike's only backing Howie because he's his baby bro.

Ash thinks it was a concussion that made me dream up the beast. I wish. Then I could shrug it off. Forget about it.

But I've got a real bad feeling, that the beast isn't going to let me forget.

Sixteen

Dad had to flatline the furnace so he could fix it. Now the windows have frosted over, and the only heat comes from the little fireplace in the living room down the hall. Dad's sleeping on the couch tonight, huddled by the fire.

'Put some layers on,' he keeps telling me. 'You're making me shiver just looking at you.'

Maybe I've got a fever or something, but I'm not feeling the freeze. Dad dug up a sleeping bag for me to stay near the fire with him. But even though the thermometer tells me I should be wearing a parka to bed tonight, I'm fine with my T-shirt and sweatpants.

I can almost see my breath in my room. Crashing on the bed now, I stare up at the water-stain on the ceiling that looks like Medusa, the chick with the reptilian hairdo. I've got this wicked headache jabbing tiny ice-picks into my brain. There's no way I'm going to be able to fall asleep with that beast running wild out in the night.

The Provincial police came out yesterday while I was in Barrie swapping horror stories with Howie in the hospital. He's back at home now, recovering. Dad showed the cops around the huts and the surrounding ice, trying to figure out why it gave. But nothing makes sense. The hut is still anchored there in place. It's not like the whole thing went crashing through. The surface has frozen over again, erasing any sign of the breaks. The fishing hole Dad made was a standard auger-drilled, basketball-sized hole. Nothing looked suspicious.

The weather conditions have been ideal for a good freeze, with the ice a solid twelve inches, strong enough to hold a small car. He even drilled a test bore to confirm the thickness. There haven't been any thaws since winter set in, no rains that might weaken the surface. And no signs of pressure ridges where the ice can buckle up if the currents underneath are strong enough.

On the day Howie went through the ice, a bunch of kids had been out in full hockey gear, playing a game of shinny just a stone's throw from the huts.

The cops are calling it a freak accident. The ice can be unpredictable.

Nobody's blaming Dad, except Dad. Like it's his fault.

A few times I came *this* close to telling him what really happened. But no matter how I play it out in my head, I can't see him buying it. Dad lives in the real world.

Last week, so did I.

Shifting my head on the pillow, I glance at the window and see the pane glazed over with frost. Tomorrow, Dad has to pick up a new regulator for the boiler.

He's a mechanical magician. He can fix anything. That's how he met Mom.

Dad was working a summer job at an auto body shop. Mom came in after a fender bender to get some work done. This was when they were still in high school. Dad hammered out the dents and did a patch-up paint job to cover the scratches.

'Then when I came to get my car, he tried to pick me up,' was how Mom told it.

'*She* was the one hitting on *me*, big time,' was his version.

Mom rolled her eyes at that. 'I'd broken my pinkie finger crashing the car, and it was in a splint. So he said to me: "I can fix that too." Then *Slick* here took my hand and kissed the splint.'

'Hey, we were a full service shop.'

'And I told him it still hurt. He said it's a daily treatment, gotta come back for more. I said: "Can I have my hand back?" He goes: "Can I have my heart back?"'

I can't imagine him making moves, acting slick. But this was in his prehistoric youth, when he had a wild streak that was gone by the time I came along.

'After that,' he said, 'she started stalking me. Kept coming back with new dents and scrapes.'

'So I was a bad driver.'

'Or a bad liar.'

Anyway, that was their 'how we met' story.

Dad's always had a feel for machines. If he can get his hands on something, he can fix it. Worst thing for him is being helpless. Like he was with Mom. Having to wait and watch her suffer.

I sigh. Stop thinking so much! I'll never fall asleep.

But as I stare at the ceiling, I find myself drifting off. It's like there's a strong current running through my head, with a powerful undertow tugging me down.

My eyes close in one long blink.

And they open on darkness.

What the—

I'm gone from my room, lying out in the open under a midnight sky. A sky deep with stars. I sit up with a gasp, looking around, expecting to find my bed under me. But I'm laid out on a slab of ice. No, not a slab, a whole field of ice, stretching away to frozen hills and bluffs.

I'm barefoot, and still in my T-shirt and sweats. But I'm not feeling the cold. Not a shiver.

I get up and do a three-sixty, taking in the view. The polar landscape is coloured in shades of blue. By the starlight, I make out massive mountains in the distance. No trees, no lights anywhere, and nobody but me.

I'm dwarfed by the scale of this place.

Where the hell am I?

Then I hear a cough. I swing around, searching the dark. There are breaks in the ice field where jagged rocks stab up like rough gravestones.

I consider calling out, but who knows what'll answer?

I wait, holding my breath. Another cough. Close by.

Stepping carefully with my naked feet on the slick ice, I do a wide circle around the nearest gravestone. Not wanting to surprise whatever it is, or be surprised.

Nothing behind the first rock. Moving on to the next, I get halfway around and see a crouching figure. Takes me a second to recognize it.

'Howie?'

He squeaks, swinging toward my voice. 'Who-who's there?'

'It's me. Danny.'

Howie lets out a shaky breath, but stays huddled

against the boulder.

'What're you doing here?' I ask. Maybe a dumb question. I mean, what am I doing here? And where's *here*?

'Hiding.'

'From what?'

I glance around, searching for any movement in the ice-scape.

'I don't know,' he says. 'It just felt like the right thing to do.'

With Howie, hiding's always the right thing to do.

'Where are we?' I sit next to him and lean back on the rock.

'Don't know,' he says, looking up at the sky. 'For sure, a long way from home.'

I follow his gaze, taking in the blackness thick with stars. A full moon is rising above a distant mountain range, shining down on the ice world with a cool blue glow. 'Weird.'

'Definitely a long way from home.'

It looks amazing, but none of it feels real. It's like some billion dollar special effects, with awesome visuals. I can feel the rough surface of the rock against my back, and hear the hollow rush of wind blowing past our hiding place. But where's the cold?

I shake my head.

'We're dreaming, right?' I say, figuring it out now. 'I mean, *I'm* dreaming. I guess you're not really real.'

'Who's not real?' He hugs his knees to his chest.

'Well, I'm dreaming you, right?'

He gets a worried frown. 'I thought I was dreaming you.'

'Wow, you just blew my mind,' I say, sarcastic. Then I decide to try something, and give him a punch in the shoulder.

'What'd you do that for?'

'Did you feel it?'

'Yeah. You feel this?'

Howie jabs me in the ribs with his bony elbow.

'Yeah. Quit it.'

He rubs his shoulder. I rub my ribs.

'So, what did that prove?' he asks.

'Nothing, I guess. Except maybe that we're a couple of idiots. Lost in space.'

I try to laugh, but my throat is too tight and dry.

Howie clears his throat.

'Some primitive cultures believe in shared dreams,' he tells me. 'Like as part of a . . . a spiritual journey.'

'Fascinating, Yoda. What is this? *National Geographic*?'

'Just trying to help.'

If I have to get stuck in a dream with somebody, why couldn't it be Ash?

'You know,' I say, taking in the view, 'when I'm having a dream, I usually don't realize it's a dream.'

'Me neither.'

'This feels different. Kind of, I don't know, *wrong* somehow.

I notice Howie shivering.

'You cold?'

'No. Just . . . scared, I guess. You?'

I run my hand over the sheet of ice we're sitting on.

'Cold? No. Should be, though. It must be fifty below.'

'So, what do we—' he starts.

But he's stopped by a noise. I hold my breath, ears wide open.

A clicking sound.

'Do you hear—' Howie says.

I put my hand up to quiet him. I hear it all right. That clicking is strangely familiar.

Claws. Digging into the ice.

I peer around the edge of the rock. Nothing but ice. Frozen hills and bluffs beyond. Glaciers looming in the distance under the midnight sky.

Then by the light of the stars and the blue moon I catch sight of it. Stalking across the frozen field about fifty yards away.

As I watch, pressed tight to the rock, the beast rises up on its hind legs, towering above the rocks poking up through the ice. Its enormous head sways, like it's scenting the air. Clouds of steam blow from the long slits of its nostrils.

Scenting. For us.

I slip back out of sight. Howie stares a question at me.

My lips to his ear, I whisper: 'It's here.'

His shivering gets worse, but he stays quiet.

Think! I tell myself. Quick!

The gravestones stick up across the ice field, with clusters here and there. I spot one of these crowded spots off to the right, in the opposite direction from the beast. I point it out to Howie.

Let's go, I mouth.

He nods. I have to help him to his feet. Howie's shaking so bad, I don't know how he's going make it if we have to run.

I peek around the boulder, and see the beast roaming on all fours, weaving through the maze of stones.

As long as we can keep out of sight, dodging from rock to rock, maybe we can put some distance between us and that thing. I grab Howie by the elbow and set off for the thickest cluster of stones.

We run silent, my bare feet and Howie's socks soundless on the ice. It's slick, like running on wet glass. Howie keeps slipping and almost going down.

Reaching a tall cluster, a kind of icy Stonehenge, I lean to look past the corner.

Nothing. Good. I can pick out the rock where we started out, black against the deep blue of the ice.

If we can keep moving . . .

I go stiff as the beast comes into view and bends close to the ground right where we were.

Picking up the scent.

It lifts its head, showing a glint of teeth. The wind carries a low growl to where we're hiding.

I slip back behind the rock. Howie's eyes are shut tight, and I have to pull him from his grip on the stone. Even with my knees like rubber, I hurry him through the maze. Twisting and turning, yanking him along.

Behind us the clicking nears. Long claws tapping and scratching across the ice.

The growl shivers through my ribs.

'Quick,' I breathe to Howie.

We come to a tight crowd of stones where we have to slip single-file through the gaps. These crevices are way too narrow for the beast. It'll have to find a way around.

Howie holds my arm as we make our way through the maze.

Suddenly we break out into the open, and I skid to a stop, breathless.

The ice cuts off in a sheer drop ahead. The end of the world.

Slow, careful, I inch up close to the edge.

Down below – way down below – is what looks like open water. At the base of the cliff there's a lot of sharp, jagged rocks.

'We're dead,' Howie says.

He's beside me, taking in the lethal drop. I'm about to answer when I see a pale form outlined against the starry sky behind us.

From its perch on top of the standing stones, the beast is watching. It couldn't fit through the maze, so it climbed over.

'Howie.' My voice cracks.

He turns and sees.

It watches. No hurry. We're cornered.

Howie's wheezing little whimpers.

Think! I shout at myself. Think of something. Anything!

But there's nowhere left to run. Nowhere but—

'Let's jump.' I think it and blurt it in the same second.

'What-what?' Howie shoots me a look like I'm crazy.

'When you fall in dreams you wake up, right? It's the vertigo, or whatever, makes you wake before you hit the ground.'

Or before we hit those rocks at the bottom of the cliff.

'What . . . what if you're wrong? What if we don't wake up?'

I shake my head, eyes locked on the beast.

'Dreams can't hurt you.' But even I'm not buying it. 'Anything's better than staying here.'

The growl picks up. My whole body shudders.

Howie moans. 'I can't.'

Maybe the beast senses what we're thinking. It tenses, ready to leap.

Gotta do it. Now!

So I shove Howie over the edge of the cliff. There's a half-second where I take in the shock on his face as he tumbles backward into nothing, reaching out to grab on to me.

I jump after him, before I can think and freeze up.

Over the edge, into the night. I'd scream if I could, but the speed of the fall rips the breath out of me.

The beast's outraged roar follows me all the way down.

In the blurring rush I catch glimpses of Howie tumbling toward the rocks.

Wake up! I shout inside my head. Now!

But the rocks rush up, the wind buffeting against me.

Howie, a pale blur in his pyjamas, hits the rocks.

I killed him! Killed Howie! Killed myself!

Then I hit.

I shock awake like I'm being electrocuted. A strangled yell dies in the back of my throat. I stare blindly around the room, still feeling the wind tearing at me.

The light's on. There's no wind. No falling.

It takes me a minute to convince myself of these things. I'm here. Awake. Alive. Safe.

Safe?

I swing my feet to the floor just as my cellphone rings. Getting shakily to my feet, I glance at the clock. Two in the morning? I grab the phone and see the caller ID.

'Howie?'

'Danny, you there?' He's breathing hard.

I still feel dizzy, my heart machine-gunning in my chest. I collapse on the bed. 'Guess so. What's going on?'

'This is going to sound weird. Really "out there".'

I know what he's going to say.

'You had a dream?' I ask.

He lets out a shuddering sigh. 'Yeah. With that thing, you know . . .'

'I know.'

'It was chasing us,' he says, a tremble in his voice.

'I know. I was there.' I rub my eyes. 'This is not good.'

'You're telling me? Why did you have to push me?'

'It worked, didn't it?'

Howie gives a weak, nervous laugh. 'Yeah. But, a little warning next time?'

We're both quiet, thinking.

'What the hell's going on?' I ask him, and myself. 'Am I going nuts?'

'If you are, I'm riding shotgun.'

I look down at my hand and rub the blue dot there with my thumb, like I can rub it away.

'Remember Ray Dyson?' Howie asks, out of nowhere.

'Yeah? What about him?'

'Well, I was thinking. Maybe the same thing that got us, got him too.'

I pause. 'But that was a dog that bit Raid, right? Made him sick.'

'Nobody's sure what it was. There were all these rumours going around. I heard they couldn't find any bite marks on him. They thought he was making the whole thing up, till he started showing symptoms.'

'Symptoms of what?'

'You heard what people were saying. Rabies. West

Nile virus. Lyme disease. Or none of the above.'

I remember that picture in the paper of Ray running away from the hospital in his pyjamas, into the night.

'You know before he freaked out, and they stuck him in the hospital?' Howie says. 'When I ran into him in the washroom, Ray was delirious. He kept saying how he thought he'd got away, but *it* was only letting him think that. He said it was coming back for him.'

'*It?* What the hell is that thing?'

No answer from Howie.

I've got a million questions.

Like, where was Ray running to? Was he trying to escape? To hide? To die?

And if the thing that attacked him was the same beast that got me and Howie, then how long before we go running into the night?

Seventeen

I ditch school and head for Howie's. He's still recovering, hiding away in his room.

It's been a couple days since our shared nightmare. Whenever I start doubting it really happened, there's Howie on the phone wanting to talk about it. This morning he called before breakfast and said he wanted to show me some stuff. He wouldn't tell me what, said I had to come over and see. So I called Ash for a ride, and she's ditching with me.

These backroads are a mess. Every rut and pothole her motorbike hits sets off a minor explosion inside my skull. The headache I've had since my fall in the ditch is flaring into a migraine. The million-watt glare of the sun reflecting off the snow needles the backs of my eyes.

At the Slater house, Howie's mom answers the door.

'The boys are upstairs,' she says. 'Don't wear Howie

out. He needs his rest. He was up most of the night.'

Me and Ash go up and find Howie in front of the computer. Pike's sitting on the bed. At the sound of the door opening Howie swings around, jumpy as always.

'Hey, Howie. Feeling any better?' I ask.

'My head's pounding. I ache all over. I'm going on next to no sleep. And, oh yeah, and I just got a nasty paper cut.'

'I guess that's a no,' I say.

I find an extra chair and collapse on it. The place feels like a greenhouse. He must have the heat cranked up. I take off my jacket and drape it over the back of the chair. I'm aching from my skull to my toenails, a dull throbbing that feels kind of like the flu.

Me and Howie agreed to keep our nightmare between us. It's just too weird. And that's saying something, on top of everything that's happened.

'Howie, you want another Tylenol?' Pike asks. He's been staying off school to bodyguard him.

'I'm already overdosing on that stuff. It's not making a dent.'

'You should eat something,' Pike tries.

Howie grunts a no. Slouching in his seat, you can see the bones of his shoulders through his T-shirt, looking like he forgot to take the hanger out when he put it on.

'So, what are you working on?' I nod toward the

computer, and the books and printouts strewn around it.

'Tell you in a sec. But first, I need you to do something for me.'

'Like what?'

He picks a glass off the filing cabinet beside his desk. Inside, there's a thermometer.

'Stick this in your mouth. Don't ask me why, just go ahead.'

I take the glass, looking dubiously inside.

'It's clean. I rinsed it off. Come on, stick it in. And I'll show you some stuff I dug up. It'll blow your mind.'

I give in and stick it under my tongue.

'You sure that's the *oral* thermometer?' Pike asks, grinning.

'Don't listen to him,' Howie says, pulling together pages of printouts. 'I got this stuff off of the *Barrie Examiner* website. Their back issues go back more than seventy years to when the newspaper started up. I dug around to see if there were any other reports of animal attacks around Harvest Cove – bear, cougar, wolf or whatever.'

I'd say our attacker falls into the 'whatever' category.

'Then I noticed something in the write-up on Ray Dyson's disappearance. They said that rabies had been ruled out, and that there hadn't been a human case of rabies in Harvest Cove in fifteen years. I went in the *Examiner* archives to check that old case out, and found this.'

He hands a page to me. Ash reads over my shoulder. It's dated January twelfth, fifteen years ago. There's a story on the aftermath of a nasty blizzard. Downed power lines, blocked roads. A photo shows a guy skiing down the middle of some street in Barrie.

'So it snowed,' I mumble around the thermometer.

'Under that,' he says.

Beneath the blizzard story is a small picture of a teenage girl. *Have you seen Brianna?* the headline asks.

The article talks about Brianna Watts, of Harvest Cove. After contracting a suspected case of rabies from an animal bite, she'd undergone a series of injections to cure her. But now she'd gone missing. Last seen on the night of January ninth. Her younger sister said they were watching TV when Brianna just got up and walked out of the house into the blizzard, in her pyjamas, without a word. Brianna's mother said: 'She didn't take her coat, her keys, her bag, anything. I can't think what's happened. She's been sick this past week, recovering from her infection. She's had the chills real bad, and just hasn't been in her right head.'

I glance up at Howie. 'Did they find her?'

'Not a trace. She just *vanished*. No sign of foul play,

so it was treated as a missing persons case. A possible runaway. But there's more.'

He hands me some pages.

The next one goes back twenty-one years. February first. *Local Boys Report Bear Attack*, the headline says. Two brothers, thirteen and fourteen, claim they were attacked walking home after a hockey game the previous night. They describe a large white bear that chased them down. The brothers say they managed to scare it off somehow, suffering only scratches and bruises. Provincial police are sceptical, noting that polar bear sightings are extremely rare this far south, and the brown bear population should be inactive, in the middle of their hibernation cycle. Also, the boys' stories and descriptions of the animal are inconsistent. Police have issued a 'Bearwatch' alert for Harvest Cove and neighbouring counties.

Turning the page, I find another article about those same brothers. February twelfth. *Brothers go Missing*, it reads. Possible runaways. There was a history of domestic abuse between the parents. But the mother said that had nothing to do with her sons going missing. 'My boys wouldn't leave me,' she told the paper. 'Every family's got its problems, but there's no way they'd just up and leave. Doesn't make any sense.' The article mentions the brothers had both been home sick from school that week.

There's a follow-up story with photos of the brothers, giving their heights and weights, and a number to call.

'How about these guys?' Ash asks. 'They ever show up?'

He shakes his head. 'A few years later they did some age-enhanced shots of them, how they'd look now. Still nothing.'

I do a quick flip through the dozen or so pages in my hand.

'How ma—' I pull the thermometer out. 'How many of these are there?'

'Too many,' Howie says. Then he nods toward the thermometer. 'What's it say?'

'It says . . . Hold on. This thing must be broken.'

Ash grabs it from me to take a look.

'Wow,' she says, seeing the reading. 'It's definitely busted.'

Howie shakes his head. 'We've got another one in the downstairs bathroom. It'll say the same.'

'True,' Pike puts in.

Ash frowns at the thermometer, then at Howie. 'You'd have to be a corpse to have this temperature.'

'Touch him,' Howie tells her.

'Huh?'

'Just touch Danny's hand.'

'Okay,' Ash says, like this is some kind of trick.

I hold my hand out as if we're going to shake. She reaches to take it, a puzzled smile on her face.

She grabs it, and then gasps, pulling away.

'What?' I say. 'What's wrong?'

I glance at my hand. It looks normal. I rub my palms together, feeling nothing strange.

'You're freezing,' Ash tells me.

'Huh? I don't feel anything weird. But *you* feel like you're running a fever or something.'

With all the commotion the last few days, me and her haven't had any time to get up close and personal.

'It's not her,' Howie says. 'It's you. And me. Don't you feel . . . different? You know, since you got bit?'

'Different? Like how?'

'Like, I don't know . . . changed?'

Howie's a major hypochondriac. He's got a medical guide to symptoms and diseases that he uses like a bible. He diagnoses himself with something new every week.

'Changed into what?' I ask.

'I think it's like what happened to Ray.'

'Ray had rabies, or Lyme disease. And he went nuts, or whatever.'

Howie shakes his head. 'I think he got bit, just like we did. Like they all did.' He nods towards the printouts I'm holding. 'And it did something to him.

Infected him, or poisoned him. Something. Can't you feel it?'

I don't feel anything, I want to yell at him. I'm not different. I'm the same old idiot I was a week ago. I want it to be true. *But*.

'You should go to the hospital,' Ash says. 'Both of you. Get checked out. Get them to run some tests.'

'Lot of good that did Ray,' Howie mutters.

I shuffle through the pages, shaking my head. 'I don't know, man. This sounds like one of your weird conspiracy theories.'

'Hey, you saw that thing too,' Howie says. 'And those pages you're holding – that's a lot of missing kids for one small town.'

I catch the date on one of the printouts. 'Nineteen forty-eight?'

I scan the write-up on some fourteen-year-old who ran away in the middle of a cold snap.

'How long has this been going on?'

'Who knows?' Howie shrugs. 'At least as far back as I could find in the *Examiner* archives.'

'How come I've never heard about any of this?' Ash shuffles through the articles.

'Most of the cases were written off as runaways,' Howie tells her. 'There were never any signs of foul play.

And no bodies ever showed up. Just *poof*, and they were gone.'

We're all quiet for a while. Ash keeps going through the printouts, while I'm trying hard to poke some holes in Howie's crazy idea.

'So, what, all these missing kids got bitten by that thing?' Ash asks.

Howie nods. 'Bit. Infected. Changed.'

'But you and me,' I say. 'We're still here. We got away from it.'

'It *let* us get away.'

'I still say you guys should go to the hospital,' Ash tells us. 'Whatever's wrong, maybe they can help.'

'Right.' Howie shakes his head. 'Like they cured Ray Dyson? They'd just stick us in quarantine. If they had anything, or knew anything, they would have used it on Ray. They gave him rabies shots because they thought it was a dog that got him, and he showed some of the right symptoms for it. But then they said the bloodwork came back negative.'

'What kind of symptoms?' I ask Howie.

'He had headaches, chills. Hallucinations. What else? Insomnia, photophobia—'

'Photo-what?' I break in.

'Extreme sensitivity to light.'

This sounds way too familiar.

'So,' Howie says. 'How you been feeling?'

Like crap, but I don't want admit it.

'You've got the chills, right?' he asks. 'How about the headaches? Insomnia? Photo—'

'Okay, already. Yeah, I'm feeling bad. Could just be the flu.'

I start pacing. There's a maze of stuff on the floor – boxes of junk, a telescope, mountains of books, old jam jars full of dried insects. Hard to breathe with all the dust and heat. 'Man, it's like a sauna in here.'

'Are you joking?' Ash says. 'It's freezing.'

I notice she still has her jacket zipped up.

'Sorry,' Howie says. 'I had to kill the heat and crack the window open. I was going to pass out.'

I go stand by the window, soaking up the breeze blowing in. 'I don't get it. That thing had us both, could've just taken us right there – me in the ditch, you on the lake. Instead it only bites us, or stings us, and lets us go? What's that about?'

'Maybe it likes to play with its food,' Pike says.

'Funny.' Only I'm not laughing.

'No, really,' Pike goes on. 'See Agent Orange there?' He points to the stuffed cat on the top shelf across the room. 'She was a great mouser back at Gagetown. Caught six in one day. She was a killing machine. But if you watched her hunting, it was total torture. I mean, she'd catch the mouse, lick it a few times then let it go. And when it tried to make a run for it, Agent Orange would leap on it again. Catch and release. Till the mouse gave up and just lay there, waiting for her to snap its neck.'

Playing? That's one game I'd rather skip.

'So, what do we do?' Ash asks Howie.

He always has the answers, but now all we get is a heavy, helpless sigh.

In the silence, my mind goes round and round, chasing its tail. Its little mouse tail.

'How long was it?' I say finally. 'Between when Ray said he got bit, till he went missing in action?'

'Two weeks.' Howie's already way ahead of me.

I do the math – from the night I got bit till now.

Seven days left.

Eighteen

Small towns have strange acoustics. Whispers at one end of town are heard sharp and clear at the other end. If somebody gets caught screwing around on their husband or wife, gets pulled over for drunk driving, gets caught shoplifting at the Red and White, gets fired, gets pregnant, gets head lice – then you can be sure the news will whip through Harvest Cove like a tornado on steroids.

But that's for the small stuff. The everyday embarrassments and misdemeanours.

For the big stuff, it's like the whole place has gone deaf. The way Fat Bill could prey on young guys for years undetected. The way nobody knew Jan Sorenson, the old man who's been running the Harvest Cove gas station forever, had also been beating his seventy-year-old wife for forever. Not till after she died from internal bleeding, and the cops pulled her records at the Royal

Victoria Hospital. They showed she'd been treated for breaking just about every bone you can break, going back nearly forty years.

Everybody hears whispered gossip and rumours clear across town. But nobody hears the scream next door.

'Man, this town is a hole,' I say, looking at the pages and pages of research Howie printed off for me, like it's a school assignment.

'A black hole,' Ash agrees.

I'm in her room, with my *homework* spread out on the floor. She's sitting beside me on her workout bench, going over the evidence.

Ash's room is so *Ash*. With free weights scattered on the floor waiting to stub your toes, dirty laundry covering every surface, and posters from slasher movies and punk bands as wallpaper. A bulletin board on the back of her door shows her workout stats, body weight and mileage. Hanging off a nail on the wall is an army helmet.

I point it out. 'One of your dad's?'

'Yeah.' She takes it down and shows it to me. *CAPT ANIMKEE* is markered on the canvas sweat-guard inside the rim. 'See that?' She pokes her finger at the coating of dust on the metal. 'That's real authentic Afghanistan desert dust.'

Ash rubs the grey chalk between her fingers,

with a small smile. Proud of her dad.

There's a knock at the door.

'Yeah?' Ash calls.

Her mother pokes her head in. 'Dinner's ready. Are you staying to eat, Danny?'

'If that's okay,' I say.

'Of course. Come while it's hot.'

Dinner turns out to be meat loaf and mashed potatoes. The loaf is huge and there's a mountain of taters, enough for a whole platoon. But when Ash and her dad start chowing down it goes fast. They eat like somebody's got a stopwatch on them. No talking. No coming up for air.

Ash's mom, Laura, has strawberry-blonde hair, bright hazel eyes and a spatter of freckles across her nose and cheeks. I don't see any of her in Ash. Those Indian genes were way too strong for the pale, freckled Whitey genes.

'I picked up a bunch of those pocket warmers,' Laura says to Ash's dad.

'Don't need them,' Nick says.

'I'm not going to have you losing a finger to frostbite. I'm very fond of those hands.'

'Mom,' Ash says. 'Trying to eat here.'

'Nick's going on patrol,' Laura tells me. 'Up in Northern Ontario, with the Second Rangers. What are you guarding us against up there, anyway?' she asks her husband.

'Hell if I know. Terrorist polar bears?' He forks a baseball – sized scoop of potatoes into his mouth.

'The Second Rangers is made up of Cree and Ojibwa,' Ash says. 'They work better with the locals up north. You know, show them some friendly faces.'

'Red faces,' Nick adds.

'Yeah,' Ash says. 'And, they know the land.'

'That's not my land,' Nick puts in. 'I'm no Inuit. I was born and raised on the Grassy Narrows reservation, just west of here. And I got the hell out of there fast as I could. That's why I joined the army – my ticket off the *rez*.'

The loaf is quickly reduced to its dry end-bits, and the mountain of taters to a speed bump on the way to dessert.

'I was telling Danny before about your Windigo ghost stories,' Ash says.

'Not stories,' he corrects her. 'They're real as rain. If a Windigo catches you, he'll swallow you whole.'

With a peach pie heating up in the oven, everybody pushes back from the table, making room for their expanded guts.

'You want a Windigo story?' Nick looks at me and stretches his legs out. 'I got one for you. The

Windigo who liked white meat.'

'Nick,' Laura says, 'not everyone gets your sense of humour like we do. We're your family, so we have to. But Danny's a civilian.'

He grunts in pretend disgust. 'You want to hear it or not?' he asks me.

'Sure.' I mean, what am I going to say? I just hope it doesn't end with him jumping up, shouting 'Kill Whitey!'

'Way back, at the beginning of the white invasion . . .' he starts off.

'Here we go,' Laura mutters, touching his hair as she passes by, making him grin up at her.

'Way back, there was a great shaman who could see the future. He told his people when the snows would come, when a child would be born, when another tribe was planning to attack. One day he was struck down by a dark vision. He had looked deep into the future and seen the end. End of the tribe, of the *manitou* –'

'Spirits,' Ash explains.

'– end of the land itself,' he keeps going. 'A great evil walked the world. And it had a white face. The shaman saw that these white men would cover the land, infesting it like lice. And feed off it till there was nothing left but the bones of the earth. So he went into the woods and asked the manitou if they would join him and fight for the land. But they told him that the only thing that could defeat such a great evil was an even greater one. And the shaman knew there was no evil greater than the Windigo.'

Ash is slouched down and stretched out just like her father. She must have heard this story before, but she's soaking it up like I am.

'So,' Nick says; 'the shaman decided to make himself a Windigo, from scratch. Taking in a newborn whose mother had died in labour, he raised it to be his child, a child of the night. The shaman went out in the dark of a new moon to one of the invader's settlements and caught himself a white man. Then he cut him into pieces, and fed him to the child. He had to chew the flesh himself, because the baby had no teeth, then spit the meat in its mouth.'

'Pie's ready.' Laura closes the oven. 'How big a slice you want, Nick?'

He holds his hands wide apart.

'Danny?'

'Just a sliver, please,' I say, this story being kind of an appetite killer.

She passes out the plates.

'So,' Nick continues, around a peachy mouthful. 'The baby grew fat and strong, fed only on the palest of flesh. When its teeth came they were like a wolf's. Its fingers grew claws long as a bear's, and white fur ran in a mane down its back. It became Windigo. When it was big enough to hunt on its own, the shaman set the Windigo loose on the white man. And its hunger had no end.'

'Sounds familiar,' Laura says, kissing the top of his head.

'But there was no end to the whites, either. They bred like rats, spreading disease and death where they went. The Windigo feasted on them. But when the invaders learned the nature of this beast, they organized a hunt, and set a trap for it. Using a pale-skinned albino man, they lured the Windigo into a clearing in the woods. They had been chasing it for days, and the Windigo was starving. Blind with hunger. It could smell the delicious flavour of that flesh, white as new snow, and could not resist.'

Nick pauses to fork in another hunk of pie. I've barely touched mine.

'The Windigo ran into the clearing, toward the albino who was tied to a post in the centre. Then the men hiding in the trees opened fire, shooting the Windigo so many times its white fur ran red with blood. It escaped, and got away from the hunters. But now *Death* was chasing it through the night. Before, Death had been its hunting companion, ready to share in the feast of the Windigo's victims. Now Death was the hunter. The Windigo returned to the shaman, its father.'

Nick licks his fork.

'And the shaman, seeing the future – the end of his tribe, of the manitou and the land itself – gave one last gift to his child. From his medicine chest, he took out the skin of a white man he had taken years ago, when his dark vision of the endtimes had first come to him. Stripping off his clothes, he dressed himself in the white man's skin. And he gave himself to his starving, dying child. One last meal before Death took them both.'

Laura starts to clear the table. 'And what's the moral of that story?'

As she passes Nick, he gives her butt a pat.

'The moral is, stick to red meat,' he says. 'Better for you.'

She laughs. Ash smiles, shaking her head.

Nick gets up and stretches.

'Danny,' he says. 'Grab your boots, and come on out back with me. I want to show you something.'

So me and Ash go join him on the back porch.

'No, just Danny,' he tells her.

'Dad,' she says, in a warning tone. Then she speaks in Indian, something quick and tongue-twisting.

Nick responds with more Ojibwa, sounding like he's

trying to reassure her. She doesn't look convinced, but he grabs a flashlight, puts a hand on my shoulder and guides me across the back yard to a wooden shack with a small chimney.

'Finished it in October. Before the ground hardened.'

I hurry to keep up, shooting nervous glances to the dark edges of the snowy yard. Where anything could be hiding.

The thought strikes me, as Nick leads me into the darkness, that this guy has actually killed people. Ash told me he shot some Taliban guys over in Afghanistan. She said he got pretty twisted up over it, which is why he transferred from active duty after his last tour ended and came to CFB Borden. Where the only killing you do is killing time.

So I'm a little nervous about what he wants to show me. And why Ash had to stay behind.

He reaches the shack and flips a wooden latch to open the door. 'Watch where you step. Floor's kind of rough.'

Nick gestures me in first, shining the light into the cramped interior. I find benches jutting out from the walls.

'Sit.' He squeezes in and sits on the bench opposite me. It's tight in here and our knees are touching. There's a strong pine smell in the shack, undercut by a deep smoky odour.

'What do you think?' He plays the light around.

'I think . . . I don't know. What is it?'

'A sweat lodge. A midget one. But still, up to Ojibwa code.'

I see a pit at the rear and some large, flat rocks. There's a big empty pot next to it.

'Ash uses it when she needs to make weight, or work out some knots. I use it to . . . clear my head.'

He switches off the flashlight, but leaves the door open. I can make out the bulk of his shadow, but not his face.

'So,' he says, after a brief silence. 'You and Ash? What's that?'

'I-I don't know,' I mutter, half wishing I could see his face, half glad he can't see mine.

'I see how you look at her. She feel the same?'

'I guess so. Maybe.'

His knees bump mine as he shifts on the other bench, making me flinch. I can feel his eyes on me. Does he call this a sweat lodge because he brings people out here to sweat them?

'What's said in the lodge, stays in the lodge,' he says. 'Clear?'

I nod, then realize the gesture is invisible in the dark. 'Sure.'

He's quiet for a long moment, sweating me.

'I always wanted a boy,' he says finally. 'Laura wanted a girl. But instead, we got Ash. I took her hunting, took her to the fights. Put her to bed with war stories. Laura got cheated, never got the girl she could go shopping with, dress up and do – you know, female stuff.'

It's so close in here, maybe it's better not being able to see each other. Like confession.

'So,' he goes on. 'I was getting worried I'd messed her up. Hadn't let her be a girl. But now, you show up. She's never done that before. Brought a guy home.' He taps the flashlight on the bench. Then he chuckles. 'Heard she knocked you out, first time you met.'

'She knocked me stupid. My brain didn't clear for days.'

'Yeah.' I can hear him smiling. 'That's good. So you know who's boss?'

'Like she's going to let me forget?'

Nick snorts, then gets to his feet. The flashlight comes to life. He's shaking his head, grinning.

'She's going to eat you alive,' he laughs, reaching over to squeeze my shoulder. 'Hey, you're freezing, Danny. Better get you in, get you warmed up.'

'Yeah.'

Stepping out into the snow, I feel a blast of winter wind. I'm sure the wind chill's sub-zero, but for me it's like a summer breeze.

I'm a stubborn guy, but there's only so long I can stay in denial. Something's definitely wrong with me. Howie asked if I felt *changed*. But changed into what?

What did that freaky thing do to us? And why?

Pike said maybe it was just playing with its food.

As I follow in Nick's bootprints in the snow, I look up to see Ash and her mother moving around in the warm light of the kitchen.

If I'm going to get eaten alive, better if Ash does it. I can think of worse ways to go.

Nineteen

It's real late. The deep dark dead of night. I'm fighting sleep, pacing my room, scared of what's waiting in my dreams. I've got so much caffeine pumping through my veins my heart's banging off my ribs like a caged animal.

Dinner at Ash's place was weird. But not bad weird. Being with Ash and her mom and dad I saw how they fit together. The way they move around each other, the little touches. How they fill in the spaces between the others' words, finishing their thoughts. Making fun, inside jokes, speaking in their own code.

Sitting with them after dinner, it hit me – this used to be mine. Me, Mom and Dad. We had this.

There's a line from a poem we read in class: *When people die, worlds die with them.*

I shake my head, trying to lose this feeling.

When I got back from Ash's, I found a bright red envelope on the kitchen table. Obviously a Christmas card. From Aunt Karen, Mom's kid sister.

'Came this morning,' Dad said, sipping his beer.

He was crashed on the couch watching some Clint Eastwood western. They're all pretty much the same – man with no name rides into town, kills bad guys, rides out. He lives nowhere, owns nothing, always on the move. Sounds familiar.

Dad was doing his trick where he rolls a bottle cap over his knuckles, like you do with a quarter. Back and forth, as a gunfight blazed on TV.

I turned the envelope over and over. Finally I gave up and tore it open. A Christmas card. Harmless enough. But something slipped out, falling on the floor in front of the couch. We both looked down.

A photo. My heart skipped a beat. Dad stopped rolling the cap. For a moment, neither of us moved. Then Dad picked it up.

A summer snapshot of a day at the beach back in Toronto. I remember it so clear, like I just stepped off that beach a minute ago. Me and Mom are taking turns diving off Dad's broad shoulders into the cool water of Lake Ontario. He's standing neck-deep, letting us use him as a platform.

It's Mom's turn. The camera catches her laughing hysterically, balancing on Dad's shoulders. All eyes are on her. You can see the back of my head as I dog-paddle nearby. Dad's got his hands on her calves, keeping her steady. He's looking up at her perched there. She's shiny-wet in the bright sun and squinting against the dazzle off the water. His mouth is open, telling her to . . .

'Jump,' Dad mumbled to the photo, caught in the same time warp as me. The ghost of a smile tugged at the corner of his mouth.

Dad held the photo tight, bending it.

Then I noticed a spot of red on his other hand, a drop of blood trickling from his closed fist.

'Dad. Your hand.'

Took a second before he saw the blood. Opening his fist, I saw where the bottle cap had bitten into his palm.

I grabbed a box of tissues and handed him a wad, taking the picture from him. I slipped it in my pocket, out of sight.

While Dad soaked the blood up, I got him a fresh beer and me a Coke. We watched the rest of the movie, even though I knew how it was going to end. We didn't talk much. Just sat there, getting through the night together.

Now I put the photo with some others I keep buried in a drawer. I only take them out when I get scared I'm going to forget something about her. Something small but key. I can't look at them too long.

On the back of the beach shot, Aunt Karen's written: *Here's a piece of summer to keep you warm this Christmas.*

I pace over to the window. The glass is frosted with a thin skin of ice. I lean in close to steam the window with my breath, to melt the frosting so I can see out. And as the ice crystals dissolve under my breath I forget where I am.

I remember breathing on another window, forever ago.

It's spring and Mom sits by the living-room window of our apartment in Toronto, looking out at the new leaves on the trees. So new they're still unfolding from their buds. The window is shut tight. Mom goes from sweating to shivers so quick I can't keep up, piling blankets on, taking them away.

She's right up close to the glass now, breathing on it. Her exhale breaks into a racking cough that makes me cringe.

'Danny?' she says, in a voice like a croak.

I go to her. 'You cold? I'll get you your comforter, fresh from the dryer.'

Mom likes the blankets just out of the dryer, all heated up. We're doing laundry every day. Mom can't keep anything down and messes up her sheets, pyjamas and things. 'Not cold,' she whispers. 'The glass. Fog it up for me, Danny-boy.'

'Ah,' I smile, realizing what she wants.

I lean over beside her and steam a patch of the window with my breath. Mom draws in the mist with her finger. She's kind of slow, so I keep fogging it back up. When she's done, she leans back to consider her masterpiece.

There are two small stick figures, side by side, holding hands. One is Stinkboy, my alter ego, with his pointy teeth and squiggly stink lines rising off him. With him is a long-haired version, with matching smell squiggles.

'Who's that with Stinkboy?' I ask. 'He got a date?'

The doodle is starting to fade so I exhale, bringing it back to life.

'That's the other me.' Mom's pale lips curve in the tiniest of grins. 'Stinkgirl. They're made for each other.'

She squeezes her eyes shut with a shiver.

'Cold,' she whispers.

'I'll get the comforter. Be right back.'

I rush down the hall and grab it. When I get back, Mom's leaning her head on the window.

'Here.' I lay the cover gently in her lap. 'Nice and toasty.'

Her cheek has wiped off some of the fading doodle. Reaching to pull her away and set her back into

her chair, I sense something's different. She feels ...
empty somehow.

'Mom?'

I take her hand and press my fingers against the inside of her cool, frail wrist. I feel for the smallest flutter, the faintest beat. I wait and wait.

'Mom?'

So quick. In the half-minute it took me to get her comforter. She was just speaking to me. She said my name. I can still hear her saying it.

Kneeling on the floor, I don't want to do anything or call anyone, don't want to leave her side. I lay my head down in her lap.

It's warm, from the comforter. But also, I need to believe, warm from her.

Now, my breath has melted the icy glass from white frost to black night.

I back up and collapse on the bed, suddenly too weak to stand.

It's so dumb. Me and Dad have spent all this time running away from anything or anyplace that would remind us. Most of our stuff is in some storage locker in Toronto. But the danger isn't in the old stuff or the familiar places. It's inside our heads. And there are a million triggers that'll bring it all back.

Fog it up for me, Danny-boy.

And all our running brought us here. Somewhere to hide. Somewhere safe.

Right!

Twenty

'So, what did you come up with?' I ask, sitting down beside Ash on the foot of Howie's bed.

Pike drove us over here after school, saying Howie needed to show us his latest discoveries. He's been home three days now, getting an early start on Christmas break. Now we're all off till the new year. If we make it to the new year.

I don't think Howie's even left the house since he got back from the hospital. He's spending all his time researching on-line.

'I've got tons of stuff to show you.' Howie rummages through his desk. Books piled five deep, papers scattered.

'What happened to that mega-watt, X-ray lighting you had in here?' Ash asks. 'It's kind of dim now. I thought you needed it for your seasonal disorder thingy.'

'Seasonal affective disorder.' He shuffles through the

piles. 'Guess I'm cured. Can't take the light any more. It hurts my eyes. Another symptom.'

Even though I got a head start, getting bit a few days before Howie, this *infection* is hitting him harder. He's always like that, catching every cold, flu, strep throat and pink-eye in the county. Somebody gets the sniffles at school, Howie gets pneumonia.

He swivels around in his chair, a bunch of pages in his lap. 'This will blow your mind. Remember all those missing persons articles I downloaded? I kept digging and found even more. But here's the thing – there's a pattern.'

'What kind of pattern?' I ask.

'Get this. They all involve victims between the ages of thirteen to eighteen. And all of them went missing in the winter months.'

I think back to the pages he printed off for me. I'd noticed they were all teenagers. But the winter thing slipped by me.

'So?' Ash says. 'Maybe they ran away from this armpit of a town. Winter's a bitch up here. Can you blame them?'

'We're not talking runaways. These guys just *vanish* – like off the face of the earth. They never come back. Never heard from again.'

'Okay. So where you going with this?' I ask.

'I've got a theory. The thing that attacked us got them too. Infected them, or whatever you want to call it. Let them go. And then, for some reason, they gave themselves up to it. Most of these articles talk about the missing kids just walking off in the night, in the middle of winter. Like Ray Dyson did. Not taking anything with them, not putting on shoes or jackets or nothing. And then *poof*, they're gone.'

Everybody's quiet.

I'm not liking Howie's theory. 'What else you got?'

'I think this *beast* – like you call it – only comes out in the winter. That's when it hunts, right? I think maybe it needs the cold.'

Pike sits on a corner of the desk, rubbing his mohawk, listening close.

Howie keeps going. 'But the disappearances don't happen every winter. I think that's part of why nobody's made the connection before. They only happen in the coldest winters, years apart sometimes. Look, I made up a graph to prove my theory,' he says, bright-eyed.

I have to hold back a smile. Only Howie could get excited over a graph. 'Let's see.'

It looks like something from a textbook. He must have whipped it up on the computer. It shows a squiggly line with spikes running from left to right, kind of like the readout on a heart monitor.

'Help me out,' I say. 'What am I looking at?'

He leans in to point.

'This shows the numbers of local missing teenagers over the past sixty years, as far back as the records went. See how the numbers spike some years, and flatline in others?'

'Yeah, okay.'

'The spikes happen in those years with the coldest winters. The flatlines are when the winters were warmer than average.'

I notice a change in the more recent years near the end of the graph. The gaps between the spikes are bigger, with longer stretches of flatline. Like a slowing heartbeat.

I point this out to him. 'You think maybe the beast is slowing down?'

Howie shakes his head. 'I think it's more likely because the last twenty years have been the warmest in centuries. Global warming. Easy winters.'

'Easy?' Pike nods toward the open window with the polar breeze blowing in. 'This place could use a little global warming.'

'But compared to how it used to be,' Howie says, 'there's been more early thaws. Thinner ice. A couple years ago the lake didn't even freeze over completely. A century ago, they used to harvest ice blocks till the end of March. Now, you can't even skate out there past February most years.'

'But this winter's different,' I say.

'It's a bad one. Just how the *beast* likes it. And because it's had to wait so long between cold snaps, it's built up a hunger. Usually there's only a couple kids go missing in the bad winters. But this one – first Ray, now you and me. I think maybe it's starving.'

'Feeding frenzy,' Pike says.

'But if it's in a *frenzy*, or whatever,' I say, 'why did it let us go?'

Howie shakes his head. 'Still working on that.'

I study the graph, with the line tracking the missing teenagers looking like a heartbeat. When really, it's not tracking life, but death.

'Where does it go, then,' Ash says, 'when it's not winter?'

Howie shrugs. 'Could be it holes up somewhere to sleep through the warmer stretches. Like in a reverse hibernation, waiting for the temperature to drop low enough for it to come out. But that's a guess. This,' he taps the graph, 'is no guess. This is proof something's going on.'

Ash gets up and stretches her back with a groan. 'I don't know, Howie. All I see is a squiggly line on a page. What's the rest of this stuff?'

She glances at the pile of paper he's set down beside the keyboard.

'Research. I've been looking into something called cryptozoology.'

'That's not a word,' I say. 'You made it up.'

'No way. Cryptozoology. It's real. It's the study of mythic or hidden creatures. Like the Yeti, or the Sasquatch.'

I give him a look. Howie's gone off the deep end. 'You're talking about Bigfoot? I thought we were being serious here.'

'I'm dead serious.' He pulls a page out of the pile and hands it to me. 'I found this on one of those sites.'

The printout is grainy, showing a crude drawing made on some rock surface. But the image stops me cold.

The beast. I see the thick curves of those enormous legs, the bulk of its body, and the long spiked claws on the paws. The head is turned to face me. The teeth are long daggers in a ferocious grin. Two little lines for the slit nostrils. And big round circles for those bulging eyes.

'That's it!' I say.

Ash and Pike crowd around to look.

'Where's this picture from?' I ask.

'It's a petroglyph,' Howie says. 'A native rock painting. From an old Cree settlement on the north shore of Lake Simcoe.'

I can't take my eyes off it. Even drawn in a basic outline it gives me a shiver.

It's real. It's really real.

Strange that it takes this cartoon cave scribble to make it all sink in. But now, I'm buying Howie's crazy theories. My powers of denial can't stand against the weight of his *proof*.

'Wait a minute.' Something nags at me. 'From when? That Cree place, how old are we talking about?'

Howie takes a deep breath. 'That painting's been dated at about a thousand years old.'

I'm shocked speechless.

'This thing's been around here forever. I found some Cree legends that talk about an evil spirit haunting the lake in the winter.'

He shuffles through more papers. 'Here it is. The Cree have a couple of names for it. *Powatamwitekew*. I guess that's how you say it. It means *eater of dreams*.'

Howie catches my eye. I know we're thinking the same thing. Our shared nightmare, being chased off the ice cliff.

'And they also call it *Oskankaskatin*,' he reads. 'Means *bonechiller*.'

There's a long silence as that sinks in.

'So do the Indians talk about people going missing?' Pike asks.

Howie nods. 'There's some stuff about this spirit stealing the souls of the young. It lures them off into the dark, and, uh . . . swallows them whole.'

'If it's been around all that time,' I say, looking up from the page, 'just think of the body count.'

He nods grimly.

There's something else that's been worrying me, ever since the Indian ghost story Ash's dad told me. The one about the Windigo who liked white meat.

'The missing victims you identified. Were they all white, like you, me and Ray?'

Howie gives me a puzzled frown. 'Um, no actually. In the pictures that went with the articles, there were all kinds of victims. White, black, hispanic. And, according to the Cree stories, a lot of Indians. Why you asking that? You think this thing has a grudge against Whitey?'

I shake my head, a little embarrassed. 'No, it's just . . . nothing.'

Ash catches my eye, giving me a small grin. 'Dad's story got in your head, didn't it?'

'Little bit.'

'But, you know there are lots of Windigo stories. They don't all go for white meat.' Ash takes the printout from me for a closer look. 'Maybe this thing got some of those stories started.' She turns to Howie. 'Is there anything on those crypto sites that tells you what to do when you've been bit by this freak?'

Howie shakes his head. 'They just record some of the rare sightings over the last century. These sites are filled with weird creatures.' He swivels around to his computer, clicking through some bookmarks. 'Most of this stuff is just ghost stories, popular myths, and drunken hallucinations. You have to wade through a lot of junk to find anything credible.'

On the screen, images of giant furballs like the Sasquatch and Yeti flicker past. Sea serpents, giant thunderbirds, snakes with wings, and other dreamed-up mutants.

'How does any of this help us?' I ask.

Howie shrugs. 'It doesn't. We're still screwed. But at least we know a little more what we're up against.'

'What we need,' Pike says, 'is a big-ass *stickybomb* to blow this freak up.'

'*Stickybomb?*' I ask.

'They were invented in World War Two.' Pike gets that gleam in his eyes when he's talking about his favourite subject. 'It's a kind of grenade they used to blow up tanks. You needed the bomb to stick onto the tank to do any real damage, so they coated them with glue. I always wanted to try a stickybomb.'

I leave Pike to his daydreaming and go look out the

window. It's getting late. 'No way I'm walking home in the dark. Can I bum a ride off you, Pike?'

'You can drop me off, too,' Ash says.

'What am I, a taxi?' he grumbles. 'You're paying gas money.'

'Put it on my tab,' Ash tells him.

I notice an open library book on Howie's desk. I lean over for a closer look. 'What this?'

'That's supposed to be a depiction of Hell,' he says.

It's a full-page illustration of the Devil, showing him as a Giant, frozen waist-deep in a lake of ice. His big, all-white eyes leer down at the damned. He's holding two people up to his mouth, stuffing them in.

'I thought Hell was supposed to be one big human barbecue,' I say.

'Yeah. But in the deepest, darkest pit there's a lake of ice. And the Devil's stuck in it.'

I look at the drawing, holding back a shiver.

'What are you thinking now, Howie?' I ask, raising my eyebrows. 'First it's Bigfoot, then a Windigo. Now it's the Devil?'

'You saw that thing, close up like I did. You tell me.'

I can only shake my head.

'Windigos and Bigfoots are bad enough. But how do you beat the Devil?

Twenty-One

I stayed up all night, with the help of a six-pack of Cokes and late-night TV. I'm dead on my feet. Probably not the best condition for operating heavy machinery.

I'm pushing a snowplough around the marina parking lot. The snow started after midnight and kept up till dawn, piling knee-high drifts against the house.

Why we need to keep the lot clear, I have no idea. Nobody's around to see it but us.

The sub-zero temperatures this morning can't touch me. I'm out here with no hat, no gloves. The wind chill's just a summer breeze.

You'd think the shudder and shake of the snow-spitting monster under my hands would keep me focused. But my eyelids keep blinking and forgetting to rise again.

It can't be more than a few seconds that I nod

off. I'm snapped awake by the grinding, cracking sound of the blades chewing up a bush at the end of the lot. The funnel shoots out splinters and wood chips, making a racket.

I try and pull the plough back, but it's stuck. So I kill the power and go around to yank some twisted branches out of the rotor.

I'm bent over struggling with this mess when I hear the breathing behind me. I freeze. The breathing is heavy and quick. Not human.

It's coming closer. I flinch at the brush of warm air on the back of my neck. Spinning around, I tip and fall back in the snow.

Piercing blue eyes stare at me from the white-furred face of an Alaskan husky two feet away. The dog pants steam into the air. And he's not alone. Four more huskies zero in on me.

'You must be made of hot dogs.'

There's an old man in a stained Budweiser T-shirt and raggedy jeans standing in the path I've just cleared. It's Mangy Mason himself. Never seen him up close before. It ain't pretty.

I get up slowly so I don't set off the dogs.

'We're all meat,' he says, scratching deep in the bush of his beard, white as the fur of his dogs. He takes his time digging around, like he's searching for something.

'You aren't, are you?' he asks, as I back up a bit.

'Aren't what?'

'Made of hot dogs,' he snaps.

Hard to tell if he's joking. Word is he's harmlessly demented.

'They smell something on you,' he says, a suspicious edge to his voice.

The huskies are sniffing the air in my direction.

'I don't know what they smell, but I'm not hiding any hot dogs.'

Mason finds one of the many holes in his T-shirt and sticks a finger through for a good scratch. There's a worn and fading tattoo on his right biceps, of a Celtic cross. I don't know how he got to be so old dressing like that in this cold.

'Why you ploughing the field?' he asks, like I'm the crazy one.

'Just a . . . miscalculation.'

I reach down to untwist the branch that's wrapped itself around the rotor, hoping he'll wander off.

'Ah.' He steps closer. 'That's why my dogs got stuck on you. I see you got bit.'

The branch snaps off in my hand. It takes a second for what he said to hit me.

'What did you say?'

'The dogs can scent it.'

'Scent what?'

Mason just stands there staring. The huskies fix their blue eyes on me, like they're starving and I'm lunch.

'You met much of the local wildlife?' he asks.

'Besides your dog-pack? No. Hey, come on. What are you talking about?'

He digs his long-nailed fingers into the coats of two of his dogs, giving them a good scratch. They lean into him.

'It likes them young,' he says, his eyes going distant now, not seeing me, the dogs, or the snowy lot. 'It took Rod McLean, my best friend in . . . ninth grade? We traded hockey cards. He was a Leafs fan, but I loved the Habs. I saw Rocket Richard play one time at Maple Leaf Gardens.'

'*What* took your friend?'

His eyes pull into focus. 'What bit you?'

He points at the little blue mark on the back of my right hand.

I'm stunned. He knows!

'Tell me!' I say. 'What is that thing?'

'A ghost, with teeth. A demon.'

More riddles and nonsense.

'That doesn't help me at all.'

'You want help?' His lips curve in a cold smile. 'There is none.'

The dogs start to stray. Mason moves along with the pack, clomping through the snow in a pair of decomposing sneakers, and no socks.

I try and think of something to say to get him to talk some sense.

Before I can come up with anything he looks back over his shoulder. 'Want some advice?'

'Yes! Anything!'

'Run.'

Twenty-Two

Squinting against the sting of blowing snow, I hang on for my life. The motorbike hits a rut, rattling my spine.

I can feel Ash's body heat through her leather jacket. Her sweat-damp hair clings to the back of her neck. After working out at the gym on base, my arms are so sore I can barely hold on. I have to lock my fingers together to keep from getting torn away by the wind.

Working out with Ash is lethal. In the gym she's a drill sergeant, and expects me to keep up. She even skips rope like a maniac, the rope whipping around in a near-invisible blur. I don't spar with her – I learned my lesson the first time. But I held the punch-mitts up so she could work on her combinations. They're like oversized catcher's mitts, for catching jabs and uppercuts. Then it was on to the speed-bag for focus and co-ordination.

My speed-bag was stuck in the slow lane, while hers was rattling off the wooden railing with a machine-gun rhythm.

I went to the gym not for the exercise, but to get my mind off this past week. And off my run-in with Mangy Mason this morning. I'm still trying to make sense out of his rantings. So I escaped the madness for a couple hours.

And now we're racing through Harvest Cove to her place, the pack stuffed with our gear bouncing off my back. The world is white on white. I focus on Ash's crow-black hair, and the warm tan of her neck, to keep from going snowblind.

Turning off the road, we climb a low hill and her place comes into view. Ash pulls in beside her dad's pick-up truck and kills the motor. In the sudden silence, I hear the sound of wood splitting. There's a thud and more cracking, carried clear on the frozen air. Nick must be chopping wood.

Getting off the bike, Ash sniffles. 'My face is numb.'

'Yeah? Can you feel this?' I steal a quick kiss. Her lips are fever-hot on mine.

'Yeah.' She grabs my butt. 'Feel this?'

But before I can take things any further, she heads for the front door.

I follow her inside, kicking my boots off on the mat.

In the kitchen, she takes a pitcher of protein shake out of the fridge.

'Want some?'

The mud-coloured stuff is supposed to taste like chocolate, but really it's more like chalk.

'Here.' She hands me a glass. 'You need your amino acids. Gotta get some meat on those bones.'

She pokes my bony chest. Tossing the backpack on the counter, I choke down a few swallows. She chugs her glass dry. Unzipping her jacket, she throws it over the back of a chair, then stops to sniff herself.

'Man, I stink. Should've showered at the base. I'm gonna scrub down. Be back in five.'

'Need someone to hold the soap?'

'Right,' she snorts. 'I've got an axe-wielding father outside.'

As if on cue, I hear the crack of another log splitting.

She disappears, and I force down another gulp of amino-acid mud. Then she pokes her head back in and I look up in time to catch her T-shirt flying at my head.

'But you can hold that. Just don't get it all sticky.'

She's gone before I can think of a comeback. I see a flash of her brown shoulders, and her naked back. Enough to melt some of the ice in my veins.

I sniff the shirt. It *is* pretty funky, but in the best way. Then I shoot a nervous look at the window over the sink, half expecting her axe-swinging dad to be staring in.

Stuffing the shirt in my pack, I pour the rest of my shake down the drain and wash away the evidence.

It's way too hot in here. I keep trying not to think about it – my *infection*. Hoping it will go away. Stupid, but I don't know what else to do.

I need air. Cold air. I grab my boots and head out the back door.

Ah! I fill my lungs and clump through the snow over to Nick at the chopping block, clearing my throat so I don't surprise him. Never sneak up on a guy with an axe.

He turns to look. 'Hey, Danny. You look beat.'

'Just back from the gym. Trying to keep up with Ash.'

'You want a workout, give this a try,' he says, weighing the axe in his hand. 'Then you'll feel the burn.'

I can see the steam rising off his head, sweat slicking his face. The sleeves of his flannel shirt are rolled up past his elbows.

'You planning a bonfire?' I ask, surveying the big pile of firewood he's hacked up.

'Just want to be sure there's enough for while I'm gone.'

His regiment heads out tomorrow to patrol Canada's northern reaches on a six-week tour. Gotta keep an eye on those terrorist polar bears, and make sure Santa's elves aren't planning a holy war.

'You're gonna miss Christmas,' I say.

He shrugs that off with a grim smile. 'Nothing new. I grew up on the *rez*, Danny. We missed every Christmas.'

What do I say to that?

I've been meaning to ask him about some stuff. But he still scares me sometimes. He's got this way of looking at you, stony and intense, seeing right through you. Most times, I know he's just playing with me, the way Ash does. Seeing if I've got any fight.

This is my last chance before he leaves. If Howie's right, and the clock on us is running out fast as he says, this could be my last chance *ever*.

'That story you told the other night – about the Windigo. It got stuck in my head.'

Ever since Howie dug up the Indian rock painting, that ancient monster mug-shot, I've been wondering about Nick's Windigo. Not that I'm thinking his bloodthirsty cannibal is what attacked me and Howie. I'm sure that was just a ghost story, mixed with a 'kill whitey' fantasy. But what stuck with me was that stuff about the evil of the white invaders. The shaman creating his Windigo to slaughter the whites – one evil fighting another.

Evil is just beyond anything I can wrap my mind around. I could never imagine it as a living, breathing *thing* – until that night in the ditch.

'Don't worry,' Nick says. 'A Windigo wouldn't go for you. You wouldn't even make an appetizer.'

'Yeah, guess not.' I give him a weak laugh. 'But, where do you think those stories come from? Are they totally made up, or are they based on something real?'

'Sounds like you want to get deep.'

With a flick of his wrist, Nick throws the axe down, the blade biting into the chopping block with a thump.

'What do you say we get out of this wind?'

He leads the way across the yard toward his sweat lodge. It looks rough, with the bark left on the logs. But when you get up close you see how well built it is, the wood fitted tight to keep the steam inside.

The door opens with a groan.

'The cedar's stiff with the freeze.' He waves me in. 'This cold snap lasts much longer, we're gonna see some trees splitting. When the sap inside freezes solid, it cracks the trunk right through. They explode. Sounds like a forty-calibre shot.'

I sit by the shallow pit at the end, where some large flat stones are set above a hollow dug out for the fire, breathing in the pine and woodsmoke.

Nick leaves the door wedged open so we're not left

completely in the dark. He leans back and stretches his long legs out as far as he can.

'Took a sweat last night. To clear my head before going up north.'

'Did it work?'

Those ink-black eyes fix on me. 'No. There's only so much you can sweat out of you.'

I find myself holding my breath till he breaks his stare.

'What's on your mind, Danny? Looks like you haven't slept in a while.'

Is it that obvious?

'What's said here, stays here. Remember?' he says.

I nod, leaning forward with my elbows on my knees. The intense scent of the pine sharpens my brain.

'You really believe in any of those things – Windigos, evil spirits, stuff like that?'

'I grew up on those stories the way you grew up on sitcoms and MTV. Back at Grassy Narrows, my grandmother is a storyteller. She can make you see things that aren't there. Make you believe.'

Nick's quiet for a moment, staring into the shadows.

'But growing up, I never saw anything like the creatures in my grandmother's stories. Never saw a manitou, a thunderbird, or a Windigo. No matter how hard I tried.'

He smiles, remembering. After a moment the smile dies off and his features harden.

'When I hit eighteen I went in the army. To get off the rez, see the world. I was still green, on my first tour with *CANBATT*, a Canadian unit of the UN peacekeepers during the Balkan War. On a raw January morning, we walked into this little hill village in Bosnia. Wasn't much left of the place when we got there. The houses were burned down, and still smoking. But no bodies. Not a soul.'

He speaks in a hushed tone, as if this place really is some kind of confessional, where secrets are told and kept.

'Guess the Serb troops saw us coming, and didn't have time to clean up. At the edge of town we found a freshly dug trench. It looked like the Serbs were getting ready to fill it in when we ran them off. That's where we found the villagers. Men, women, kids. The bodies were covered in morning frost. We secured the site and waited for the UN inspectors to come in and document it all. You know, ethnic cleansing, war crimes. It wasn't the last mass grave I saw over there. But it cut me the deepest. All those bodies, piled like they were nothing. A couple days before they were breathing, talking, laughing. And now they were dead, for nothing. For hate. So, do I believe in evil spirits?'

Everything goes quiet now, holding its breath – the wind, the crows, me.

'Evil takes different shapes, Danny. But it's as real as rain.'

There's a moment where I almost let out *my* nightmare story. The need to make my own confession is so strong. But something in me holds back. It's like Nick has his nightmare, and I have mine. They belong to us. And I can't just give him mine so he can make it go away.

Then the moment's gone. Nick groans and rubs his face.

'I'm starving,' he says. 'How about you?'

'I could eat.'

Nick shoves the door open, letting in a flood of light. I step outside after him, blinking in the snow-glare.

'Should be half a turkey left in the fridge.' He starts toward the house. 'But we might have to wrestle Ash for it.'

Turkey sounds good. Wrestling Ash sounds better.

Twenty-Three

When I get home from Ash's place I promise myself I'll just rest a minute. I won't close my eyes. Just need to lie down before I collapse.

My eyes are so dry and scratchy, feels like there's sand under the lids.

The window is wide open, letting in a delicious sub-zero draught.

I've got the core temperature of an ice cube, a never-ending headache, and my night vision is getting so good I can practically read in the dark.

What weirdness is going on inside me? I'm turning into some kind of polar vampire.

The ceiling light is bright as a summer sun. Feel like I'm getting a burn just lying here.

I'm squinting under the glare when the light turns blue.

My first thought is: I didn't know it could do that.

My second is: oh crap!

Because I'm not in my room any more. Somewhere between blinks, I fell asleep. And now I'm – where?

This room looks oddly familiar. A counter runs along the far wall, holding an aquarium and a terrarium. At the back there are glass cabinets with jars of chemical powders and liquids.

It's the science lab at school.

The fluorescent lights glow blue. I'm lying on the counter that the teacher uses for demonstrations. As I sit up, I see I'm actually laid out here on a large metal tray that takes up most of the counter top.

A giant version of a dissection tray.

I twist around to see behind me, making sure I'm alone in the room. Lined up on the counter beside the tray are surgical tools – scalpels, clamps and a hand-held circular saw. Remembering my autopsy dream, I reach up and check my head. My breath shudders out of me when I find it intact.

I drop from the counter to the floor. I'm barefoot, wearing the T-shirt and boxers I fell asleep in. I crack the door open wide enough to peek down the hall.

All clear.

But I feel this shivering dread, the way a mouse must feel when the shadow of a hawk passes over it.

Get out! Quick!

I start toward the back stairs. The blue lighting flickers and sputters, throwing wavy lines along the walls and floor. It's like the lake has risen up and drowned the town.

I wish Howie was here, like the last dream.

Passing a classroom, I look through the window in the door and see kids sitting at their desks. They stare ahead, frozen and unblinking. All of them have shaved heads. All are missing the tops of their skulls. The bone has been sawed off clean, exposing the wrinkles and folds of their brains.

The acid burn of bile rises in my throat. I'm about to turn and run when one face stops me.

In the front row there's a girl with big round eyes, wearing only an oversized T-shirt that hangs to her knees, like she's dressed for bed. I know her face from somewhere.

Have you seen Brianna? One of the stories Howie found in the papers. A missing girl from years ago. I remember those big eyes staring out of the picture.

She's here. And the other kids, what are they? More of the missing?

Brianna's eyes shift. Her stare locks onto me. I gasp, an electric shiver shooting up my spine.

The terror in those wide eyes goes beyond anything

I can grasp. They beg me with mute panic. Help me! Save me!

Then I hear the scrape of a door opening below. I break away from Brianna's stare. The clatter of something coming up the front stairs echoes off the walls. Claws on concrete!

My bare feet slap on the tiles as I speed past the other classrooms, not daring to look in.

Just as I reach the end of the hall, the doors behind me are thrown open. I risk a glance and see the beast at the far end, crouching to fit under the ceiling.

Its mouth stretches wide in a roar that blows the doors to the back stairwell open.

I stumble down the stairs, my bare feet hitting hard on the concrete. Wincing as the pain shoots up my shins. I thought you're not supposed to feel pain in dreams. That's like a rule.

I hit the back doors, crashing them open, and take a few steps into the dark before I notice something strange. Where's the parking lot? And the baseball diamond behind the school? I shoot a glance over my shoulder and see . . . nothing.

The doors are gone. The school is gone.

Where?

Turning around, I see bare trees, grey smudges in the winter night. Beyond them, the dark skeleton of the old ice factory looms over the shore of the lake.

Miss Mercer brought us out here, on the crappiest field trip ever. In Harvest Cove, this passes as a historical monument.

Why here? Not that dreams are supposed to make sense, but why this place? And where do I run? No way I've escaped that thing.

I shuffle my feet in the snow, not feeling the freeze. Think fast! It's a half-hour walk to the marina house from here. Quicker across the cove on the ice. I can just pick out the pinprick lights on the twin docks.

A roar rips through the night, staggering me. A pale figure emerge from the rotting frame of the factory.

It always finds me.

The beast takes its time. It brought me here, where it's in control.

My heart pounds adrenalin through my veins, screaming at me to run. My legs are tensed and shaking, begging to make a break for it. But my body has quit taking orders from my brain.

The beast is ten feet from me. The slits of its nostrils open and close, trailing clouds of vapour.

I see myself in the curved mirrors of its eyes, tiny and helpless. Small moans rise from deep in my throat, but my jaws are locked so tight they can't get out.

That warped, snow-pale face leans in close. The wide

mouth parts slightly, showing a glint of the blades inside. It seems to sniff, tasting my fear.

Then a low sound rises from the depths of the beast, almost a purr, shivering my eardrums. A purr, but something more. For a moment it seems like the beast is trying to speak to me. But in frequencies only a dog could make out. And in a language so alien.

Whispers murmur at the edges of my mind, words just out of reach. I feel the strangest sensation inside. My body stays locked in place. But it's like something has reached through flesh and bone, and taken hold of me.

In those round silver mirrors, I see my face clenched. The tendons on my neck stand out, straining.

I feel myself move forward, even with my body frozen stiff.

I'm being pulled. *Out*.

The purring resolves into something familiar.

Words. Thousands of words, crowded together in a confused jumble. But not just words.

Voices. So many, breaking over me.

Then a fist of ice reaches into me and yanks me inside out. It feels like the night wind is blowing right through me for a moment. Like I'm a ghost, nothing but vapour.

And with a dizzying snap, I'm staring at myself

again. But not at the reflection in those mirror eyes. I'm looking at myself from the outside.

Through eyes that aren't mine.

I feel nothing now, bodyless.

The voices shout at me from all directions, trying to be heard. Desperate.

I look helplessly at the empty figure of Danny Quinn.

I see my eyes, wide and blind with panic. And in them I catch another reflection mirrored not in silver but in my own blue eyes. The beast's looming face in miniature, mouth stretched open, showing all those razor teeth.

Trapped behind the beast's eyes, I can't look away.

It lunges forward and my view twists wildly.

When the beast pulls back, I can see clear. And a scream I have no real voice to make rips through to join other screams. I'm not alone here, in this endless dark. Not the only one made to watch the slaughter.

My scream gets swallowed by my pillow. I have to push up on my elbows to breathe. The sound dies to a whimper in my throat as I recognize my room.

I try not to blink, scared of getting sucked back into the nightmare if my eyelids close even for a millisecond.

Rolling out of bed, I lean against the wall, panting. With shaky hands I feel my face, making sure it's still there. Then I hold them out and look at them.

No blood. I'm okay. I'm okay.

I keep telling myself that, getting a grip.

I hear the low murmur of the TV down the hall. Dad's up late as always. I'll go join him on the couch in a minute, and we'll get through the night together.

When I was little and I'd cry out in my sleep, Mom would come and wake me gently. She'd listen to my drowsy retelling of the bad dream, and tell me it was safe now. She said she'd guard me, sitting next to me on the bed, until I was settled in sweeter dreams. There are nights when I'm surfacing from one dream before diving into another, that I imagine I can feel her there. Feel the weight of her pressing down the mattress, feel the warmth coming off her.

Even with all our drifting these past couple years, she seems to be able to find me, in whatever strange new place and strange new bed I'm in. Just thinking of her now calms me down a little. I'd give anything to have her here. Anything and everything. Guarding me.

These nightmares are the beast's playground. Torture chambers it builds inside my brain for its own amusement.

I'm still catching my breath, leaning on the wall, when my cellphone rings.

I see the name on the cell's screen.

'Howie?'

'Danny. I was calling to wake you.'

'Why?'

'I was there. I saw what happened.'

'You were where?'

'I saw it chasing you,' he says. 'In the school, then out by the lake.'

I sag down on the chair at my desk.

'Where were you?' I ask. 'I didn't catch sight of you.'

Howie's quiet a second, just breathing.

'I was right there,' he says finally. 'Trapped inside that thing's head. Seeing out of its eyes. I saw what it did to you. That was the worst thing ever.'

I glance at the window, half expecting to see something staring in at me.

'You know,' I say, 'something weird happened. Well, even *more* weird I should say. Right before it . . . you know, attacked me. It was like I got sucked out of my body. Into its head. And then I was watching through its eyes, what it did to me.'

For the longest time, all I hear is Howie breathing on the other end.

'They're all in there,' he mumbles.

'What?' I press the phone tight against my ear.

'All those kids. The disappeared. I could feel them all crowded inside its head. There were so many.

I heard their voices, all talking at the same time. Didn't you hear anything?'

'I heard.'

'Ray Dyson was there. I could hear his voice. He thinks he's lost somewhere. Kept asking where was the way out. But nobody was listening. They were all just talking over each other.'

I slouch in the chair, staring blankly at the picture above my bed, of the horses pulling blocks of ice from the lake a hundred years ago. A century is nothing to this beast. The Cree Indians were being hunted by it a thousand years ago. A thousand years of victims. Of voices.

'What did the Indians say about it?' I ask. 'Stealing souls?'

'And eating dreams.'

'How did you get out? How did you wake up?'

'When it started ... eating you, I freaked. Just went over the edge. Guess the shock was enough to wake me up.'

I feel a winter breeze coming in the window, licking at my bare feet. Feels good. Too good.

'Why doesn't it finish us off?' I ask. 'I mean, there's nothing we can do to stop it. But it keeps toying with us. These nightmares are like wet dreams for this thing. It gets off on them. Why not just kill us and get it over with?'

Since that first nightmare, the autopsy, it's like the beast has been dissecting our minds. Finding where it hurts, feeding on our fear.

'I've been thinking about that,' Howie says. 'With Ray and the other missing kids, there was a couple weeks between when they got bit and when they disappeared. Maybe whatever that beast infected us with takes time to work. You know, to change us.'

Now that Howie's talking science, he's sounding calmer.

'Change us into what? Human ice cubes?'

'Don't know. I'm still working on that. Whatever's going on inside us, I don't think we're *ready* yet.'

Ready for *what*?

'But there's more,' Howie says. 'I was in its head for a while before it started hunting you. And when I was looking through its eyes, I think I saw where it goes.'

'What do you mean, where it goes?'

'Where it's holed up, in the daytime,' he says. 'And through the summers, I guess. Where it hides. I can find the place. We can find it.'

'Huh? And do what?'

He's sounding very un-Howie-like. Normally he jumps when the phone rings. Now he wants to find this killing machine?

'What're we supposed to do?' he asks. 'Just wait? Ray waited, and look what happened to him.'

I can only shake my head. If Howie's calculations are right, then I've got maybe four days left. And this infection seems to be working even faster on Howie.

'Gotta do something,' he says, almost pleading. 'We can find it.'

I open my mouth to tell him he's crazy. But he's right, we can't just wait. His idea is beyond nuts, but it's all we've got. So I heave a heavy sigh and ask:

'Where?'

Twenty-Four

'What the hell is that?' I ask, getting in the back seat with Ash.

Pike's behind the wheel of his junker, with some kind of futuristic spy-gear strapped on his head. It has two short cylinders poking out like binoculars over his eyes.

'Night-vision goggles,' Pike says. 'We're going hunting, aren't we?'

'You bust those, Dad's gonna kill you,' Howie tells him, riding shotgun.

'You worry too much, bro.' Pike fools with the controls on the side of the headgear. 'I can see everything with these babies. See body heat, see through clothes. Damn, Ash, don't you ever wear a bra?'

'You want to lose some teeth?' She leans forward.

'They can't see through clothes,' Howie says. 'If you set them on infra-red they track body heat signatures. But you can also set them to pick up on ambient light.'

'You're going to have to dumb that down a bit,' I say.

'Okay. They catch even the faintest existing light, like from stars or light pollution off cloudcover, and amplify it a thousand times brighter. Makes even a moonless night look like daytime, but on a green planet.'

Pike keeps playing with his new toy. 'What do you say I try driving with these on?'

'You got a death wish,' Ash says. 'Save it for yourself. Let's get moving.'

Pike pushes the goggles up onto his forehead and we pull out from the marina lot.

Me and Howie had to give up our secret about the shared nightmares. It was the only way to explain how we knew where to find the beast. I was scared we might lose Ash and Pike with this new symptom. But Pike was easy, saying: 'Great. Let's track it down.' Ash held back judgement. 'I don't know. Weirder and weirder.'

But she's here. Not going to miss a fight.

'What did you bring that for?' Pike glances back at the small rifle in my lap. 'That wouldn't stop a squirrel.'

I snuck it out from the rack in the marina house. I feel better just holding it, even if it wouldn't make a dent in the beast.

'Now, *this* will do some serious damage,' Pike says, holding up a double-barrelled shotgun he's got stowed between the front seats.

'You got the safety on?' Ash asks.

'Of course. I may be a gun nut, but the Captain taught me to respect my firearms.'

Ash brought along a thirty-two-calibre rifle she uses when she goes deer hunting with her father.

It's weird, I never even touched a real gun till I got stuck out here in the *big empty*, where everybody's got some kind of firearm. Now I know where all those buckshot holes in the 'Welcome to Harvest Cove' sign come from.

While other people are home drinking eggnog, roasting chestnuts and watching Charlie Brown pick out his sad-ass Christmas tree, we're out hunting a demon.

We follow the dirt road along the shore till the hulking skeleton of the ice factory comes into view.

Its black bones are just visible in the moonlight. I can see easy in the dark now. Last night, I got up to take a leak and was walking back from the bathroom before realizing I hadn't even turned the light on. Usually I have to fumble to find the switch. But now I almost see better the lower the light. Photosensitivity, Howie calls it. Freaky, I call it.

'You sure you can find the place?' I ask Howie.

'I can find it.' His voice is quiet. Shaky.

We bump over frozen muck as we drive up to the factory. Pike stops and kills the engine. For a minute, there's no sound but us breathing, and the creaking of the rotting structure. Seems like one stiff wind could topple the whole thing.

'Well,' Ash speaks up. 'If we're gonna do it, let's do it.'

Pike nods, looking ridiculous in his goggles. 'Okay, boys and girls. Lock and load.'

I open the door and step out. The wind off the lake feels like nothing to me, but Ash zips her jacket up to her chin.

She sweeps her flashlight beam around in the murk. I'm seeing okay, but she must be near blind without the light. Her and Pike check their guns one more time, so I make like I'm doing the same. But I barely know how to shoot the thing.

'Stay close, bro,' Pike tells Howie. 'Which way?'

Howie points over to where the bluffs rise in dark humps past the factory. With Pike walking point and Howie right behind him, we crunch through the shallow snow.

After almost falling on his face a couple times, Pike pushes his goggles up on his forehead. 'They don't read the ground too good.'

We come to the first of the bluffs. It stands about four storeys high, jutting out on the lake.

'Over to the right,' Howie says. 'Should be a way through.'

We find a cleft, a deep cut in the rocks as if a huge hatchet had chopped down on it. We climb through to a little clearing between two tall bluffs.

'Dead end.' Ash pans her light up the rough rock-faces.

'No,' Howie whispers. 'This is it. Turn off the light.'

Ash kills it, and we all look around in the dark.

The two bluffs shelter this hollow like rocky hands cupped around it. At the far end the clearing opens onto the lake. Behind us, the walls join again. A nice little hideaway.

'Nothing here but rocks, Howie,' Ash says. 'Maybe your dream was just a dream.'

He stands there searching the surrounding walls. Right about now I'm hoping he's wrong. This thing wants to stay hidden? Let it.

Howie shudders. 'We better hide!'

We scan the dark for any moving shadows.

'Now!' he whispers.

I feel an electric prickle along the back of my neck. 'Do what he says!'

Pike finds a boulder by the rear of the clearing, big enough to give us some cover. We crouch down and wait.

Pike lowers his night-vision gear into place.

For a minute there's nothing but the sound of the wind.

'There!' Pike whispers.

Shadows are shifting over by the left rock wall. I strain to see what's moving. Then a pale figure squeezes itself out of the stone, and stretches up to its full height.

My breath freezes in my lungs. Ash stiffens. Howie leans against me, shaking. The beast moves away from the wall and tilts its head to look at the sky.

Howie gasps – only a hush of breath, but loud in the still silence.

The beast's attention snaps away from the sky.

It turns to scan the clearing, studying the bare trees and brush, the rough walls of the bluffs.

We crouch lower behind the boulder. The only thing saving us is we're downwind of the beast, with the gusts coming off the lake.

Those eyes, shining in the starlight, slowly pass over our hiding place.

That stare lingers on our boulder too long. A shiver of icicle fingers runs along my scalp. My leg muscles tense up, and the crazy urge hits me to stand up and be seen. My calves cramp with the struggle to keep from rising. Fear twists my gut. The walls feel like they're closing in on us. This whole place is a trap.

Then the beast's stare moves on.

I almost collapse with the release of the pressure, clinging on to a crag in the boulder to keep still. Howie sags against me, and I put my free hand on his back to hold him up.

The beast turns away from us and starts moving on all fours. It picks up speed, passing out of the hollow onto the ice and disappearing in the night.

I let go of the breath I've been holding, leaning on the boulder. There's dead silence for a minute.

'That was . . . extreme,' Ash mumbles.

Pike pushes his goggles up and stands. 'That's one giant, butt-ugly killing machine.'

We all rise. My legs are so shaky. Howie braces himself on the rock to stay vertical. More disturbing than seeing that thing again was the urge I felt to stand and show myself. I'm starting to understand why all those missing kids walked off into the night.

'Where did that thing come out from?' Pike asks.

He starts walking, holding his shotgun with one hand on the barrel and the other cradling the trigger guard, ready if the beast returns.

We follow. My attention is split between the bluff and the gap leading to the lake. Pike stops in front of a deep shadow cut in the rock. A cave. About seven feet tall and five wide. Big enough for us, but a tight squeeze for the beast.

'What do you think?' Pike asks, probing the blackness with his goggles. 'Let's take a look.'

Nobody rushes to agree with him.

'Come on,' he says. 'We're armed and dangerous, right?'

'I'll go in with you,' Howie says, surprising everybody, maybe even himself.

We all stare at him.

'I need to see,' he says. 'To know what we're dealing with.'

'What if it comes back when you're in there?' Ash asks.

Howie shakes his head. 'It won't be back for a while.'

'How do you know?' she says.

'I just do,' Howie mutters. 'When it's this cold out, it likes to run.'

There's a long silence. He led us right to the beast's front door. So maybe he's getting some kind of insight into its head, as it sinks its claws deeper into his. But I don't like how he's acting. Like that thing has got a spell on him, making him forget he's a born coward.

'I'll take point,' Ash says. 'I've got the light.'

'Stay real close to me,' Pike tells Howie.

I take up position right behind Ash.

We step into the mouth of the cave. In the history of bad ideas, this has got to make the top ten. But I'm feeling the pull of the place just like Howie. The need to know.

It's not a cave, but a tunnel, slanting down.

The ceiling's high enough so we don't have to crouch. Ash's light shines on a skin of ice covering the walls. Our footfalls echo loudly in the hush.

A minute goes by and we're still descending. How deep does this hole go? The floor turns slippery, coated in an inch of ice, and I have to brace myself on the walls. The rocks are smoothed out, and the floor is pretty even, as if this tunnel was dug on purpose. Like it's been here a while.

'Do you see that?' Ash's voice bounces off the walls.

'See what?' I ask, my heart seizing up on me. I bump into her when she stops.

'There's a bend in the tunnel,' she says. 'And a blue light farther on.'

I see it now, a dim glow leaking from around the corner ahead.

'Let me go first.' Pike squeezes past her. He goes around the corner, looking surreal with the shotgun held ready and the lenses of his goggles flashing blue. Pike thinks he's in a movie. He's loving this.

I can't tell how far down we've gone. We could be deep beneath the bluffs, or under the floor of the lake even.

The rest of us move toward the bend. Before we reach it Pike calls: 'Clear!'

Taking the turn, all I see is the blue glow. It shines off the ice of the tunnel and reflects back.

Then I see the cave.

It's about the size of a basketball court, with a ceiling that stretches up fifteen feet maybe. The walls glow blue. A thick mist clings to the floor, swallowing my feet.

'What is this place?' I say, then cringe at the echoes: *'isthisplace isthisplace'*.

The others are wading through the mist, exploring.

Howie reaches out and touches the far wall, then checks his fingers to see if any of the glow rubbed off.

'Why's it shine like that?' Ash whispers, trying to avoid the echoes.

Howie turns to us, his face dyed pale blue. 'Could be some kind of phosphorescent mineral deposit. Beautiful, don't you think?'

'Maybe it's radioactive,' Pike says, wandering away from us. 'Don't be taking any samples for your collection.'

'It's creepy.' Ash pokes it. 'And freezing. This whole place is way below zero.'

'When you go this deep,' Howie says, 'this far north, it's always freezing. Summer can't reach down here.'

His voice is almost dreamy. No shaking. No panic. I don't like it.

'Hey, guys,' Pike calls.

His echoes thunder off the ceiling, multiplying into a whole crowd of voices.

He waves us over, deeper into the cave.

'Keep it down,' Ash hushes him.

Pike's standing by a low rise in the floor. The mist drifts in lazy swirls above it.

'Find something?' Howie whispers.

Pike nods, his shotgun cradled in the crook of his arm, one foot resting on the rise. He looks alien in the eerie glow, with the goggles resting against his forehead, and his mohawk dyed electric blue.

'Take a look, bro.' Pike bends over the mound and sweeps his hand through the mist, clearing it away.

I see what the mound is made of.

Bones!

I blink, stunned.

So many of them. Heaped four feet deep in places. The rise stretches all the way to the cave wall.

Human bones!

I'm guessing the smaller ones are from fingers and toes. The bigger ones from arms and legs. Some ribcages, pelvis bones. Skeleton hands reach out here and there. But what tells me these are all human are the skulls.

Some with missing teeth, some missing lower jaws. All with their tops cracked open, like something hammered through the bone. Or chewed through.

Pike steps up onto the mound, climbing it.

I watch him, speechless.

'Get off there!' Ash says.

The mass shifts under his feet, with the clacking of bone on bone.

Pike looks out over the mound. 'There's a hollowed-out part in the middle. Like a nest or something.'

'Not a nest,' Howie says, gazing at the waves of mist swirling over the bones as if hypnotized. 'I think it sleeps there,' he whispers.

A bed of bones.

I finally find my voice. 'I've seen enough.'

'Yeah,' Ash says. 'Let's go!'

Pike climbs back down, scattering a few bones.

'Okay.' He moves up beside Howie. 'Time to retreat.'

Howie gives him a reluctant nod, like he wants to keep poking around down here.

We turn, leaving the mist to cover the dead.

Halfway to the tunnel entrance, Pike shouts: 'Look out!'

His voice ricochets off the walls. We spin around.

At the other end of the cave, a huge pale figure crouches in the mist, watching us. Pike lifts his shotgun.

'Wait!' Howie puts his hand on Pike's arm. 'Hold on. Something's wrong. Look at it.'

Look at what? I want to scream. Shoot! Now!

'I'm looking,' Pike snaps. 'What the hell?'

'That's not it,' Howie says.

Pike's locked on the target with both barrels. 'What're you talking about?' He fights to be heard over the confusion of echoes. 'I see it!'

I'm waiting for that thing to leap and tear into me.

Then something clicks inside my head. There *is* something wrong.

The beast's mouth is wide open, but filled with shadow. No teeth. And the eyes – empty sockets stare back at me. The whole thing looks hollow.

'Wait!' Howie says, digging for something in his pocket.

He comes out with a pen. We watch in disbelief as he winds up and throws it across the cave.

His aim is good. The pen hits the crouching figure and bounces off, falling to the floor. The impact shakes loose a minor avalanche of dust.

Ash lowers the barrel of her rifle. 'What is that?'

'I think it's just a shell,' he says.

'A shell?' Pike asks.

'Trust me. Let's take a look.'

Pike nods. 'But you stay behind me.'

Pike leads us across the cave. The closer we get, the more it does look hollow. Empty.

Pike edges up close enough to give it a kick. His boot makes a dull thud, like kicking an oil barrel. It shakes loose more powdery dust. He shoves the barrels of his shotgun right through one of the eye sockets.

Howie reaches past him to knock on it himself, an amazed look on his face. 'Some animals discard their shells when they get old, or when they outgrow them.'

Pike kicks it again. 'That's no shell. More like armour. I don't know if buckshot would even make a dent.'

I don't care what it is. I'm having a heart attack just being this close to it. The eye sockets are empty but the shadows filling them are still watching.

'Let's get out!' Ash says.

'Right.' Pike puts his hand on Howie's shoulder and leads the way back to the cave entrance.

My foot snags on something in the mist, and I freak when I can't see what it is. Lifting my foot, I find it's just a piece of cloth. I hold it up in the blue light. It's a shredded leg from a pair of pants, stiff with dried mud. The material is thin, with a drawstring inside what's left of the waistband.

'Hospital,' Howie says.

'What?'

'You know, those pyjamas they give you to wear.'

Then it hits me – this is what Ray Dyson had on when he ran off.

'Ray,' Howie whispers.

That's not mud crusted on the material.

Howie says it: 'That's blood.'

I drop the pyjamas into the mist. What else is hidden down there?

'Go!' I shout.

We break into a run.

The way up seems longer than the way down, the tunnel stretching on endlessly. Did we make a wrong turn? What if we get lost down here? This was a *bad* bad idea.

Ash's light scatters confusing flashes off the wall ice. Nothing looks familiar. The only sound is the rush of our feet, the echoes chasing us to the surface.

Finally, I smell fresh air. I have to hold back from shoving Howie aside to escape. I stumble out into the night, so relieved I forget the beast isn't down in that cave. It's out here somewhere.

'Get moving! We're easy targets here.' Pike starts us across the clearing.

We run to the cleft in the rocks that leads us out of the hideaway. My heart surges when I catch sight of the car. Never thought I'd be so happy to see the crapmobile again.

We pile in. Pike guns the engine, the tyres spinning in the snow. We're speeding and motionless at the same time. Like in the nightmares, where I'm running and running and getting nowhere. No escape.

Because that thing isn't just out there in the dark. It's inside my head. There's no way I can shake it.

Then the tyres catch and we shoot off. Nobody says anything. We just watch the patch of road ahead lit by the one working headlight.

We came here tonight looking for answers. For some way out of this nightmare. But there is no way out. All those missing kids. All those bones.

Me and Howie are next.

Twenty-Five

'Let me get this straight,' the cop says. 'There's some monster out here, hunting down kids and killing them? That about it?'

It's the morning after our trip underground, and we're all standing out by the ice factory, on the snowy shoreline. Officer Baker of the Ontario Provincial Police frowns at us with his bushy black eyebrows. He thinks we're nuts. Can't blame him.

'Not a monster,' I say. 'But some kind of . . . wild animal. We can show you where it's holed up. Seriously.'

I called the number on Ray Dyson's 'missing' flyer, asking for the cop who visited the school last week. It was my idea, a desperate one, so I'm spokesman for us. I was kind of vague on the phone, thinking there was no way I'd get him out here if I spilled the whole story up front. So I just said I found something connected to Ray Dyson's disappearance, and could he come meet me out by the factory. He wanted to know more, of course. But I told him it was something he had to see in person.

'You found a piece of bloody clothing?' Baker says now. 'Belonging to Ray Dyson. But you left it behind?'

This is like the third time we've gone over that part.

'Right,' I tell him. 'I dropped it. Down in the cave.'

I've told him that much, but left out the heap of bones and skulls. Gotta ease him into it.

Baker scowls at me, then at each of us. He grabs a small flashlight that's hooked to his belt and turns it on.

'Let me see your pupils,' he says, stepping up close.

'Huh?'

'Eyes forward.'

'I'm not high. This is for real.'

He shines his light in my eyes. With my photophobia, the beam feels like tiny hot needles stabbing through to the backs of my eyes. I flinch, taking a step back. But I guess he doesn't see anything strange because he moves on to Pike.

'Next!'

One by one he goes through all of us. Ash just grits her teeth and looks pissed off. Howie squints and cringes like me.

'What now?' Pike speaks up. 'A breathalyser?'

'Shut it,' Baker tells him. 'So, you got something to show?' He turns to me. 'Show it!'

'Over this way,' I say.

I start leading us over the hill to the bluffs looming against the shoreline. The new snow has filled our tracks from last night, making it slow going. The whole landscape is painfully white to my tender eyes.

The wind cutting in off the lake must be brutal, but not to me. Can't tell if my fever-freeze is getting worse. I keep checking my body temp and it's scary low. Like I should be laid out in a steel drawer down at the morgue.

I don't need our old tracks to find the way. It's imprinted on my brain, like everything about our trip underground last night.

'How far?' Baker grumbles behind me.

'Just past this ridge.'

We make the short climb and cross through the cleft in the rocks into the clearing.

'Over here.'

I rush ahead. Approaching the rock-face, I stop and search the bluff. I take a few steps farther along it, sweeping my eyes over the wall in front of me. The tunnel is . . .

Where is it?

I back up from the wall, trying to orient myself.

No. No. This can't be right.

The tunnel opening is gone.

'Howie?'

He comes over and searches with me.

Where is it? I want to ask him. But I can't say that with the cop staring at me, arms folded.

Things look different in the dark. Maybe I got turned around the wrong way somewhere.

'This is the place,' I mumble. 'Right?'

'Yeah.' Howie walks along the wall. 'It . . . it should be here. Right under this overhang. I remember the formation. We're like standing directly in front of it. There must be some kind of door or something.'

Stepping up close, I look for any signs of cracks. Nothing. I try leaning my weight against the rock-face in a couple places. But it's solid.

'It's here,' I tell Baker. 'I swear. There's a tunnel. We went inside. And down . . . to the cave.'

I trail off, turning back to the wall and giving it a few more shoves.

Come on! This is not happening.

'Game's over, kids,' the cop says. 'I don't know what you're playing at here, but I'm not amused.'

I give the wall an experimental kick. 'It's not a game. This is for real.'

Pike and Ash are standing back. They're looking for the opening too. But from a distance. They see where this whole thing is heading.

Officer Baker rubs his forehead under the brim of his hat, like we're giving him a migraine.

'Listen,' he tells us. 'I know everybody's shaken up by Raymond's disappearance. But whatever you think is going on here, I'm not getting it. I'll let it slide this one time. But don't pull this crap again, guys. Hear me?'

He starts to walk away. I want to tell him to wait, the tunnel's got to be here somewhere. If only I'd kept that torn leg from Ray's pyjamas, with the blood, then I'd have proof Baker couldn't walk away from. But I've got nothing.

I look around at the guys for some help. Ash gives me a sympathetic shrug. Pike shakes his head, like he knew this was a bad idea. Howie paces back and forth in front of the blank wall.

The tunnel was here. Now it's not.

I guess when you've been hiding out for a thousand years, you get good at it. If you can make all those kids disappear, and do it so nobody even realizes they've been taken, you must know a few tricks.

And this one is the perfect vanishing act.

Twenty-Six

When I get back to the marina I sneak past Dad. He's in the garage, using the table saw to cut new boards for the dock. I go in the side door and head upstairs.

It's been getting harder to hide what's happening to me. I mean, I've got the skin tone of a corpse, ghost-pale bordering on blue.

After a late dinner last night, I was drying dishes when Dad went to put his hand on my shoulder, leaning over to grab a sponge. I flinched away from him like he was holding a blow torch. Didn't want him touching me, because then he'd feel the freeze and know something's seriously wrong. He gave me this look.

'I, uh . . . strained my shoulder working out,' I told him. 'It's just real sore.'

'You should ice it down,' he said.

'Right.' Just what I need.

So I'm keeping my distance from Dad. There's no way I can explain. And I don't want to end up as some lab rat in the hospital.

Upstairs, I take a quick sub-zero shower to clear my head. This cold fever is getting worse.

In my room, I stand in front of the open window. It's just a little after four in the afternoon and the sun is dying. I watch the twilight take over the cove, colouring the snow and ice a steely blue.

After our spectacular crash and burn with the cop and the disappearing tunnel, we drove around a while, going nowhere.

Pike was pissed off. 'That's it. We tried it your way. Now we do it my way.'

'What's your way?' I asked.

'Nuke that mutant freak. What we need is one of those bunker-buster bombs. There's one that weighs ten tons. They call it a *Grand Slam*. It can plough through reinforced concrete like it was butter. Or a thermobaric bomb. They're real smart, they detonate twice. When the bomb hits, first it blows out this incendiary mist that fills the bunker – or cave. Then the second detonation ignites the mist. If we had one of those we could barbecue this freak.'

'Let's talk real,' Ash broke in before he started frothing. 'We need a new strategy.'

The talk went around and around, like our driving, getting us nowhere.

The cops were our best shot. We could've handed the whole crazy thing over to them. They've got the manpower, and the firepower, to deal with it.

Now we're on our own.

Outside my window the darkness deepens, the blue landscape shading toward black. Another day gone. How many left before me and Howie go running off into the night? Two, maybe three?

There's got to be another way. I'm coming up empty. So I call someone with an IQ.

'Hey, Howie. What're you up to?'

'Danny. You know, research.'

'Time's running out for research.'

'Yeah,' he says, sounding small and sad.

'Sorry. I'm jumpy. What kind of research?'

'Spiders.'

'Okay. What about them?'

'You know they can only eat food in liquid form?'

'What does that have to do with anything?' I ask.

'Well, when they catch their prey − flies or other insects − they inject them with digestive fluids, to break them down inside, liquefying their organs. Then they puncture the skin and suck it all up.'

'That's . . . disgusting. So?'

'So, maybe something like that's happening to you and me. When that thing stung us, it injected us with something that's been changing our bodies. Maybe it's transforming us into a digestible form. Making us edible. Might explain why it doesn't kill its prey right off. It can't eat them until they're compatible with its metabolism.'

I shake my head. He's talking about us being *digested*, like it's some science project. He should be freaking out. Like I am. But I guess you can only stay scared so long before your mind flatlines, exhausted. Whatever *change* is happening in us, it's not just our organs. If that thing owns our dreams, who knows what else it's messing with inside our skulls?

'It's a theory,' Howie says. 'Maybe it needs us iced.'

If Howie hadn't been right about so much already, I could just shrug off his theory. But it seems like the deeper the beast gets into our minds, the more Howie sees inside its head.

'But how does that help us?'

'Guess it doesn't, really,' he mutters.

I can hear it in his voice, like I saw it in his eyes earlier after our plan fell apart, that feeling of doom. Looking in the mirror after my cold shower, I could see the same thing in my own eyes. Something I saw in Mom's too, near the end.

'Why us?' I ask. 'I mean, was it all just about us being in the wrong place at the wrong time? Or were we, you know, chosen?'

'I've been wondering that myself. How does any predator select its prey? Sometimes it's convenience. Something tasty wanders by, they snap it up. But the higher you go up the food chain, the predators become more selective. This thing is at the top of the chain, above Man even. It's got a very particular taste in victims – humans, thirteen to eighteen. But why us? Who knows, maybe we've got a special pheromone scent, maybe we have elevated levels of some hormones, or other chemicals in our brains.'

I know he's thinking what I'm thinking. All those skulls in that bed of bones, with their tops cracked open.

I groan. 'So we're special.'

'Maybe it's just got good taste, eh?'

'Yeah, right. Hey, make sure Pike keeps an eye on you.'

I don't like the way he's sounding. Too calm. Very un-Howie-like.

'You think I'm gonna go AWOL, and disappear in the night?'

'Kind of, yeah.'

'Don't worry. Pike's got me on lockdown. Can't even

go take a leak without an escort.'

'Good.'

'But who's keeping an eye on you?'

Looking out my window at the deepening shadows, I know exactly what's keeping an eye on me.

Twenty-Seven

Howie told me where to look. I follow First Line past the overgrown railroad tracks that lead to where the Fraser Mill stood, before it burned down twenty years ago.

I keep going, walking under the power lines that run north from the big transformers in Barrie.

About a half-mile past the mill, I find what Howie said to look for. Hanging from the junction at the top of a utility pole, a black cable snakes down from the power lines above. When the cable reaches the ground it runs away from the road toward the lake, disappearing under the snow.

I start backtracking it, having to kick through the snow every few steps to make sure I'm not going off course. I keep an eye out for any movement, even though it's bright daylight and I should be safe. All I see are a few crows, inky shadows against the pale sky. The landscape stretches white and untouched.

Mom loved being the first to break new snow. She'd rush me out to the park in the morning after an overnight snowfall. She'd say we were like those guys who walked on the moon, because we were stepping where no one had set foot before.

'Their shoeprints are still up there,' she told me. 'There's no wind on the moon, nothing to move the moon dust. So those footsteps are just like they left them. Forever.'

She would have loved all this new powder, fresh and waiting. Too bad there's no such thing as *forever* on Earth.

The cable crosses a low hill. From the top I see where it ends.

The trailer rests on cement blocks, the last shreds of paint peeling off its siding. Miles from anything.

Just how Mangy Mason likes it.

This morning, I told Howie and Ash about my semi-deranged conversation with the guy.

'Mason's a nut,' Howie said. 'But he's been living on the cove for longer than anybody. Maybe he knows something. What else we got?'

'Worth a shot,' Ash agreed. 'I'll come with you and watch your back.'

I said I didn't want to spook the old guy. From what

I hear, Mason never talks to anybody if he can help it.

'I think we bonded,' I told them. 'I should go alone.'

Starting down the hill, I see where the cable runs right under the trailer. Howie told me how Mason keeps getting busted for bootlegging electricity off the power lines.

A few years back, the Feds tried to kick him and his trailer off of what they said were public lands. Then Mason turned out to be not so nutty. He claimed 'squatter's rights'. He's been living there for fifty years. So the Feds decided to wait him out. The guy is ancient, and walks around in the middle of winter in a T-shirt. He isn't knocking on death's door, he's pounding on it.

I don't see any sign of him as I approach the maze of garbage surrounding his trailer. Dozens of car tyres are stacked in piles, like he's building a fort. Deceased fridges and stoves huddle under coats of snow, with a weather-eaten couch and recliner nearby to sit and enjoy the view. He's even got a satellite dish (for decoration?) on the roof. And flapping high above it all is an upside-down Canadian flag on a tilted steel pole. Flying the flag the wrong way up like that is supposed to be a sign of distress. He's got that right.

I have to watch where I'm stepping to avoid all the yellow stains in the snow from the dogs. The door to the trailer is wide open.

'Hello?' I call in.

The lights are on, and I think I hear the low mumble of a TV.

'Anybody home?'

Three furry white faces appear in the doorway, with three sets of ice-blue eyes studying me. I see the dogs asking themselves: *is this food?*

'You still breathing?'

I spin around.

Mason has snuck up on me, silent in his ragged sneakers. He's wearing cracked sunglasses held together with tape, and his half-shredded Budweiser T-shirt. Two more huskies stand with him.

'Still breathing.'

He spits into a nearby drift, and climbs the steps into his trailer. 'Not for long. You smell ripe.'

Smell ripe? The stink coming off this guy makes my eyes water.

'Can I talk to you a second?' I ask.

There's a clatter of metal from inside, then the grind of a motor.

'Won't do any good,' he calls back.

The dogs bump me as they go in.

Maybe this wasn't such a hot idea. But I came this far. 'I just wanted to ask you—'

'What?' he snaps. 'Get in here, or get lost. In

or out. I don't talk through walls.'

I step into the dim interior, where it smells like something was left to rot.

'Lunchtime.' He sticks a can of dog food under the mechanical opener. Mason grabs a hub cap from a teetering stack on the counter and plops the contents onto it, then sets the cap on the floor for his mutts. He does this a few more times, until everybody's happily gorging themselves. The rotting remains of past meals are shoved against the wall.

He grabs a couple of paper plates and cracks two more cans. The dog food glorps out onto the plate.

'So,' he says. 'Turkey Delight, or Liver Feast?'

It takes me a second to realize he's offering *me* a choice.

'No, I'm good.' I hold back a gag. 'I had a few Milkbones on the way over.'

That's supposed to be funny, but he only frowns like *I'm* the unstable one here.

'More for me.' He tosses his sunglasses on the counter and grabs a fork.

Mason sits on a stack of four mattresses that takes up the end of the trailer. A TV rests against the wall at the foot of the bed, like he warms his feet on it at night. CNN is on, covering some war.

'The other day, when we were talking,' I begin. 'You know, about the local wildlife? You said something took your best friend, back when you were a kid. What did you mean by that?'

He chews, watching troops in some bombed-out hellhole.

Is he even listening?

Then he sets his fork down and rolls up the right sleeve of his T-shirt. He bares his biceps and the big faded tattoo of a fancy cross he's got inked there.

'See that?'

'Yeah. Nice cross.'

'It's a Celtic cross. A ward, a protection,' he snaps, eyes intense. 'I gave myself God's mark so the Devil couldn't claim me.'

'Right,' I mutter. We just took a sharp turn into crazytown.

'Take a close look. Do you see?'

'Yeah, sure.' I glance at it and nod.

'No you don't. Look into the eye of the cross.'

I'm getting this creepy feeling, like he's trying to hypnotize me or something – *stare at the eye, you're getting sleepy* . . .

But all that's there in the centre is a clear patch of un-inked and wrinkly skin. Nothing more than—

In the middle of the *eye* is a small blue dot.

Just like the one on the back of my right hand. Like the one on Howie's neck.

'You got stung? When?'

He scratches deep in his beard with the fork.

'Fifty, fifty-one years ago.'

His mark looks as fresh as mine.

'But, how? I mean, I thought if you got bit then it took you. Like you said it took your friend.'

Mason considers the chunk of Liver Feast on his fork, a distant look in his eyes. Then he fills his face with it.

'Rod McLean,' he mumbles. 'We were playing a little night shinny out on the ice, by the light of the moon. I was up a couple goals, when his slap shot knocked one of the tin cans we were using for goalposts flying. So he skated off to find the puck, and I got the cans set up again. Then I heard Rod shout. Thought he was just horsing at first. I skated over toward the sound of his voice. And then I saw it.'

He licks his fork clean, remembering.

'The demon had him flat on his back on the ice, holding him there. It looked like something the Devil had bred in his zoo of damned souls. Rod was out cold. Dead, for all I could tell. I held my hockey stick ready to swing when the demon looked my way. Then it was on me.'

Mason holds his arm out, showing his cross and the blue dot in the eye.

'Got me right through my winter coat. Knocked me out. When I came to, Rod was shaking me awake. The demon was gone. Didn't know why we were still breathing. Rod, he got sick a few days later. Me too, only not as bad.'

'What happened to him? Your friend?'

'Rod got sick. Then he got better, for a while. The doctors thought it was tetanus, or blood poisoning. But they couldn't explain why he had ice in his veins, why he was so cold, but not shivering. They gave him drugs for it, thought he was getting better. But the demon got inside his head. Got in mine, too. You know what I'm talking about. The whispers. Voices so close, like somebody's breathing the words in your ear. But nobody's there.'

He stares at me for a moment. 'Not yet, eh? Soon, you'll hear them.'

I get this shiver, like a spider crawling down my spine.

'Rod was a tough kid, but he couldn't take it. And one night, in the middle of a January cold snap, he took off. He shared a room with his little brother. The brother told me later, the last thing he heard Rod say was. "I'm coming. I'm coming." Like he was answering someone calling him.'

Mason throws his empty cans onto the pile on the floor.

'And?' I ask.

'And, nothing. Storytime's over.' He stands up. 'Get the hell out.'

He waves at me like I'm a mosquito. I start backing out of the trailer. 'What about Rod?'

'They never found a trace of him.' Mason hustles his dogs out along with me. 'Come on,' he tells them. 'We've got work to do.'

I step back into the fresh air.

'I don't get it,' I say as he follows me out into the snow. 'You're still here. You survived. How come?'

His huskies watch him like they're waiting for the answer with me.

'What did you do?'

'I ran,' he says. 'Rod was gone, and I knew where. Knew he wasn't coming back. When I started hearing the whispers, I knew there was no fighting it. I was next. So, I ran as far as I could. Ended up in Toronto. Far enough. I still had the ice in my veins, still had the *chill*. But the whispers went away. And the dreams.'

Mason looks at the frozen lake where ghost squalls of windblown snow chase each other.

'Came back here three years later. Thought I'd imagined it all. But Rod was still gone. And when winter came that year, the dreams came with it. Only not like before. I could feel the demon sniffing around me in the dreams, feel it watching. But something was changed inside me. And it didn't want me any more.'

'Why? What changed?'

'I changed. I wasn't a kid any more. It only takes them young.'

'Why?' I feel like I'm on the brink of some discovery.

'How the hell do I know? God works in mysterious ways – so does the Devil. All I know is the demon leaves me alone now. I don't have what it needs. But you do.'

A shiver spider-crawls down my back.

Mason walks away with his dog posse.

'Run while you still can,' he calls back. 'Like I did. Before it's too late.'

Twenty-Eight

There's no answer on Howie's cell, or his home number.

Got to see what he makes of Mason's story. Maybe with this new info he'll come up with something.

Back at the marina house, I pace around my room and keep trying his cell. Maybe there's a tiny bit of hope. Mason found a way to escape his death sentence. So it can be done.

I slouch back in my chair. Ash called me late last night, checking on me. She wanted to brainstorm, figure out a plan. But I was too freaked to focus.

'You never get scared?' I asked her.

She's always so cool, even after what we saw down in the cave, after she'd seen the beast with her own eyes.

'Sure. But you can't let it show. Life's a fight, Danny. You let them see you're scared, you've already lost. You got to eat the fear. Never let them see where it hurts.'

Right there is the whole history of Ash. Why she's unbeaten.

My phone rings, startling me. The screen says: *unknown caller*.

'Hello?'

'Danny, it's Pike.'

'Hey, man. I've been trying to get Howie. What's—'

'I'm calling from the hospital,' Pike says. 'It's Howie. We couldn't wake him up. Doctor says it's some kind of coma. They think it might be a relapse, from the hypothermia. But they don't know what's really going on. You should see him – his lips have gone blue.'

'I just talked to him on the phone this morning,' I tell Pike. 'He didn't sound so bad.'

'I found him on the floor in his room, unconscious. I couldn't get him to wake up. Man, I don't know what to do.'

I've never heard Pike sound like this. Helpless. The flicker of hope I was feeling a minute ago has been snuffed out.

'Keep an eye on him,' I say. 'In case he tries to run away, you know.'

'Right. I know. I'll be watching him close. But we gotta think of something.'

'Like what?'

'Like how do we kill that thing?'

This *thing* has been around for a thousand years! How do you kill the unkillable?

'I gotta go,' Pike says. 'I'm not letting him out of my sight.' He hangs up.

I stand staring at the phone. We're screwed! We're dead!

That thing is so deep inside our heads. It owns us.

Mason told me – I smell ripe. We're both ripe, me and Howie.

Our time's up.

Mason's a nut, but he's also the only one who ever escaped that thing. *Run*, he said. *While you still can.*

Something tells me it's too late for Howie.

So, sick with fear, I do the only thing I can.

I run.

Twenty-Nine

Sitting on a stump in the trash-strewn field by Highway 11, I watch the sparse traffic speed through this big stretch of nothing toward Toronto. Across the road is the Last Stop Convenience Store. The Greyhound bus stops there twice a day.

Shouldn't be long now.

A pick-up truck whips past. I check my watch. I check to make sure I've got my cellphone in my backpack. Then I check my guts for the hundredth time.

Do I stay, or do I go? Fight or flight?

But my brain keeps stalling. I hiked all the way up here ready to leave. Now that I'm here, I really don't know.

It's just – I'm sick of running. Leaving everything and everybody behind. Starting over again, just when I think I've found something worth staying put for.

Something like Ash. I know what she'd say – flight is not an option. But she doesn't know what it's like to have that thing inside your head, its poison in your veins.

The last couple days I've held back from touching her knowing I'd give her the shivers.

'Must be like kissing a snowman,' I said, when she pulled me in close.

I could see the worry shading her eyes even as she smiled. 'More like licking a Danny-flavoured popsicle.'

Ash is fearless. Unbeaten. We could have been something.

I squint into the blowing snow, searching for the Greyhound. The road is still empty.

Dad's going to be. I'll call him from the bus, or when I get to Toronto. Aunt Karen is always saying I can come stay anytime.

But Dad will think I'm abandoning him, talking off like this. Three days till Christmas too. The worst time of year for us, when everything reminds us of Mom, and missing her eats us alive. Only way we get through it is together.

I've got to come up with something to tell him – anything to keep him from dragging me back here.

Fight or flight?

Flight worked for Mason, kept him alive.

I remember how it felt, the night in the clearing out in the bluffs as we watched the beast emerge from its tunnel. That insane urge to rise from our hiding spot, to stand and give myself up. Like it was calling, and I couldn't help but answer.

Mason talked about the whispers. *Soon, you'll hear them.* Right now the beast seems to be focused on Howie. But when it's done with him, I'm next. Even now, in the light of day, I feel the pull of something. Like a lake current trying to draw me back to shore. I can still resist it, but what happens when night falls and the beast wakes.

Poor Howie. Never caught a break his whole life, so scared of his own shadow he's got a restraining order against it. Now he's lying in the hospital.

And what's ripping me apart is that I know what's happening to him right now. Inside his head.

He's in the beast's world. Trapped there. Dreaming its dreams. Can't wake up. Can't escape.

I can see him, too scared to jump off the edge of the cliff and wake up. Too weak to tear himself free of the nightmare. Before, I was there to give him a push, show him the way. Now he's alone.

I watch the highway. Where's the bus? Come on already.

But I'm so tired of running. Drifting from town to

dreary town. If Dad stays still too long the past crowds in on him. Eats him up.

But there's nowhere we can run that's far enough. No place we can hide it won't find us. Even here, at the end of the world. Nightmares always track you down.

Get on the bus. Don't look back. Looking back is lethal.

Through the blowing snow, I see the Greyhound coming down the hill.

I grab my pack, startled by the sudden appearance of the bus. Guess I was beginning to doubt it would ever come.

This is it. Stay or go?

If I leave now, Howie's dead. That's a fact.

There's no cure for this thing we've got. And by Howie's calculations, I can count the time we have left in hours. But what good is me dying with him going to do?

I stand on the shoulder of the highway, watching the bus approach.

Pike wants to kill it. Kill a predator that's survived a thousand years without a scratch.

I go to step out on the road and cross.

Do it. Do it!

But my feet aren't moving.

I can't leave Howie locked in that nightmare. I know

what it's like to be left behind. Can't do that to him.

And who's next, after I take off? Pike? Ash?

She's been trying to show me how to fight. But I'm no scrapper. What I really got from her, what stuck with me, is her *drive*. There's no quit in her. Flight is not an option.

The bus pulls up in front of the store, idling.

Last chance.

Some things you can't escape by running. However this is going to end, it ends here and now.

I stay on the shoulder until the Greyhound pulls away. It goes down the snow-blown highway, between endless white fields.

I let out a deep sigh. But I'm not sorry.

I turn from the highway and the bus shrinking in the distance. It'll be a hike back to the marina. Give me time to psych myself up – to grow some balls, as Pike would put it.

Where I'm headed, I'm going to need them.

Back into the nightmare to get Howie.

Thirty

'Where have you been?' Dad asks, as I sneak into the house with my backpack.

'Just out.'

He's sitting at the kitchen table with his toolbox, working on a blender.

'Where's you find that?' I ask.

'I'm just fixing it for somebody.'

I notice a couple of empty beer bottles on the table. Nothing strange about that. But there's red lipstick on the mouth of one.

'Somebody *who*?' I ask, knowing already.

Dad pretends not to hear. But then he sees me picking up the lipsticked empty.

'The woman from the Red and White.'

'Andrea?'

'I believe that's her name,' he says, shuffling parts around.

'So. You like her?'

Even with doom and panic creeping up on me, I can't help a small grin.

Andrea won't give up. First it was bringing over the blinking midget Christmas tree. Then, the casseroles and lasagnes. Nice tries, but they got her nothing more than a grunted 'you shouldn't have done that'. But this is genius. The way to Dad's heart – get him to fix stuff. He's a born fixer. So that got her in the door, even got her a beer.

Dad gestures at my backpack. 'What's all that?'

Think fast. 'The gym. I was working out.'

'Well, your friends have been calling. What's wrong with your cell?'

'Battery must have died.'

Really, I just turned it off. I was planning a clean getaway and didn't walk anybody talking me out of it.

Dad grabs a paper towel to wipe some grease off his hands. 'I hear Howie's back in the hospital.'

'Yeah.'

'Poor kid. You think it's serious?'

Dead serious. 'Don't know.'

'How *you* feeling?' Dad frowns. 'You look beat.'

'Uh, yeah. Intense workout.'

'You're really pale.' Dad presses the back of his hand to my forehead. I'm not quick enough pulling away. A startled look flashes in his eyes. 'You're freezing.'

I step back. 'It's like thirty below out there. I'm fine, just got to warm up.'

'I'll turn up the heat.'

'No!' I say, way too loud. I'm already baking in here. 'I mean, I'll put on a sweater or something. Don't worry about it.'

But worrying is what Dad does best.

'Okay,' he says. 'But watch out, eh? Maybe there's something going around.'

Right. Something with eight-inch teeth and a taste for teenagers.

I start down the hall to my room.

'I'm gonna heat up some meat loaf,' he says. 'Want some?'

'Did you make it?'

'No. She did.'

'Sounds good then.' I head for my room. 'But I'm just going to take a nap first.'

Andrea's wearing him down. It's funny, here's Dad finally showing some signs of life, and here's me showing signs of death.

Not so funny.

I close my door, crack the window open and strip down to my boxers and T-shirt.

Outside, the late afternoon is starting its long

blue fade into night. I take in a deep breath to cool my lungs.

This is it.

If you try real hard to fall asleep, it ain't going to happen. But I am deliriously drowsy.

I stretch out on top of the covers. The only light comes from the blue of the winter sunset. Blue like the glow in the beast's cave.

Deep breaths. I try and slow my heart, making an effort to release the tension in my muscles.

I give it ten minutes. Lying still. Breathing easy. And another ten.

No good. I'm weak with exhaustion, but my brain just won't let go and fade to black. Maybe because it knows what's waiting when it does.

Giving up, I open my eyes . . .

And see myself reflected in the ceiling above. I gasp. The water-stained ceiling is now a mirrored surface. I sit up, blinking in confusion. The whole place is mirrored – walls, floor, my bedroom door.

I go to swing out of bed. The desk, the lamp and the pile of school books all shine with a metallic smoothness. The bed under me too. I touch the sheets, with the reflected image of my hand meeting the real thing. I half expect the sheet to crinkle up like tin-foil. But it still feels soft.

Any move I make is thrown back at me from every surface in the room.

I'm in the dream. On the beast's turf.

And I remember why. I'm here for Howie.

Move fast! Before it catches my scent. If it hasn't already.

I look out the window. The world outside is still caught in a blue twilight. The Cove is the same. Snow and ice, and skeleton trees.

I brace myself with a breath of frosty air. Then I call out.

'Howie!' My voice carries over the empty landscape. No answer. This dreamscape is as stiff and lifeless as an unshaken snow-globe.

He's gotta be here somewhere. We shared the nightmare before, and I found him. So I can find him again.

I hope.

Pulling my head back in, I listen hard. There's a hush of sound, like a breeze drifting through the house. But it's something more . . .

Whispers. Coming from somewhere on the other side of my bedroom door.

I go over to it, keeping my eyes on the knob so I won't get distracted by the images bouncing back at me from every direction, imitating every little move I make.

Reflections of reflections.

The door opens on a hall of mirrors, lit by winter blue. The whispering rises. Too many voices talking at the same time.

'Howie!'

Nothing.

'It's me. Danny.'

Moving into the hallway I make the mistake of looking down. The floor seems to drop out from under me, with nothing solid to support me but my own reflection.

I take a step, watching the sole of my bare left foot meet its twin rising up on the flipside. I get the weirdest sensation that I won't fall as long as I have the reversed images of my own feet to walk on.

I take baby steps, while the whispers rise and fall as if they're wandering the house. Searching.

'Howie!'

The murmur goes quiet. Something heard me. Then it hits me – maybe *I'm* what the voices are searching for.

I look up from my strange balancing act to see steam pouring out of the open bathroom door ahead. I glance in. The condensation has fogged up the silvered walls inside. Something's been scribbled on the clouded walls.

DANNYBOY   DANNYBOY   DANNYBOY DANNYBOY DANNYBOY.

Over and over, in rows reaching from floor to ceiling.

What Mom called me.

I forget to breathe. The beast has been dissecting my memories, finding out where it hurts.

I force myself to break away.

But there's nowhere I can look that I don't see myself looking back, wide-eyed and desperate. These mirrors are like the beast's eyes. If I stare into them too deep, or stay in here too long, they'll swallow me up.

Focus!

This dead silence is electric, like the moment between the flash of lightning and the thunder.

If I was Howie, where would I hide? He's just too good at hiding out, been doing it half his life. So the only way I'll find him is if he comes to me.

'Howie!'

As I step into the living room, the silver surfaces trick me with my own reflections staring back.

There! Something moving in the corner. I swing around and find a girl, maybe thirteen, in pink pyjamas. She's hunched over, hugging herself. Her eyes lock onto mine. The girl's lips move, but I can't make out what she's saying. Whispers.

I step closer, straining to hear. Then I realize she's standing *inside* the wall. I see my own reflection behind her. There's two of me, but only one of her. She's trapped in the wall.

Her lips move again, her voice barely a whimper.

'Show me. Show me the way out.'

And she reaches her hand to me, as if I'm going to take it and lead the way.

I can't help flinching back, scared what might happen if she touched me.

She's one of *them*. The missing.

'Show me.'

'I don't – I can't.'

Then I catch more movement. Over there, staring out from the silvered curtains, two guys lean together. They look familiar. Where have I seen them? Then it comes to me. Their pictures were in the *Examiner* archives. Runaway brothers from half a century ago.

'Take us with you,' the older brother's voice echoes, calling from a deep place.

Every second more rush into the living room, racing along the walls. I jump when I see an Indian girl appear beneath my feet, staring up like she's looking through a glass-lidded coffin. She's got on an animal-hide dress and speaks in a language that sounds something like Ash's Ojibwa.

These ghost reflections crowd in. Dozens and dozens. Voices begging, desperate . . .

Take me. Save me. Show me.

So many. The mob keeps growing, shoving and

pushing each other, trying to get my attention.

They want me to take them out of here. Howie said they don't know they're dead. He's got a living, breathing body to return to. There's nothing for these lost souls to go back to but a pile of bones.

I stumble around, expecting to feel hands grabbing at my ankles, pulling me under. I duck my head at the figures swooping over the ceiling like diving bats.

'Danny?'

I stop cold.

'Danny, over here.'

I track the voice to a corner. Howie's crouched low, in his hospital pyjamas. Knees hugged up against his chest, he's making himself small to avoid the crush.

I run over to him, ignoring the rest.

'Howie! I came to get you. Let's go.'

I bend next to him.

'Can't,' he says, from the other side of the mirror. 'I'm stuck in here.'

'It's just a dream.'

He shakes his head. 'It's more. It's where the beast keeps . . . them.'

The others press in closer now, but he keeps his eyes on mine.

'Forget them,' I say. 'Just focus on me. Think! Use

your brain. What ... what do I do? Can I use something to break you out of this?'

The wall looks like a mirror. It should shatter if I hit it hard enough.

'Won't break,' he says. 'But maybe . . .'

'Maybe what?'

Howie presses his palm against the inside of the wall. 'Try and grab my hand.'

He kneels there, waiting for me as the crowd gathers to watch.

Okay. Here goes. I tap the wall with my fingertips. The contact makes ripples in the surface, as if it were almost liquid. I pull back, startled.

'I felt that,' Howie gasps. 'Push. Push on through.'

I take a shaky breath then lean forward, shoving my hand wrist-deep into the silver. So cold it burns. I flinch back, but Howie's got hold of my wrist now and I have to pull his weight too. The bones of my hand stiffen into icicles. The others crush in, clawing at my wrist, trying to grab on. Screaming faces shove forward, their features twisted with fear and desperation. Their weight threatens to drag me in deeper.

Straining against it, I crash backward on the floor. Something lands on top of me.

I roll out from under it.

Howie lies on the floor beside me, shaking like he's having a seizure.

The whole place shudders. Earthquake, or dreamquake. Like something just woke up.

I scramble over to Howie. 'Just breathe. Breathe.'

It takes an effort to get him to sit up.

'We gotta get out of here,' I say. 'Gotta wake up.'

He pushes himself to his knees. 'How?'

I feel a shudder in the floor beneath me. Something's pounding up the stairs.

'Get up!' I grunt, heaving Howie on his feet.

His legs are shaky, but we gotta go. Now!

'Where . . . ?' he says.

I have no idea. I mean, no matter how far we run, we're still in the nightmare, right?

But then I flash on the last time we got stuck together, on that moonlit ice field.

I aim him toward the hall. 'Go!'

I half shove, half drag him. I don't look back. The ghosts trapped in the walls scatter like fish smelling a shark in the water. The beast is closing on us.

We race down the hallway toward my room. The floor seems to stretch under us. It's like we're running in place. But I put on a burst of speed to close the distance.

A thunderous roar hits me from behind with a shock wave. We skid the last few feet into my room.

I kick the door shut. Like that's going to stop anything.

'Out the window,' I gasp.

Howie stares back at me.

'Don't think. It worked before. Jump!'

It's only a two-storey drop to the ground. That's got to be enough to break us out of this. I grab his wrist and pull him over to the window.

I'm ready to heave him out if I have to. But Howie climbs onto the ledge. He leans out, and takes one last look at me before letting go.

The door explodes inward.

I scramble onto the ledge, whacking my head on the sill. Without thinking, I throw myself out into the blue twilight.

As I lunge forward, something grabs my ankle. Claws rake my skin, trying to get a grip. My momentum breaks me free and I'm falling fast.

I wake convulsing on my bed, gasping for air. I'm fear-blinded for a moment, not sure where I am. In the dream or out. I swing my legs over the side of the bed and sit there, shaking until my head starts to clear.

I check my ankle, expecting claw marks and blood.

Not a scratch.

The voices are gone. Those lost souls begging me to show them the way out. They don't know there's nothing for them to come back to. Just scattered bones.

I think Howie got out okay. He should be waking up in his hospital bed right about now.

One tiny victory.

I just bought us a little time. Maybe another day. If I can make it through the night. It'll have to be enough. We need to make some plans. Gotta think.

What's next is going to be hell.

Thirty-One

'Can you hear me?' Pike says, leaning in close to the speakerphone.

'You don't have to yell,' Howie's voice comes through. 'Just talk normal.'

'Okay, so everybody's here,' Pike tells him, sitting down in the swivel chair at Howie's desk.

We're all in his room, while he's lying in a hospital bed in Barrie. He snapped out of the coma same time as I was waking up in my room. And after a long sleepless night we're both still breathing.

'So, what's the plan?' Ash wants to know. 'And don't say let's nuke the thing. Stick to reality.'

'This is the plan.' Pike holds up two sheets of paper. 'Me and Howie worked it out at the hospital.'

They show some basic drawings scribbled in pen.

'What's it supposed to be?' I ask.

He hands one page over. 'A map of the area

around the tunnel entrance.'

Ash leans in to take a look. I can see Howie's handwriting marking the points on the map. It shows the stretch of shoreline, from the abandoned ice factory to the bluffs. There's the clearing hidden between the rock walls. The tunnel entrance is marked as a little door at the base of one wall. A small circle indicates the boulder we hid behind. At the top is the lake, with the gap between the bluffs opening onto it.

'We're gonna set a trap,' Pike says. 'And slaughter it.'

'How?' Ash asks. 'That thing's got some heavy-duty body armour. Take a lot to bring it down. I've got my deer rifle, and maybe I can get hold of my dad's shotgun. But is that gonna even dent it?'

'Way ahead of you.' Pike's got a crazy gleam in his eyes. He hands over the second page of scribbles. 'This is the plan.'

It's a map of the tunnel, from the entrance at the base of the bluff down to the cave.

Two black 'X's are drawn just past the last sharp turn before the tunnel opens onto the cave.

'What do the "X"s mean?' I ask.

'That's where I'm going to leave a couple of Christmas presents.'

'What kind of presents?' I say.

'Show them,' Howie's voice comes out of the speaker.

'Right, bro,' Pike calls back.

He grabs something small off of Howie's desk and tosses it to me. It's some kind of electronics, the size of a quarter with tiny wires hanging loose from the bottom.

'What's this?' I jiggle it on my palm.

'A blasting cap.'

I stop jiggling.

'We needed some serious ordinance,' Pike says.

'What's ordinance mean?'

'Stuff that goes *boom*.'

I try to keep my hand from shaking, try not to breathe on it.

Pike takes it back. 'Don't worry. It's harmless. Not hooked up to anything. Yet.'

'Where'd you get that?' Ask asks.

'Same place I got this.' Pike goes over to Howie's closet and pulls out a duffel bag. He's more gentle this time, making me even more nervous. Setting it on the floor in front of us, he unzips it.

Holy crap!

Resting on a cushion of towels at the bottom of the bag, sealed in bright orange wrappers that are covered in warnings and 'skull and crossbones' symbols, are about two dozen sticks of dynamite.

'Where did you . . . ?' I whisper, trying not to make

a sound. My heart's beating so hard it feels like it's going to crack a rib.

'You know how they've been clearing land for those new greenhouses up north of the cove. The quickest way to clear stumps is to blow them. Lot of stumps around here.'

Through the end of summer and into fall we'd hear the distant booms of the clearing going on, echoing like thunder. Felt like living on the edge of a war zone.

'They quit clearing for the winter, but left the goodies behind in storage. The security's a joke – one old guy in a trailer watching TV.'

Howie's voice speaks up. 'It's the only way, guys.'

'Anybody got a better idea?' Pike zips the bag up.

This is nuts. But me and Howie are out of time, and this is all we've got.

'Okay. I'm in.'

Ash nods. 'Me too. So what's the deal?'

Pike taps the tunnel map I'm holding. 'The "X"s show where I'm going to plant my IEDs.'

'Your what?' I ask.

'IEDs,' Howie says. 'Improvised Explosive Devices.'

'I'm going to rig up a couple of land mines. I've been thinking it through.' Pike warms up to the subject. 'There's different ways to go – a trip-wire mine, a remote detonator, or a pressure mine. Trip wires are tricky, and they take time to set up. With remotes you can set them off with cellphones, but our target lives underground and I doubt a signal could get through all that rock. So that leaves pressure mines – you just need to plant and activate them.'

I look from the map to the duffel bag holding enough explosives to maybe level the house. Then I meet Pike's eyes. This is his dream. He knows they're never going to let him in the army. He's just too psycho. This is it for him. His shot. His war.

'Tricky,' Ash says. 'This isn't blowing up pumpkins on Halloween.'

He shakes his head. 'It's just a bigger pumpkin. On Halloween I used timers, made from cheap digital watches to set the charges. Worked beautiful. But a pressure mine is the way to go here. Nobody screws with my bro. I don't care if you are a killing machine from hell. You're going down. Right, bro?' he says, leaning over the speakerphone.

'Right,' Howie replies, sounding very far away.

'Why set the mines there?' Ash asks.

'Remember how just before you get to the cave, there's a sharp turn in the tunnel? Then you see that blue light? When the beast comes home, it'll take that bend and before it knows what hit it, it's blown to bits. Won't even see it coming.'

She nods. 'And how are you supposed to get in there to set this all up?'

Pike scratches his mohawk. 'That's where you guys come in. Everybody's got a part to play. I'm *demolitions*, of course. Ash is the lookout, guarding my back. And Danny . . .'

I brace myself.

'Danny's the bait.'

Thirty-Two

The sun disappears behind the cliffs on the far shore. I watch the sunset even though the light hurts my eyes, because it might be my last.

We're waiting for dark. Won't be long. The winter night comes on fast. No clouds tonight, and no moon. Not a problem for me. I can pretty much read in the dark now.

What is a problem is my driving skills. Or, lack of them. I failed my test twice at the DMV back in Toronto.

Which is why I'm real nervous about my part tonight.

Pike's junker is parked by the old ice factory. Sitting beside it is my ride for tonight, a Yamaha snowmobile I borrowed from the marina. It can do sixty miles an hour. Better be enough.

Driving it over here with Ash holding on in back of

me, there was way too much spinning and fishtailing. I almost flipped it climbing one of the low hills leading up to the bluffs. And I even did a full three-sixty doughnut, not on purpose.

'Man, you stink!' Ash said, when we stopped for a breather halfway to the factory. 'And I'm not just talking about your driving. That's some serious stink coming off you.'

I'm wearing a filthy T-shirt and sweats I pulled from the dirty laundry. My workout stuff.

'Part of the plan,' I said. 'You know, to lure it out after me. Gotta give it the scent.'

'I guess.' She wrinkled her nose. 'Maybe we won't need the TNT. It'll just choke on the smell.'

'Right. I'm laughing on the inside.'

She was trying to get my mind off all the stuff that could go wrong tonight. Trying to distract herself too. She was jumpy all day, since we set everything in motion. Scared more for me than herself.

I guess I really have turned into *Stinkboy*. Mom's doodle on the bathroom mirror. My evil twin.

And I remember what always happened to Stinkboy – getting shot, stabbed, burned and bombed. No happy endings for him.

'You want me to go with you?' she asked, squeezing me tight from behind, resting her chin on my shoulder.

'I could do the driving. Pike can watch his own back.'

'Then we'd both be dead meat.'

She shook her head. 'Ain't that easy to kill an Indian.'

I met her eyes, so dark and sure. I wished I felt like her – invincible. I looked down at the thin line on her lower lip where it got split. Scarred but unbeaten.

Every day I fall deeper for her. Wish I had more time.

'No way,' I said. 'I gotta do this myself.'

I leaned in close and gave her my icy kiss.

With that decided, I fired up the engine and steered us across the ice to the factory.

Right now, Pike's tinkering with the *twins* in the trunk of his car. That's what he named the two mines he's rigged up. Orange sticks of dynamite bundled together with duct tape, a mess of copper wires and some flat metal discs he calls 'pressure triggers'.

Pike steps back from the trunk.

'Everything good?' I ask, hushed, like anything above a whisper might set the *twins* off.

He nods. 'Relax. I haven't attached the blasting caps yet. I'll do that when I plant them in the tunnel.'

'Just try not to blast your nuts off while you're down there,' Ash says. 'I don't want to have to explain all this to the Captain.'

'Don't worry about me. I'll take care of my end. How

about you, Danny?' He inspects the snowmobile. 'How does it handle?'

'Real slippery.'

'You got the fun job,' he says. 'The chase scene.'

The wind off the lake picks up. Ash and Pike turn their backs to the chill. The dimming light paints us all in blue.

'How long now?' I ask.

Pike looks up at the sky, where the first stars are starting to show. 'Soon.'

Here's how it's supposed to go. *If* we can pull it off. *If!*

I'm the bait. We know the beast can sense us – me and Howie – the ones it's bitten and infected. We're bonded with it. So, I'm supposed to lure it out. Like waving a hot dog at a rabid pit bull. When the beast shows, I'll hop on the snowmobile and speed my butt out of there, with the beast in hot pursuit. Then I lead it away from the clearing, heading in a straight line across the cove, over the lake, back to the marina. Home sweet home. Once I get back there I'm safe. I mean, the beast wouldn't even be able to fit through the door. And Dad's there. This will work. It has to. But the doubts are crowding in on me now.

While this is happening, Pike's down in the tunnel setting the mines. Ash is watching his back by the surface entrance, armed with a single-barrelled shotgun and one of her dad's handguns.

Simple plan, right? But what sounded so solid this afternoon, safe in the light of day, is starting to look like one of the top ten worst ideas of all time.

Still, we're here. Out of time, and out of options.

I was going to leave Dad a note. You know, for if things go bad and I don't make it back. Didn't want to just disappear, like the others. I tried, but I couldn't figure how to explain it all. He lives in the real world. All I came up with was: *Dad, I'm sorry*.

This better work. I don't want to hurt him more.

I wish I was with Howie right now, safe in a nice quiet room in the hospital, watching sappy Christmas shows on TV, waiting for all the craziness to be over.

'Weapons check,' Pike says, getting up from the snowmobile. 'How are you for ammo?' he asks Ash.

'Two magazines for the semi-automatic. And a pocketful of shells for the shotgun. Can't see needing any more than that. If things get that bad, we're screwed anyway. What do you got?'

Pike ejects a fully loaded magazine from the stock of his own pistol and blows on it, like there might be a speck of dust that would ruin his aim.

He pats the chest pockets of his thick jacket. 'Four

mags of twelve. And shells for my double-barrelled. How about you, Danny?'

'Huh?' I'm blinking stupidly at the sight of all that firepower. 'Oh, I brought a rifle from the marina.'

I've got it strapped onto the side of the Yamaha's seat. I brought it more for moral support than anything. All a twenty-calibre is really good for is squirrel hunting.

'I loaded four shells,' I say. 'That's all it holds. Besides, I'm not the Terminator. I can't be driving and shooting at the same time.'

Pike nods. 'Okay. Get ready to move out. Be full dark soon.'

He goes back to the trunk and loads the mines delicately into his backpack, wrapping them in towels he's brought to cushion them.

'So what happens if this plan doesn't, you know, work?' I ask. 'What if that thing doesn't take the bait?'

Pike gives me a wink. 'Then we go to the back-up plan.'

'There's a back-up?'

'Don't worry. I got it covered.'

He lights up with his deranged grin, like a magician guarding the secrets behind his tricks. He grabs his night-vision goggles from the back seat.

'Ash. Here you go. There's no moon tonight, so you're gonna need these.'

He hands them over and runs through the settings with her.

'Thermal is useless with this freak,' Pike says. 'No body heat. So just keep it set for ambient light.'

Ash straps them on and looks around at us. 'You guys are all green. Like radioactive.'

'Try magnifying,' Pike says. 'Focus on the factory.'

Ash reaches up and adjusts something, looking off into the ruins of the ice factory.

'Wow, yeah,' she says. 'I could see a mouse fart at fifty feet with these.'

Ash makes a slow turn, scanning the landscape. 'Very cool. Very—' Then she freezes up. 'There's something out there.'

'What? Where?' Pike asks.

'It's moving!'

He whips out his pistol. 'You better not be screwing with—'

'Shut up! It's coming this way!'

'I can't see nothing.' Pike sweeps his aim at the surrounding darkness. 'From where?'

She points. We strain to see.

With my hypersensitive eyes I pick out the figure moving toward us.

'Hold on!' I say. 'Don't shoot. It's too small. It . . . It's . . .'

I can't believe my eyes. He's running down the dirt road, so small he's in danger of being swallowed up in the blackness.

'Howie?' I call.

He's barefoot, wearing his hospital pyjamas.

'Bro, what are you doin'?' Pike goes to meet him, shoving his gun in his pocket. 'You're supposed to be in the hospital. How did you get out here?'

Howie just stands there looking dazed, panting white clouds into the frosty air. Pike puts a hand on his shoulder, making Howie blink and focus on him.

'It's calling me,' he gasps.

His voice is breathless but calm beneath. He's pretty far gone. Under the beast's spell, as deep as Ray Dyson was when he ran off.

'You're not going nowhere,' Pike says. 'You're going to wait right here.'

'Can't . . . can't help it,' Howie wheezes. 'It's calling.'

Pike's got his flashlight out and sweeps the beam down to Howie's bare feet in the snow. They're chewed up and bleeding from the long run. All the way from Barrie. That's an insane marathon he's just done. But he's not feeling the bloody mess of his feet.

He's only feeling the *need*.

'Bro, look at you,' Pike says. 'Get in the car, and wait

here. Don't worry. I'm going to end this. It'll all be over real soon.'

Pike steers him into the back seat. Howie's so dazed he doesn't fight it. Pike shuts the door gently and leans on it a second, looking in at Howie staring off into space, hearing whispers.

'Guys!' Ash says. 'Heads up. Something's coming this way.'

What now?

'There's more than one.' She's got her goggles aimed in the direction Howie came from.

Pike grabs his shotgun and cradles it in one arm while he scans the darkness of the dirt road with his flashlight.

'Hold your fire,' a voice calls out. 'I won't bite. But they might.'

Pike's light finds a thin bearded figure, surrounded by half a dozen wolf-like ghosts, near invisible in the snow.

'What the hell is this?' Pike says.

'Mason?' I step forward. 'What are you doing here?'

He stops ten feet away, his huskies huffing steam into the frosty air.

'My dogs caught a scent up on Cove Road. They started tracking. I came along for the ride.' He looks past us at the car, and Howie in back. 'Oh, yeah. That's what they caught wind of. He's pretty ripe.'

'We don't got time for this crap,' Pike snaps. 'Listen, old man. Go be crazy somewhere else.'

Mason ignores him, his focus locked on me. 'Guess you didn't run.'

'Guess not,' I say.

'Dumb move.'

In the glare of the flashlight Mason looks skinny and pale, like a walking corpse. He ran away a lifetime ago, and survived – as this wrecked ghost. He stares into me with those haunted eyes.

Before I know what I'm saying, it comes out. 'You want to help?'

'Help what?'

'We're gonna end this thing tonight. We're gonna to kill it.'

Mason barks out a laugh. 'And *I'm* the crazy one here?'

'What do you say?' I ask him. 'You in or out?'

He digs his long nails into the fur of his huskies, shaking his head. Then he shrugs. 'Why not. It doesn't want me. It's your funeral. So what's the plan, General?'

Pike's pissed at the delay, but says the dogs might be useful. I sketch out our plan real quick. Mason's doubtful, but gives an impressed grunt when he gets a peek at the mines in the backpack.

'Tell you what,' he says, 'I can be your eye in the sky. I'll get up high and lookout. Let you know if the demon doesn't take the bait. I can climb up top of the bluff there. See for a long ways.'

'See in the dark?' Pike says.

'I see better in the dark than you see in the light.'

'What about the dogs?' Ash asks.

'They stay with me. They're shy when it comes to demons.'

Mason searches his pockets, emptying out all kinds of crap on the roof of the car – dog biscuits, sunglasses, a can opener, a switch blade.

'Here we go,' he says finally.

Before I can see what he's found, a noise rips through the night, making us all jump. It cuts off after a second. Mason grins at us, holding up a small air horn.

My heart's ramming against my ribs. 'A little warning before you do that?'

'Then where's the fun? So, I'll use this to sound the alarm, something goes wrong.'

Pike grabs his pack from the trunk. 'Let's get moving! Danny, you might want to take the snowmobile down to the shore, and come in the clearing from the lakeside. I saw you drive in here. I don't think you can make these hills.'

'Right. I'll go around.'

He settles the pack gently against his back, not wanting to wake the twins inside. Then he knocks on the car window to get Howie's attention. It takes a moment before Howie turns a blank stare on Pike.

'Stay here,' Pike tells him. 'Stay!'

Howie just blinks back, lost in the whispers.

Pike turns to us, shaken by Howie's state. But he chokes it back. 'It's time. Let's send this freak back to Hell.'

He leads the way into the low hills that border the bluffs. Mason and his pack trail along after.

Ash puts a hand on my shoulder and gives me a little shake. 'You can do this. Straight line across the ice. Hit the gas and don't let up. Hear me?'

I nod, totally numb.

Ash leans in quick to kiss me, and gives me a little punch in the chest goodbye. I watch her go. Then just as I'm turning toward the snowmobile, she calls back.

'*Netaga waab minodoo*. Kill the white devil.' What her dad shouts to get her pumped up during a fight.

I give her a grim smile and nod, before walking over to my ride. Passing the car, I glance in at Howie. He's staring straight ahead, eyes empty, locked in a trance. His time's up. Inside his head he's already gone.

If this doesn't work, I'm next.

I straddle the Yamaha's seat and turn the ignition.

The headlight comes on, the motor roaring to life.

Kill the white devil.

I squeezing the accelerator on the handlebar and the snowmobile jerks forward. There are no seatbelts on these things, so it's just hold on for your life. I lock my legs in place and pull out slow. It's a gradual slope down to the ice. I coast along, carefully making the transition from solid ground to solid ice. Then I rev the engine, testing myself with a burst of speed. Okay so far, but so far nothing's chasing me.

To my right the shore humps up into the looming bluffs. To my left there's nothing but the expanse of the lake, stretching off to the far shore. Nothing out here but me and my racing heart.

I skid along till I come to the gap that leads into the clearing. I let the engine idle for a moment before I pass through, remembering a line from a poem Howie told me. About how written on the gates of Hell it says: *Abandon hope, all who enter here.*

Twisting on the seat, I glance back, searching the darkness for the faint lights on the marina docks. There they are, so tiny in the distance, like the wind might blow them out leaving me lost in the blackness. Those frail lights mean safety. Get to them before the beast gets to me.

I let out a shaky breath, and rev the Yamaha up the

steep snowy incline and into the clearing, my eyes wide as they'll go, ready to run.

My gaze goes right to where the tunnel entrance should be. But all I see is the unbroken face of the rock wall. Maybe a good thing. At least it's not already out, waiting for me.

I do a U-turn on the snowmobile, aiming its headlight toward the gap and the lake. Then I pry my hands from their death grip on the bars, so stiff my knuckles pop as I shake them out. Getting off the seat, I leave the motor idling, its low grumble comforting. I'm not going to be one of those horror movie retards who can't get the engine started.

My breath catches as I see a flicker of movement across the clearing. I strain to make it out in the murky shadows. Then I recognize Ash and Pike stepping through the cleft, and I can exhale.

I wave. They wave back. Taking a few steps away from the snowmobile, I scan the wall for the tunnel mouth.

I pull my cellphone out and dial Pike. Across the clearing I hear the faint echo of his ringtone.

He picks up: 'Any sign?'

'Nothing.'

'It's probably waiting for the temperature to drop.'

Pike's right. Howie showing up means the beast is ready for its next victim.

'Any ideas?' I ask.

Before he can answer, I hear rocks tumbling. Staggering back, I search the wall for any shift in the darkness. It still seems solid.

A shower of gravel rains down from above, followed by the sound of a dog whining. I look up and see the pale phantom of Mason waving down at me. I wave back.

'That's just Mangy,' I tell Pike. 'He's in position.'

'Okay. Hope he doesn't land on me when he comes crashing down. Danny, how about you get a little closer to the wall. Give it a sniff of you. Let it know you're here.'

'You think this thing can smell through rock?'

'Howie says it can sense you guys somehow. Smell, psychic vibrations, whatever. You get close enough, it'll feel it. Give it a shot.'

Great idea! I'll just stick my head in the lion's mouth, see if it bites.

'Me and Ash are going to wait behind the boulder, okay?'

'Right. Thanks for the back-up.'

What am I doing? Did this ever sound like a good idea? Or am I just so punch-drunk from lack of sleep I never thought about it till now?

Too late to turn back. Give it a sniff? I guess the reek coming off me might just penetrate solid rock.

My brain and body are telling me to run, but I move toward the foot of the bluff.

I don't get three steps before I hear more rocks tumbling. Shooting a glare up in Mason's direction, I catch movement straight ahead of me. A chunk of the wall is shifting.

I stumble in reverse, not taking my eyes off the widening shadow. My phone clatters to the ground. I nearly fall on my butt when my heel trips on one of the snowmobile skids.

I turn to get on. Get the hell out. But my knees lock up, so sudden I almost topple over. It's like they're stuck in invisible concrete.

I feel a shiver inside my skull. Icicle fingers reaching in, freezing me in place.

I swing my head around to see the beast emerge from the tunnel. Stretching to its full height, it towers against the rock-face. It fixes me with the glimmer of those silver eyes.

Panic pounds through me. I bend back and bang my fist against the back of my right knee. It's so stiff I have to punch twice more before it gives.

I lunge across the seat of the snowmobile, flailing for the handlebars. Grabbing on, I pull myself forward on the seat and squeeze the accelerator.

With a jolt that almost throws me, the Yamaha roars

to life and lurches ahead. I gun the motor, aiming for the gap onto the lake and forgetting about the slant to the ice. I fly down the hill, going airborne for a second before hitting the ice. My chest slams forward against the bars, but my right hand keeps squeezing the accelerator. Swerving left, I zoom across the lake beneath the looming bluffs.

The noise and shudder of the Yamaha rattles my brain, blocking any thoughts that aren't my own.

The bluffs drop away to low hills at my side. I risk a glance back.

I can't believe it! Fifty feet away, coming on impossibly fast, the beast is in a full galloping sprint, sure-footed on the slick surface. Gusts of steam blow from its nostril slits.

I make myself face forward and bend low to lessen the wind drag. The skeleton of the ice factory flashes by. I pick out the marina lights. My finish line. Way *way* too far away.

The snowmobile is going full throttle and I'm keeping a straight aim. But that thing is just too freaking fast. I take a quick peek back.

It's gaining!

My fist is cramping up on the accelerator, like I can squeeze more speed out of it by brute force.

But the marina might as well be on Mars, for any chance

I have of reaching it before the beast takes me down.

My rifle is strapped to the seat. I can feel it bumping my calf. But it's useless against that thing.

I can't keep myself from looking back.

Closer! A charging white blur. Not tiring. Could probably run all night.

Out of nowhere, I see something sticking up from the ice directly ahead. The headlight flashes off the orange buoy, frozen in the ice.

Only a fraction of a second to avoid a head-on collision. I pull to the right. Just as I'm about to fly past the buoy, I see where the ice has buckled around its base.

Too late!

The front end of the skids catch on the bumps and twist the Yamaha around. It's like a giant hand reaching out to spin me.

I fight to keep my grip on the throttle as the darkness whirls around.

Can't stop! I stop, I die!

With the rear end still fishtailing wildly, I gain some traction and buck forward. I've lost sight of the beast, but I'm still moving.

Flying over the ice, I search desperately for the marina lights.

They're gone. Snuffed out. My heart seizes up. Where'd they go? I'm driving blind.

It takes a moment to find the shore, a grey blur.

But it's on my right now. I'm going the wrong way, back where I just came from. Gotta turn!

Glancing over my shoulder I see the beast on my tail, ready to jump.

Coming up on my right are the bare bones of the ice factory.

On the open ice, I'm dead.

I cut hard to the right and climb the shoreline with a teeth-cracking bounce. The steep incline threatens to flip me, but I make the top, hanging on for my life.

The factory towers up.

No time to think.

Plunging into the ruins, I dodge between pillars where the walls used to be. The ground is covered in ankle-deep snow. Good for the snowmobile skids, but bad for what might be hidden beneath, waiting to wipe me out.

I have to slow to squeeze through openings, avoiding fallen timber, ducking under beams. I twist and turn in this rotting maze. Parts of the path I take are too tight for the beast. Buying me time.

But I can't just hunker down and hide in here. It'll get to me. So I keep on, nearly getting decapitated by a low beam.

A crash behind me, the sharp crack of wood breaking.

My headlight jitters down what must have once been a long hallway, stripped to its framework.

I hear a splintering sound.

I glance back through the bare ribs of the hall. The beast sweeps its arms to chop through two by fours like toothpicks, making its own path through.

Can't shake this thing. Only one place left to run.

I see an opening on my left and swerve, shooting out into the open again. I grip the accelerator tight and whip past Pike's car, almost clipping the open back door.

I race into the hills, back to the clearing. My only chance is to get to Ash. She's got the firepower, maybe enough to scare it off. Make a stand.

I climb the first hill, close to flipping. Just as I reach the top and start down, a noise rips through the night. The blast of Mason's air horn, sounding from the peak of the bluff. It goes on and on. He's spotted me – spotted *it* on my tail.

I skirt the edge of the next rise, but then have to climb up to the cleft in the bluffs that leads to the clearing. I can't slow down, can't look back.

I push the snowmobile up. Up!

Taking the peak of the hill at full throttle, the snowmobile launches into the air, flying through the cleft and out the other side. One skid clips a rock and the Yamaha throws me.

I tumble through the air. And hit hard. Feels like my chest has caved in.

I'm rolling down an incline, skidding to a halt at the bottom. My face rests on the ground, with snow in my mouth, in my eyes. I spit out slush and suck in a breath of air.

I try and look around, deafened by the endless blare of the horn echoing off the bluffs. Then I make out something else.

'Danny!' shouted from close by.

I push myself to my knees, searching.

'Danny! Over here.' Ash.

She's moving toward me, shotgun in one hand, the other clamped around Howie's wrist. He's struggling with her, weakly. I concentrate on getting to my feet. I make it halfway up, then Ash is there to lean on.

She shouts something I can't understand past the scream of the horn. Then the noise cuts off and I make out what she's saying.

'Where is it?'

I turn to look back.

Stepping through the cleft into the clearing, the beast locks onto us.

A riot of barking erupts from the huskies on the bluff. The beast doesn't even glance up. Slowly it makes its way down to the floor of the hollow, nostrils flaring. Tasting our fear.

Howie's straining in Ash's grip, trying to break free and go to the beast.

'Hold him!' Ash pushes him at me.

I grab on to Howie.

Ash lifts her shotgun, pumping a shell into the chamber. But before she can shoot, a blast of gunfire splits the air. The beast flinches under the impact, swinging its head around to find the source.

I spot Pike, just outside the tunnel, his shotgun on the beast.

Ash gets off a shot, peppering its thick torso with buckshot.

The pellets bounce off like hailstones. All that did was piss it off more.

There's a freeze-frame moment where we realize we're screwed.

Then Pike yells. 'Move! Here! Down the tunnel!'

Down the tunnel? That's crazy! But we're cornered.

'Go!' Ash pushes me and Howie forward. 'Go!'

Pike fires off another round to cover us.

I drag Howie across to the opening in the rock-face, flanked by Ash. The entrance gapes like the mouth of a tomb.

Ash leads us into the inky black. I rush to join

her, with Howie in tow.

'Stay on the left side!' Pike runs to meet us. 'Left side! Left side!'

A white light flares to life ahead. Ash with her flashlight, showing the way.

'I'll take him.' Pike reaches out.

I hand Howie over and start down the tunnel.

'Stay left!' Pike barks. 'The mines are set just before the cave.'

Down and down and down, we stumble through the dark. Ash's light jumps around in crazy arcs.

I keep moving in a dazed panic, wondering if we've taken a wrong turn, plunging lost into the guts of the earth. My legs go on automatic, carrying me deeper. I focus on the swinging light. Don't lose her. Don't want to be alone down here.

Ash skids to a stop. I pull up, my feet skating on the slick surface.

'Hold on,' she says, breathless.

'What?' I pant.

'We're here.'

I see the blue glow and the curve in the tunnel.

She gives me a hard stare. 'Slower now. Eyes on the floor!'

I nod. The shivers running through me aren't from what lies ahead, or from the cold. The freeze can't touch me any more. What I'm feeling goes deeper. Under my skin, inside my head. Ghost whispers.

I know Howie's hearing it sharp and clear.

Pike emerges from the gloom, half carrying Howie.

Ash disappears past the bend in the rock, and I follow.

She hugs the left wall, her back brushing along the rock, moving as if she's on the edge of a cliff looking at a thousand-foot drop.

But what she's staring at are two black shadows, positioned at centre and right on the tunnel floor.

The *twins*. Duct-taped, wire-tangled bundles of death.

The floor is black ice and smooth rock. I focus on Ash's path, walking an invisible tightrope.

It takes only seconds. But seconds stretch down here in the dark. Making me sweat.

Finally, she's clear.

'Go, man,' Pike hurries me. 'Go!'

My left foot skids on a slick patch. Keeping my spine pressed to the wall, I shift my right foot over to join it.

A salty tear of sweat blurs my vision. I blink it away, and it runs down the side of my nose to hang on the tip of my nostril.

My heart trips a beat. Below me sits enough TNT to vaporize me. How much pressure to set one off?

I sniffle at the sweat, trying to suck it in. As my nose twitches, the drop falls.

Slow motion rules my world. I can see exactly where it's going to land.

Right dead centre.

I watch the drop trickle over the metal surface of the trigger. And . . . nothing.

Keep moving. I shift my feet along.

My stare is locked on my shoes when Ash takes my arm and pulls me to safety.

I look back at Pike carrying Howie past the mines. He's safe in the cave before I can blink.

'Take the right side,' Pike tells us. 'I'll take left. Stay low!'

Ash pulls me with her.

Pike takes up position by the mound of bones hidden in the fog.

He drops Howie beside him and grabs a handful of shotgun cartridges from his pocket. Ash is doing the same, the brats going into combat mode. Me and Ash are farther from the entrance. Over her shoulder, I see the beast's discarded shell. I keep my eyes on it for a second to make sure that's all it is. But it sits motionless, like a gargoyle, staring at us with those empty sockets.

When I look over at Pike, I gasp.

Howie's broken away from his side, stumbling

toward the entrance. 'Howie!' Pike drops the shotgun and launches himself in pursuit. But Howie's closing in on the mouth of the tunnel. Pike's shout echoes off the walls.

He reaches out as he runs. Too late.

Howie's about to step into the tunnel.

Then the earth rips apart.

Thunder cracks the air. Flames burst from the tunnel and a fist of super-heated air slams me back.

The earth shakes, the air too hot and smoky to breathe. I cough. Coughing turns to puking. Can't breathe. Can't see. Everything is fog and smoke.

Through the blue haze, rocks tumble from the roof, crashing on the floor without a sound. The world has gone deaf.

I squint tears out of my eyes.

Then I feel this pressure inside my skull growing stronger. With a painful pop, my eardrums screech back to life.

I crouch, moaning.

A scream of pure agony breaks against the rock walls, throwing back echoes that make me wince. I cover my ears, searching for the source.

Through gusts of fog, I make out a body on the floor across the cave. It rolls over onto its back.

Howie! Still alive.

There's blood gushing from his nose, and he's shaking with a coughing fit. But he's still breathing.

The scream shakes the stone under my knees.

Something moves in the mist by the cave entrance.

The fog parts and the beast staggers into the cave. The right front leg has been cut in half, ending in jagged spikes of bone. Its hide is scorched black on that side.

The mouth hangs open, the long blades of its teeth gleaming blue. Its scream deepens into a ragged growl.

Those silver eyes meet mine.

It rears up on its hind legs.

The beast takes a step closer, mouth stretching wide.

I'm dead!

A blast of gunfire erupts next to me. I spin and see Ash with her pistol raised. The giant flinches as bullets bounce off its chest, shoulder, forehead. Ash empties her mag on it.

The last shot catches the beast in the eye, making it screech and bow its head. As Ash's gun clicks over and over on an empty chamber, the creature howls.

A fat drop of liquid silver runs down from the left eye.

'The eyes,' I croak, voice raw from the smoke. 'Go for the eyes.'

Ash ejects the empty magazine and digs in her

pocket. She fumbles the new mag out, and drops it. It clatters on the rocks, eaten instantly by the tide of mist. Ash sweeps her hand in the fog, feeling for the ammo.

The beast steps toward us, crying a new silver tear from its wounded eye. Ash isn't going to find the mag fast enough.

Then it stops, shaking a rear leg like it's caught.

Howie's lying right in its path, coughing and hacking, eyes squinted shut. He reaches out and grabs blindly at whatever just bumped into him.

'Pike!' His arm hooks around the beast's ankle. 'Pike?'

The giant's head snaps downward.

'Pike?' Howie pleads, like his brother can still save him.

With a backward kick the giant dislodges him. Howie flies toward the far side of the cave and crashes on the mound of bones.

The beast turns to me.

I try to look away. But I'm frozen, can't even blink.

I open my mouth to warn Ash. She's still searching for her ammo.

But before I can speak, a wild yell ricochets off the walls.

Pike emerges from the mist in a burst of speed, racing across the cave. He rushes up behind the giant, leaps into the air and lands on its back.

It twists to see what's there.

Pike clings to the bony ridges of its back. He wraps his arms and legs as far as he can around it, digging his heels into the beast's ribs.

Pike's insane!

The beast tries to throw him. But Pike won't budge.

It's like he's riding the mechanical bull at the Legion Hall. Like if he just stays on long enough he'll win.

Pike said he had a back-up plan. If this is it, we're screwed.

I hear the click as Ash slaps a mag into the stock of her gun.

The beast twists, reaching back with its razor claws. Pike lets out a howl as they snag his foot, ripping off his boot. A spray of his blood runs down the beast's ribs.

Pike holds on tight, but his right hand reaches to dig in his jacket pocket.

No bullet is going to puncture that armour. The eyes are the only soft spot, and there's no way Pike can take aim at them from his position.

Ash searches for a clear shot while the beast bucks, shrieking with rage. Pike yanks something out of his pocket. Not a gun.

The beast stretches, contorting to grab the pest clamped against its spine.

Pike lifts what he's holding up to his mouth.

A bundle of dynamite, six sticks taped together. He uses his teeth to rip off a strip of paper, then slaps the six-pack hard against the beast's back. And it sticks.

Stickybomb! It comes back to me, Pike talking about soldiers using them against tanks.

Pike dodges the claws, pressing frantically at something on the bundle.

As the beast takes another swipe, Pike falls to the floor with a loud grunt. Swallowed by the mist, I make out his shadow as he crawls away. The beast turns to get him.

My eyes find the six-pack stuck to the beast. There's something attached to the bundle of dynamite and wires – a digital watch.

A timer. Counting down!

'Get down!' Ash shouts, tackling me to the floor.

The explosion cracks the earth apart.

And the world ends.

Thirty-Three

The end of the world hurts like a bitch.

I wake to darkness and suffocation. My whole body convulses. I try and suck in air, but there's only smoke and choking dust.

I'm buried alive, a thousand tons of rock flattening my chest. My body starts bucking, trying to shake the pressure threatening to crack my ribs.

I open my eyes, blind and burning with the dust.

Then a miracle. The weight of the mountain on me shifts the tiniest bit. I get a wisp of air to my lungs.

Blinking tears out of my eyes, my vision clears. I see the blue cave. The roof hasn't fallen in. Yet.

I'm not buried. It's . . .

Ash. Lying on top of me. I manage to worm my way out from under her.

She's coughing now, coming to. There's blood running from her nose, but Ash is still in one piece.

Clods of dirt and stones tumble from the roof like hail. Boulders have crashed to the floor. Something wet hits my cheek, making me flinch. I reach to swipe it off, thinking it's blood. But my hand comes away wet with water.

Water?

The roof is dripping a steady rain. In spots, thin streams are pouring down. Above the hollow space of the cave, and who knows how many feet of rock, sits the weight of Lake Simcoe.

More drops hit my forehead. Get out of here. Now!

But just as I move to get up, something stops me cold. Through the gusts of smoke I see a thick albino leg, the long spikes of its claws dug into the floor.

The beast. Still standing!

But as the mist shifts, I let out a shuddering breath, half-shiver, half-laugh. There's nothing left above the knee.

He did it! Pike killed the unkillable.

Ash sits up, spitting out the blood running down from her nose.

'Ash, it's dead.'

She groans. 'The guys?'

'Don't know. But we gotta get out. The roof is caving in.'

I struggle to my feet. Ash pulls herself up, leaning on

me. I squint through the smoke. No sign of Howie and Pike. But I see the tunnel entrance across the cave.

The hail of stones is getting worse.

Holding each other up, we stagger through the fog, tripping over fallen rocks.

I let out a yelp as a ghost rises from the mist.

'Danny!' it says.

A hand grabs my arm. I jump back, my heart seizing. Then a face leans in close.

'How-Howie?' I pant

'Help. Help me with Pike.'

Another ghost kneels beside him.

'I'm okay,' Pike mumbles, dazed. 'Just give me a sec. Man, what a ride.'

The thunder in the rocks overhead deepens.

'This whole place is coming down,' I say. 'Move. Now!'

Howie drags his brother to his feet. Pike stands drunkenly.

'Right behind you, Danny,' he says.

I lead the way, Ash at my side.

Reaching the shadow of the cave mouth, I'm in such a rush I take the first step through before stopping dead. I put my hand out to stop Ash.

My eyes strain to see through the mist. Did the beast trigger both mines, or just one? Is the other twin still waiting down there?

Howie bumps into me, giving me a heart attack.

'Go slow,' I say. 'Watch for the other mine.'

Inching along, I find a small crater in the floor from the first explosion. Then I see a shadow squatting by the wall. The surviving twin, still intact.

A crash and thud rumbles from the cave as part of the roof starts to give way.

Small rocks tumble from the roof of the tunnel. A couple bounce off my head. A stone the size of a golf ball clips the edge of the sleeping mine.

I freeze, waiting to be blown into a thousand bloody pieces.

But half a second ticks by, then a full one.

'Watch your step!' I point out the mine.

Howie nods, eyes wide.

My back to the wall, I shuffle past with Ash. I don't breathe easy again until I take the sharp turn leading away from the cave. Howie follows close, arms wrapped around Pike to keep him vertical.

Good thing me and Howie can see in the dark, because the blue glow dies off and we make our way up the tunnel in total blackness. Ash grips my wrist tight.

The way up seems longer than the way down.

'Still with me, Howie?' I call back.

Before he can answer, a violent concussion rips through the dark, whipping up the tunnel and hitting us with a blast of hot air and smoke. I'm thrown against the wall with Ash.

The second mine!

As I'm coughing out the smoke, I hear a roar from down below, rushing toward us.

I flash back to that crowd of voices trapped inside the beast's mind – the panic of countless victims. And now all those souls are making a jailbreak after an eternity of torture.

But it's not souls or ghosts I see gushing up from below. A wall of water fills the corridor, floor to ceiling, pressed onward by the weight of the lake above.

It swallows up the brothers, and I just have time to suck in a breath of smoky air before it hits.

The wave shoves me ahead of it. I hang on to Ash as the water knocks me against the rocks, spinning and pushing me upwards.

Even immune to the cold, I can feel the bite of the icy water.

The wave presses me on. My breath is about to give out when I surface near the roof of the tunnel and gulp in a lungful of air. Ash pops up, gasping.

We sputter and spit up lake water. Lost in the dark.

Something below grabs on to my leg, making me yelp. I try and kick it loose.

Pike and Howie bob up, hacking and spewing.

We dog-paddle frantically, keeping our heads above water.

How far to the surface?

Then I feel the sweetest breath of winter air on my face. We're close.

I swim ahead till my feet touch the tunnel floor. Ash follows, and we slog out onto dry rock.

A breeze brushes over me, smelling like snow and cedar. I want to lie on the floor and just breathe. But I need to get out.

Like two drunks, me and Ash stumble up the last stretch of tunnel, leaning together. Howie and Pike stagger after us.

The night sky stretches wide and bright with stars. We lean against the rock face and just breathe. A surge of relief makes me want to laugh like a madman.

But Ash is shivering real bad. I'm immune to the cold, but she's not.

'Gotta get you warmed up.'

She's hugging herself, shaking too much to speak.

Across the clearing, I catch something moving in the dark. Silent phantom shapes come toward us. It's a breathless second before I make out Mason and his huskies.

'It's done,' I call out.

Mason shakes his head. I know how he feels. I was

327

there and I can barely believe it.

Near him, I notice the snowmobile flipped on its side, but still in one piece. I can hear the purr of the engine idling.

'Howie, we gotta get her and Pike heated up quick. Can you drive the car?'

'Yeah. Where?'

His eyes are clear now, the trance broken.

'The marina. Closest place.'

'Right. Lean on me, Pike.'

The brothers start moving.

Ash hugs onto me as I walk us to the snowmobile. The headlight is busted and one of the skids is cracked, but it's still breathing.

Howie glances back.

'I'm going to take Ash on the snowmobile. Be quicker across the lake.'

I grab the handlebars and heave it over onto its skids.

'See you back at the house,' I say.

'H-hot c-coffee,' Pike stutters.

'You got it.'

I straddle the seat, and Ash gets on behind me.

'Hold on tight,' I say, looking over my shoulder.

Past Ash, I see Mason and his dogs in front of the tunnel. He's staring into the darkness. Seeing ghosts.

Ash locks her arms around me. 'Go, Danny! Fast.'

I pull the snowmobile around and head for the gap onto the lake. I take us smoothly down the incline I jumped earlier. Reaching the ice, I hit the accelerator. And we're flying.

With Ash pressed close I wish I had some body heat to share with her. But I'm only a few degrees warmer than the frigid air whipping by us.

Just as we clear the shadow of the bluffs, I feel the ice shake under us. We start swerving. I grab Ash's arms, keeping them locked on my chest.

Then, with a cracking boom the surface of the lake explodes about fifty feet from shore. Chunks of ice are thrown up, as if some giant sea creature is breaking through, making a hole big enough to swallow a tank.

My brain runs wild. All those stolen souls, suddenly freed. A horde of escaping ghosts bursting up through the lake floor, then shattering the ice.

I fight down panic, regaining control of the snowmobile. We race on, putting distance between us and the break.

I risk a glance back. The black water froths and bubbles in the new opening. Then I realize what's going on.

After the cave collapsed, and the lake floor came crashing down, all that trapped air must have been forced to the surface. Cracking the ice. The water seems to boil in the break, with huge air bubbles.

The headlight's dead, so we speed blind through the dark. Only the dock lights on the far end of the cove keep us on track. Time stretches out, and it seems like we're never getting any closer. But finally we're climbing the snowy slope and pulling up to the side of the house.

I unlock my stiff fingers from the bars, grunting as I get off the seat and pull Ash up. She leans on me as we stagger to the door.

It swings inward and Dad appears. He must have heard the snowmobile racing up.

In the spill of warm yellow light, he sees us.

'What the hell?'

All I can do is hold Ash out to him, like this is a relay race and I'm ready to drop. 'Get her warmed up,' I pant.

Dad lifts her easily. 'She's soaked through. And frozen. Upstairs. Now!'

I follow slowly, one step at a time. My boots are cement blocks. I only had enough strength to get me this far. I'm done. When I get to the top of the stairs, Dad's laying Ash down on the floor in front of the fireplace.

Leaning against the wall, I've only got a minute before I've got to come up with answers.

The truth is impossible. I was there and I barely believe it. There's nothing to show for it all, either. Any proof we had is buried under the lake, and tons of rock.

There's only one way I can think of to play this.

Dad breaks a seal of ice to get Ash's jacket zipper down.

'Danny?' Dad says. Just my name, but he's telling me I better have answers, and quick.

I take a breath. 'We fell through the ice.'

'What?' He gets Ash's arms out of the stiffened sleeves. 'Where?'

'By the ice factory.'

That sounds real. This can work.

Dad starts to say something, but right then a car skids to a halt outside.

'That's the rest of the guys,' I say.

I'm going to need to think fast to keep up with Dad's questions. But right now my ears are still ringing, everything's too bright, and the floor feels like it's tilting just a little. The wall is the only thing keeping me up.

'What guys?' Dad asks. 'What the hell—'

But he cuts himself off. 'Later. Right now, get out of those clothes. And grab something for Ashley to put on.'

I nod, pushing off from the wall, and head for my room. Dad's taken charge. This is when he's best, when there's something that needs fixing. And we really need fixing right now.

'Bring blankets,' he calls.

I do a quick change, and dig out some clothes for Ash and the guys. Down below the side door opens, followed by the thud of boots climbing the stairs. Dragging the blankets off my bed, I stop for a second and just breathe.

My heart slows. I stand still, feeling its steady beat.

For some reason, Howie's graph pops into my head. The one he made of the missing kids over the years, with a zigzag line, spiking with each cluster of lost kids. Those spikes that looked like heartbeats on a monitor. Signs of life, and death.

With the beast gone, we've seen the last spike. Now Howie's graph can end in a flatline.

And maybe all those lost souls can finally rest.

Thirty-Four

The place is so quiet. Almost peaceful, like a graveyard. Which it is. There are no markers, but somewhere beneath my feet the bodies are buried. The bones.

I walked out here all the way from the marina, through the new snow. Don't know why. There's nothing left to see.

The sun glares painfully white off the fresh powder in the clearing by the ice factory. The landscape has changed a little since that night a month back, when we nearly drowned, got blown up, and eaten. After the explosions underground, the bluff has settled a bit lower. Rockslides and tremors have collapsed the tunnel.

Nothing to show for what happened down below.

And nobody knows, except me, Ash and the guys.

I'm still kind of shocked at how the story I came up with in a few dazed seconds at the marina held up. While Dad was defrosting Ash and Pike, filling them with coffee and roasting them in front of the blazing fire, I figured out the rest of the story. It went like this . . .

When we heard Howie was missing from the hospital we went looking for him. He'd been real sick with some weird infection, confused and hallucinating. Pike thought he might be trying to get back home to the Cove. So we drove around a while, then decided to split up to cover more ground. I took the snowmobile to scout the lakeshore, while Pike and Ash searched the backroads. When I found Howie out on the ice, I called them on my cell and tried to get Howie to come back to the house with me. But he was all freaked out, seeing things. When Pike got there, he tried to talk his brother down from his hallucination. And while we were out there on the lake, trying to bring Howie in, the ice gave.

I'm sure that if you leaned on my story too heavy it would fall over. But there we were, soaked and frozen. Howie in his hospital pyjamas with his feet raw and bloody from his long run. There was the break in the ice out by the bluffs. And really, what other explanation was there?

None that would fit into Dad's *real* world.

I look at the pale winter sky. In the distance now I hear the familiar rumble of Ash's motorbike, rising and falling as she makes her way over the hills.

I told her where to find me. We're supposed to meet up with Pike and Howie at their place. Pike's got something planned. Why does that make me nervous?

Pike's still limping from the stitches he got on his foot where he was slashed. It took some quick thinking to explain those wounds. Best I could come up with was that Pike stepped on some rusty nails out by the ice factory when we were bringing Howie in. Kind of weak, but they bought it.

Something catches my eye, just inside the mouth of the collapsed tunnel. I step closer. There on the rocks lies a beaten-up hockey puck.

Takes a second before it clicks – Mason. Leaving something behind for his friend. Remembering an unfinished hockey game played on the lake a long time ago.

Makes me think of the families of the missing. I wish I could tell them, and give them some peace. But with nothing real to show it would just be cruel. When that bully Ray Dyson ran off, I said that's one missing person nobody's going to miss. But now I don't know. Even Ray had a mother.

I turn and look around the clearing one more time, before Ash arrives. The ground is blanketed in fresh powder. Snow has that magic touch, covering up all the plain and ugly things. Making everything new. Hard to believe anything bad ever happened here.

The bike's growl is getting close. Time to go.

So, what's the final score in all this mess?

Answers: Zero. Questions: Endless.

Like, what was that thing, really? Windigo? Demon? Or just some mutant freak? And why *us* – me and Howie and all the others through the years? Why did it choose us?

Maybe, like Howie says, it just had good taste.

Zero answers! That's hard to take. But at least I'm still around to ask the questions.

I stand here, untouched by the bite of the icy wind off the lake, in this unmarked graveyard. Nothing to show for the horror.

Nothing but the ice in my veins.

Ash kills the motor as we pull up to Pike and Howie's place. I get off the bike and stretch my back.

Ash removes her sunglasses. The bruises on her face have faded to yellows and browns. Her head took a wicked bounce off the cave floor, when she tackled me as the bomb blew.

'Don't stare,' she says. 'Unless you're going to do something about it.'

'Like what?'

'Like you and me back at my place later. Mom's

going to be out till late, and Dad's up north wrestling polar bears. Use your imagination.'

'I am,' I tell her, deep and seductive.

She gives me a playful punch in the chest, then we go around back to the tool shed, where Pike said to meet him.

As we approach the half-open door I hear a gasp from inside.

'Quit flinching,' Pike says. 'Or you'll ruin it.'

'How much more?' Howie's voice is tight.

'Almost done.'

Ash glances at me with raised eyebrows, then throws the door open. It cracks against the wall of the shed.

Girl likes to make an entrance.

'Break it up,' she says. 'What're you doing to this poor boy?'

I squeeze into the shed beside her. The place is cluttered with lawn chairs, barbecues and bicycle parts.

Howie's sitting on a stool by a workbench, with the sleeve of his T-shirt rolled up. His shoulder is smeared with blood and what looks like ink.

Pike's learning over him, holding a towel stained red and black. He glares at Ash. 'You almost wrecked my masterpiece.'

'What the hell?' I ask.

'Let me finish,' Pike says. 'Hold on a second.'

He sets the towel down on the bench and grips Howie's arm. Me and Ash look on as he uses a seeing needle to jab three holes in a row in the skin of Howie's shoulder. Howie winces as drops of blood well up. Then Pike grabs the small face-towel, soaked with black ink, and rubs it into the needle pricks he's made. Howie whimpers, but stays steady till it's over.

Pike looks at his bloody work. 'Done!'

Howie lets out his breath.

'What is this?' Ash asks.

Pike grins his deranged grin. 'Homemade tattoo.'

I shake my head, stunned. 'But why?'

'It was Howie's idea.' Pike pulls out some antibiotic hand wipes and starts cleaning Howie's shoulder.

'Yeah, I got to thinking,' Howie says, cringing at the sting. 'After what we went through, we should do something to remember it. What we did together. Because what we did was *big*. It was impossible.'

This isn't the same Howie who was jumping at his own shadow a couple months ago. He got sprung from the hospital after the doctors decided his condition was due to a relapse of the hypothermic shock he suffered falling through the ice. You'd think he'd be ready for the nuthouse after what happened to him. But there's this calm to him now, even some confidence. Like somewhere along the way he grew some balls.

'And I thought,' he goes on. 'Maybe years from now we might start having doubts. That maybe it wasn't real, just something we dreamed up. Or a story we told ourselves so many times we started to believe it. But if we have something physical to remember it by, then we can just look down at the tattoo and know it was real. It happened.'

His tattoo is becoming clear as Pike wipes away the inky mess.

I squint at it. Looks sort of like a number eight, only lying on its side like it fell over, and stretched out like someone sat on it.

∞

'What is that?' Ash asks.

'This is the symbol for *infinity*,' Howie says.

'Why infinity?' I ask.

Howie touches the tender red skin around the mark. It's little, only a half-inch long.

'Because it means no limits. It goes on forever. Never-ending. Never forgotten.' He gives a little shrug. 'Just seems right.'

'Howie did mine.' Pike rolls up his sleeve, showing his left shoulder. There's the freshly inked infinity loop, and right above it another new tattoo.

'What's that other one?' I ask. 'Looks like a candle.'

'It's a stick of dynamite. See, with the fuse lit. We just

gotta ink in "TNT" on it.'

'Dad's gonna love that.' Howie shakes his head. He looks at me and Ash. 'But how about it, guys? You know, Indians and Africans used to get tattoos that showed what tribes they were in, and what battles and wars they'd won. That was some weird and wild battle we fought. So let's do something to remember it.'

'Like I'm going to forget?' I say. 'I'm still having nightmares.'

Tribes, Howie says. He wants to be part of something. Guess I do too. We did the impossible – killing the unkillable. Something to remember.

'Okay, I'm in,' Ash says.

Howie turns to me. 'What do you say?'

I turn it over in my head. It's crazy, but I kind of like it. And what's a few little needle pricks after what we went through?

'Is it gonna hurt?' I ask.

He shrugs. 'Like getting stung by a bee. Or a swarm of bees.'

'Great! Well, you're doing mine, Howie. No way I'm letting Pike poke holes in me.'

I go first. If I have to watch Ash get hers before me I might chicken out.

Howie gives me an ice cube to numb the spot. Pike

fires up his lighter and heats the tip of a new needle to sterilize it.

Suddenly this seems like the worst idea ever.

But I sit down on the stool and show Howie exactly where I want mine. He cleans the spot with an antibiotic wipe.

'This is how they do jailhouse tattoos,' he tells me. 'I read how to do it on the Internet.' He uses a pen to outline the symbol on my skin. 'Perfect.'

Howie grabs a bottle of black India ink and pours some out onto a face-towel. While he's doing this, Pike sticks a bandage on Howie's shoulder, covering the tattoo still dribbling blood.

'I might need someone to hold me steady,' I say. 'Don't want a blurry tattoo.'

'I got you.' Ash comes up behind me and reaches around to grip my arm.

'Ready?' Howie asks.

'No. But do it!'

I shut my eyes and brace.

Epilogue

The Ice Age is over.

I swat away a swarm of mosquitoes as I break from the trees onto the pebbly beach. Sunlight flashes off the calm waves of the lake. The deep blue-green of the water looks like liquid heaven, calling out for me to take a dip. Stones cruncning underfoot, I stagger to a stop and bend over with my hands on my knees to catch my breath. A bumblebee glides lazily by, newly woken from its winter sleep, stunned like I am by the warm sun and the green smell of spring in the air.

I'm running the trails with Ash. No way I can keep up with her. She's running laps around me. But she shouts encouragement when she passes me by.

Stuff like: 'Move it, pussy!' and, 'Hustle, Whitey!'

Very encouraging.

I collapse on the beach and squint at the glitter off the lake. The spring thaw came late, with winter giving up slow and stubborn.

My blood still runs a little colder. The chills come and go, usually at night. Right now, after chasing Ash for the last hour, I'm feeling like an ice cube in a furnace.

Ash has her sights set on the junior provincial bouts in Toronto. The next step on her path to world domination.

She's back there somewhere, running like the Devil's chasing her.

I know the feeling.

The water looks so deliciously cool, I can't resist. Kicking off my runners, I stuff my socks in them, strip off my T-shirt and wade in waist-deep. The lake never loses its frosty bite. Never forgets it started out as a chunk of glacier.

I splash my face, wetting back my hair.

Straight ahead is the orange buoy me and Ash raced to over the ice, months ago. She let me win that time. I like it when she lets me win. We've been meeting up here ever since. This beach is our place, too rocky and out of the way for anybody else to want it.

I'm thinking of going along with Ash when she fights in the city. I can stay with my aunt. Maybe go out to see Mom's grave, and tell her where I've been, what I've been up to. Tell her everything.

I told Ash about visiting the grave to say all this

stuff. She gave me a puzzled look.

'What makes you think she's there? I mean, stuck in the ground. When you die you go free, right?'

'Is that an Indian thing?'

'Not really. Just how I see it. Seriously, why does she have to be *there* . . . and not here? Wherever you are.'

I like that idea. You die, you go free. So Mom could be wherever. Everywhere I am.

Even here, waist-deep in the lake.

The sound of rocks crunching underfoot wakes me from my sun-dazzled daydream. Ash is standing by the waterline. Her natural tan is a shade redder, and a little dusty from the trails, her face shiny with sweat.

'Slacker. You own me a mile.'

I splash at her. 'Come on in and try and collect.'

She tosses her shoes and socks beside mine, wading into the lake in her shorts and her *Stalk and Kill* T-shirt.

When she comes up next to me, she dunks her head under and whips it back, spraying an arc of water into the air. Her slicked hair is the same midnight dark as her eyes. Blinking drops away, she spouts a mouthful of lake water in my face.

'Thanks,' I splutter.

'No problem. So hey, uh . . . Did you talk to your dad? What's the word? You staying?'

Me and Dad had a blowout fight when I told him I

didn't want to go on running from place to place. Told him I wanted to stay, right here in this nowhere town. Long enough to catch my breath, anyway. Long enough to see what this thing is between me and Ash.

It would have been an even bigger blowout if Dad hadn't already been softened up some by Andrea. She's dragged him out the last couple months – to the movies, the Speedway, even over to her place for some home-cooked. He's still playing hard to get. But not as hard as he used to. She's like a dog on a bone, and the bone never wins that fight.

'It got kind of ugly,' I tell Ash. 'You know, so much stuff we never talked about. But he came around. I think he's as tired of running as I am. The marina owner says he can use Dad's help through the summer. So Dad's talking him up on it.'

Ash reaches over and gets me in a headlock. 'Knew I had you hooked. Once you go native you never go back.'

I give her a bite on the biceps to break free.

'Hey, don't go all Windigo on me.' Ash lets go.

She gives me a tsunami splash, soaking my head. Squinting the water from my eyes, I see the spot where I nibbled her. Right near her small black tattoo.

I got mine on the back of my right hand, with the blue dot left by the beast's sting caught in the eye of the infinity loop. Sometimes I feel this ghost pain there, like a splinter of ice under the skin. I have to rub it till it melts away.

'Quit thinking so hard,' Ash says, flicking water at me. 'You're gonna hurt yourself.'

I look over at her, and at the scar on her lower lip. Right. Less thinking. She's reading my mind, pulling me in close.

This will never end. This moment. This kiss.

I know, nothing lasts forever. But right now I feel infinite.